BRIDE OF DEATH

For Keith,
with my everlasting
thanks

BRIDE OF DEATH

T. A. PRATT

T. A. Pratt

The Merry Blacksmith Press
2014

Bride of Death

Cover art by Lindsey Look
lindseylook.com

Cover design by Jenn Reese
www.tigerbrightstudios.com

For information, address:

The Merry Blacksmith Press
70 Lenox Ave.
West Warwick, RI 02893

merryblacksmith.com

Published in the USA by The Merry Blacksmith Press

ISBN—0-61595-434-0
978-0-61595-434-9

Dedication

For Haddayr.

Because she's a badass.

Dear Me

Dear Me,

Marla Mason here, fresh from the grave. It's late in Vegas and I can't sleep, maybe because as far as I can tell I've been unconscious for the past month, even though I know part of me was awake and doing the business of the universe. I might as well have been in a fugue state, sleepwalking, in a walking blackout, for all the impression thirty days in the underworld made on me. I don't like losing time. It feels too much like losing part of myself. Maybe because it *is*.

I've never kept a diary before, not even as a teenage girl, but I've got my reasons for starting now. The thing is, I can't entirely trust my memory. In a handful of weeks I'll return to the other half of my life, and when I come back to this mortal coil next time, what if I'm all blank-slated again? This notebook could be the only reliable record I have. Which means I should try to *keep* it reliable. I'll do my best, but you're me, Future Marla, so I shouldn't have to tell you: trust no one. Maybe not even yourself.

Don't expect a bunch of mushy dithering introspective stuff here—spending too much time wringing my hands with indecision gets in the way of wringing necks. I'll have to write down some conversations (unless I can avoid having any), and I'll try to keep those pretty much accurate, except I doubt I'll have the patience to write down the bullshit and pleasantries. I've got a pretty good memory for what people say, when I feel like listening. It's handy for throwing words back in people's faces.

What I'm trying to say, dear possibly-brain-addled me from the future, is, I'll try to keep things as true as I can, without writing it all down so tediously that you get impatient and start to flip through the pages looking for sex and violence. (The violence will probably be along shortly, but as for the sex, don't expect too much. I'm a married woman now, ha ha, oh, gods.)

Here goes. I woke up yesterday, buried alive.

It wasn't much of a burial, very much a shallow-grave affair, and after a moment of thrashing panic I clawed my way out of a pit of dry sand and sat up. It was like being buried by kids at the beach, only with no ocean, no kids, no cooler full of sodas and sandwiches close at hand. I was in a dim room—except it was actually a *cave*—lit by a flickering fire. The air smelled like burned cinnamon and cloves. My friend Pelham sat cross-legged a few feet away from my grave, and when I sat up gasping and spitting and covered in dust he rose and brought me a porcelain pitcher of water and a cup and a rag. I washed out my mouth, spat, and wiped the dirt off my face.

"What," I said, "in the everlasting *fuck* is going on?"

Pelham tried to smile, but he could never hide his feelings from me, and I could tell he was anxious and unhappy. He'd started out as my employee—sort of an all-purpose personal assistant, valet, and occasional bodyguard—but we'd become closer since my fall from grace (and further fall into another sort of grace). He said, "Ah, perhaps it's best if I let you explain that?"

He fumbled in his waistcoat—he was dressed like an English gentleman from the 1920s despite the heat, too hot even in what should have been the coolness of a cave—and brought out a ragged sheet of paper, much-folded and stained with troubling blots of brown stuff. One of his hands was bandaged, and blood had seeped through the gauze. "What happened to your hand? Did you have a tea-sandwich-cutting accident?"

"You don't remem—no, of course you don't. The ritual required a bit of blood, that's all, nothing I couldn't spare. Here's the message you sent."

I frowned, took the paper, and unfolded it in my lap.

Dear me, it began.

> *If you're reading this, you're alive again. Enjoy it while it lasts. You're probably wondering why you can't remember anything that happened in the past month. I'm sending Pelly this message to set your mind at ease about that, even though I know it probably won't do any good. The Mister and I both agree, it's best if you just don't worry about it. You were in Hell, and you were doing Hell's business, and that's nothing that belongs inside a mortal mind. Letting you remember what happened this past month, when you were a goddess, would probably pop vessels in your mere-mortal brain anyway—the experiences just wouldn't fit in your head,*

any more than the ocean would fit in an eyedropper. Trust me on this. What happens in the underworld... well, you know how it goes.

Yours,
Mrs. Death
(But mostly I call him "Mr. Mason")

Dear me indeed.

I was starving—being in the underworld for a month will do that to a person, apparently, and don't ask me where my mortal body was while I was in goddess-form, because I have no idea how any of that stuff works. Maybe they propped my corpus up in a corner of hell's throne room, or kept it in a coffin, or maybe it was the core of my goddess-self, like the stone in a peach.

Luckily, it turned out I was wrong about the lack of a cooler and soda and sandwiches. Trust Pelham to provide the necessities. I sucked down sugary carbonation and gobbled up turkey and ham and cheese. Between mouthfuls I said, "Where are we?"

Pelham cleared his throat. "Death Valley, California."

I snorted despite myself. "Death Valley. That's cute. You have to admit, Mr. Mason can be cute. And making me crawl out of my grave, that's also funny." I paused. "Except I bet that was *my* idea. To make myself really appreciate the fact that I was coming back to life. That seems like the kind of crap I'd put someone through. What a bitch." I sighed. "I don't like thinking of myself as two different people, Pelham. Mortal-Marla and Goddess-Marla. It's messed up."

"There is certainly some mythic precedent for such duality, Mrs. Mason."

"Oh, I believe it. There's nothing so fucked up that some god or another won't try it. What's the shortest distance between me and a shower? Because I have dirt in places I shouldn't mention in polite company."

"I have an RV parked not far from the cave, but there's the small matter of... the cultists."

I swallowed my mouthful and gave him the side eye. "What cultists?"

"*Your* cultists."

"Since when do I have cultists?" I said it the way I'd say "Since when do I have lice?" or "Since when do I have bedbugs?" or "Since when do I have liver flukes?"

"They began to gather when you first departed this mortal plane, and they have awaited your return." The way Pelham twisted his hands around told me this was the source of his anxiety. "As for how they know about your ascension to goddess-hood—"

"Part-time," I said, automatically.

"—or how they knew where to find *me*... I have no idea. The cultists are tuned in to some particular psychic wavelength that lets them apprehend that portion of the supernatural spectrum that you occupy. They report visions, dreams, whispers in the night, all leading them to me, to *this* place. Some of them seem... damaged. Others seem perfectly ordinary. There is an affable dentist named Ambrose Mason—no relation, but they make much of the coincidence—who has taken on a sort of leadership role, and a personal chef, and a used car salesman who is keen to proselytize on your behalf, though I have restrained him. Such things are to be expected, I suppose, given the circumstances."

"I don't want cultists, Pelly."

"And yet goddesses of death tend to attract them."

Hell. Maybe I should back up.

The Context Problem

YES. I'M A GODDESS OF DEATH. Except right now, I'm not. Technically. Or I am, but my goddess-hood is in remission.

One thing that's harder than I'd expected, now that I'm writing things down, is trying to figure out how much context to provide. Obviously I *know* what I was doing in the underworld, I know how I became the—yech—Bride of Death, as those sexist idiots in the black robes and silver masks call me, so it's not like I need to rehash all that stuff here, for Future Me.

Except what if next time I come out of the underworld I *don't* remember the basics? What if my slate gets wiped cleaner and cleaner every time? The note I sent Pelly—assuming I really sent it—makes it sound like losing my memory of the afterlife is just a sort of cosmic nondisclosure agreement, a "there are some things woman was not meant to know" type deal. But I know better than to trust anything anybody says—especially myself.

The last thing I remember, before waking up in the dirt: I was in a hotel room in Maui, and a door appeared on the wall. Death—my husband—opened it from the inside, and beckoned to me. I stepped into blackness... and that's it.

What if the physical transition to the underworld and back again is causing me trauma? Brain lesions? Mini-strokes? Great spreading white patches in my gray matter? Most people don't go to Hell in the flesh, and it's not like there's a lot of precedent for commuters to the underworld, or part-time goddesses. (There's Persephone, of course. I wish she was still around, assuming she was ever real. I'd love to pick her brain.) Who knows what this whole part-time godhood thing is *doing* to me?

So, just in case this memory loss becomes a bigger problem, have some context, Future Me.

There's magic in the world (obviously, right). Most people are totally oblivious to that fact, but there are some people who can use that magic, occasionally for good, mostly for personal profit. Those people call themselves different things—adepts, witches, magi, whatever—but where I'm from we're called sorcerers. (It's a regional thing, like whether you call carbonated soft drinks "soda" or "pop.") For a while I was the chief sorcerer—sort of a cross between a crime boss and a secret mayor and a superhero—of a city that shall remain nameless. No false modesty here: I was pretty hot shit. I made some major moves in my day. Saved my city from magical destruction a few times, and probably saved the world at least twice. One of those times the world was only in danger because of something I fucked up, but I still count it as a win. Everybody makes mistakes; I *fix* mine. Unfortunately, that didn't stop the other sorcerers in my city from exiling me. They have a zero-tolerance policy for world-threatening screw-ups. I was pissed at the time, when they fired me and kicked me out of the city I love, but in retrospect, I see their point.

One of the biggest bits of magic I ever did involved a symbolic ritual marriage to the god of Death. It was necessary, to save my city, and for a while that "marriage" gave me certain powers beyond those of any mortal—even great sorcerers. The thing was... the marriage was a little less symbolic than I'd realized. And eventually my husband, who is literally the god of Death, started showing up, pestering me to join him in the underworld. Because it turns out being the Bride of Death isn't like being the First Lady; it's more like being the co-president. Mr. Death couldn't do his job right, because he was only *half* a deity, and I'm his other (better, obviously) half. I don't know why Death needs a formerly-human consort—it's probably something to do with the cycle of life-death-rebirth, and fertility, and the land, and seasons, and crap like that. (I'm a city girl. Don't talk to me about crop cycles.) There have been other death gods and other brides before us, because there are seasons even in the underworld, but apparently their terms of office are on the order of centuries and millennia, so I don't expect to retire for a while. Don't ask me what exactly a dualistic death god/dess *does*, either, because I've got no idea: see the previously-mentioned cosmic NDA. Apparently it's important, though. I assume I don't dress up in a latex Grim Reaper outfit and chase people with a spectral scythe, but who the fuck knows for sure?

For a while, I did a pretty good job keeping Death off my back, telling him I'd join him in the underworld eventually, we'd be together for centuries after all, so he could give me a few decades to live my life. Unfortunately, a time came when I got into the nastiest fight of my life, with a crazy chaos witch who was—I hate saying this—better than me, and I couldn't see a way to stop her without killing myself in the process. So I did what was necessary, and I stopped her from wrecking the world, and I *died.*

Now that I think about it, that was probably the *third* time I saved the world. I'm not especially noble, but weighing my life against the continuing coherence of reality wasn't such a tough choice, and I made the ultimate sacrifice, yadda yadda.

I would've asked my husband for help—being married to a fundamental force of the universe should have some perks—except for two things: I have issues when it comes to asking for help at the best of times, and I knew he'd refuse to intervene to save my life, since me being alive was a huge inconvenience for him.

After I died, my husband was there beyond the veil to greet me. He was so happy I was dead, which is not a great quality in a spouse.

I told him I wasn't done with life. If the universe needed me, the universe could damn well wait. My lifespan is a drop in the bucket of eternity, so what's the hurry? He didn't see it the same way, but he knew spending a large chunk of forever with me when I was furious and scorned would make his underworld into entirely the wrong kind of Hell.

In the end we negotiated, because marriage is all about compromise. We settled on the Persephone clause: I would spend six months of the year alive on Earth, and six months in the underworld, ruling by his side. But I'm a better negotiator than Persephone was, because *my* six months don't have to be consecutive. We settled on doing a one-month-on, one-month-off rotation for the first year, with an option to alter the structure in the future. (I got some other useful benefits, too. He wouldn't agree to let me have the powers of a death goddess in my mortal form—apparently human brains can't be trusted with that kind of power—but I scratched a couple of smaller concessions out of him.)

So there. That's why the cultists call me the Bride of Death. Even though I'm more like the co-regent. I'd beat that fact into their heads, but that would require acknowledging their existence. The problem is, when I'm cold and aloof and even mean to them, they *like* it. Death cultists are such masochists. I guess I should get back to talking about them.

The Cult of the Bride of Death

"GET RID OF THEM," I SAID.

Pelly shook his head. "I have tried. But they are religious fanatics, and you are the object of their fanaticism."

I paced around the cave, glaring at the fire raging between us and the outside world. "What's with the blazing flames? It's not hot enough here for you?"

"The ritual required to wake you involves burning certain spices and herbs."

"That explains why it smells like a bakery hit by an arsonist in here." I sighed. "How many cultists are we talking about?"

"Around two dozen. So far."

"Is there, like, a high priest, or—"

Pelham cleared his throat. "That would be me. They desired someone with a personal connection to you. The choices were me, or Rondeau, and—"

"Rondeau as a cult leader is a bad idea," I agreed.

"We discussed it, and determined that he would find it difficult to resist sleeping with certain members of the congregation," Pelham said. "He did not seem to view that as a drawback, but I did."

Rondeau is a good friend from the old days, my longtime right-hand man, from back when I ran a city. He's not a sorcerer, exactly, but he's a psychic, and an oracle generator, and a lecherous hedonist with no impulse control, and pretty rich ever since he sold off some prime real estate he inherited. Wealthy and morally-flexible and telepathic… that's a dangerous combination, but fortunately, he's too lazy to use his powers for much in the way of evil. "Is he around?" I asked.

"At a hotel in Las Vegas. He's watching the head."

I looked at him blankly. "The what?"

Pelham frowned. "You really don't remember *anything*? You didn't send us a letter when you gave us instructions about the head—you sent an emissary to speak to Rondeau, an oracle in the form of a ghostly talking dog's skull. No? Ah. I'd better let Rondeau explain it. We'll head for Vegas after you're cleaned up. But I'm afraid it might be best for you to address the cultists first—"

"There's not a back way out of here?"

Pelham shrugged. "There are rumors of extensive caves beneath Death Valley, but I do not know details, and am not equipped for spelunking at the moment."

I groaned. "I do not require cultists. I don't even like having *friends*. What do they want from me?"

"To touch the hem of your garment. To 'bask in your black aura,' as they say. To receive your 'dark blessing.'"

"Ew. That sounds like a euphemism for vampire handjobs or something."

"Indeed. They are a group of devoted lunatics who will obey you unquestioningly… probably. The 'lunatic' part may at times overrule the 'devoted' part. I can't say for sure. They spend most of their time chanting and burning things and giggling and cutting themselves."

Wonderful. "What should I do with them?"

"Whatever you will, oh dark lady." His lips quirked in a smile. I had to smile back. I remember back when I wasn't even sure Pelham *had* a sense of humor. He'd come a long way. "Perhaps you can send them on a mission to plant trees or feed the hungry—though I shudder to think of *what* they'd feed them."

"Fine, fine. I'll come up with something. After running the city for all those years, it'll be a nice change to have some *obedient* followers." Something nagged at the back of my head. "I'm in a cave in Death Valley. Why do I remember something weird about caves in Death Valley?"

"Are you thinking of the giants?"

I snapped my fingers. "Yeah! Some doctor back in the nineteen-whatevers claimed he found some crazy burial chamber full of giant skeletons and weird artifacts, right? And then scientists supposedly covered up all the evidence, because that's scientists for you, always covering up evidence."

"I discovered those stories when I began to research the site of your resurrection," Pelham said. "Some believe there are vast miles of hidden caves, containing temples and treasure rooms, beneath the valley. The claims of nine-foot-tall skeletons dressed in clothes made from animals unknown to science are… tenuous at best. Certain religious-minded conspiracy theorists believe the giants are nephilim, children of angels and men mentioned in the Bible as 'giants in the earth.'"

"Why do those people get to be 'religious-minded' and *my* followers get called cultists? My people are worshipping an actual goddess, after all, so it seems unfair to—"

Pelham cleared his throat. "They wear black robes, and masks of hammered silver, and the only reason they don't sacrifice animals *constantly* is because I told them you would disapprove of them presuming upon the power of death that is yours alone by right. They speak to the black spaces between the stars and cut abstract designs into their flesh with ceremonial daggers and drink blood. They are *death cultists*."

"Okay. Point taken. I guess I'd better go review the troops."

"Let me get my robe."

I snorted. "Really? You wear a robe? Does it have little glow-in-the-dark skulls on it?"

"I do. And it does not. I find looking the part helps keep the cultists in hand." He spoke in tones of infinite resignation. Pelham picked up a puddle of black cloth and draped it over himself, then covered his head with the voluminous hood. He looked like a background character from every 1970s horror movie about Satan worshippers.

"You lead," I said. "You look the part, at least. I'm greeting my worshippers—what an asshole thing to say, I hate myself—looking like Pigpen from the Charlie Brown comics."

"Emerging from a cave, with the dirt of the grave still clinging to you? They will be transported by ecstasy at the sight of you, Mrs. Mason."

For some reason I'd expected it to be dusk, but it was blazing afternoon, and when I emerged from the cave behind Pelham I blinked in the sun like a cartoon mole. I heard the cultists before I saw them: a whish and swish of moving robes, and voices saying, "There she is!" and "The bride!" and "Bride of Death!"

Once my eyes adjusted I could see them, about twenty-five figures kneeling or in some cases laying flat-out prostrate among the scrub growth on the ground before me. Most of them wore silver masks, simple circles blank except for two eye holes and a slit for a mouth, some surrounded by spikes that might have been meant to signify sun rays or knives or teeth. All those masks made me nervous. Even though I'd been kicked out of my city, I still had an authoritarian ruler's distrust for people who hid their faces.

"My people!" Pelham's voice was big and booming. He must have taken some drama lessons. "The goddess has awakened!" He looked at me. Pointedly.

I stepped forward. The gathering of cultists looked tiny and insignificant out here, in this dry and stony place, against a backdrop of low hills beneath a distressingly sprawling sky. The total absence of skyscrapers unnerved me, too. "So," I said. "You're my worshippers. I thought there'd be more of you."

I meant it as a joke, but they moaned with one voice, like little kids who'd just heard mommy was disappointed in them. I tried to backpedal. "Hey, it's okay, I'm new at the godhood thing, we've got plenty of time to grow..." Shit. What was I even talking about? I didn't want *more* of them. I hadn't asked for these people to come bother me in the desert, so why should I reassure them?

Pelham was wincing, and I knew I was blowing it. Once or twice in my life I've had cause to play the dominatrix, so I tried to draw on that experience. I stood straighter, put a sneer on my face, and said, "So. You think you're fit to worship me?"

"Yes, Bride!" they answered.

"Mmm. I'm not convinced."

"We will pluck out our eyes!" one shouted. "I would die for you!" called another. "Kill! Kill for you!" That last was a particularly large cultist, clutching his fists convulsively.

Way too heavy for me. "Killing and dying aren't necessary. I've got the whole death thing covered. It's kind of my wheelhouse."

"Then how may we serve you?" said one of the cultists.

There were giants in the earth in those days, I thought, and had an inspiration for how to get them out of the way, and keep them from mutilating sheep or going door-to-door handing out pamphlets about my greatness. "I have emerged from the dark caves beneath this dry valley, a place named in my honor." Kind of a stretch, there, but they didn't seem to notice. "In those caves, there are artifacts, and treasures, and the remains of ancient races that lived before the rise of man. You will explore those depths, and map the secret places there, and by toiling in the dark in my service, better come to know my nature."

Pelham cleared his throat. "Because the Bride of Death does not wish you to perish until a time of her choosing, you are to be *very careful*, and procure proper equipment before you descend."

Oh. Right. Sending dentists and car salesmen into a dark pit was maybe not the best plan for their well-being, but give me a break, I'd just crawled out of a hole in the ground. Anyway, it was bad enough being a wife; I had no intention of being a mommy too. "My high priest will give you the details," I said. I could see the RV, tan and white and as long as a yacht, parked beyond the cultists. *Shower.*

I held my head high and tried to step regally, weaving my way through the kneeling and sprawled cultists. They tended more toward averting their eyes and whimpering than trying to tug at my pant legs, so that was all right.

I opened the RV door and slipped inside. The place was tidy, as befitted Pelham, though it was also stiflingly hot. There was a big fruit basket with a card from Rondeau on the table. The thought of fresh fruit made me salivate immediately, despite how crammed I was with sandwiches, but cleanliness called more urgently. I looked at the tiny upright-coffin-sized shower and wondered how long the water tank would hold out. I figured I might run it dry.

I stripped out of my filthy clothes, knowing Pelham would've brought a clean wardrobe for me—hopefully something *other* than a black robe and a silver hockey mask. As I turned on the water, I caught sight of something written on the inside of my left wrist. Small letters, recognizably my printed handwriting, but when I rubbed at the letters, they didn't come off. Not ink, then—a tattoo. I had no memory of getting tattooed, which meant I'd acquired this bit of body art in the underworld.

The tattoo was just two words: "Do Better."

I stared at it for a while before I stepped into the trickle of the shower and closed my eyes.

Do Better.

Aw, gods. That's a hell of a thing to demand of yourself.

City of Gold

Once Pelham had mother-henned the cultists to his satisfaction, he joined me in the RV, sitting at the tiny miniature table across from me. I heard an engine start up nearby, and figured it was some of the cultists heading off to buy caving gear. Did they wear their silver masks in the camping store, I wondered? If they did, would anyone bat an eye? The desert had its fair share of weirdos, and some history of attracting cults. The Manson family had holed up in a ranch in Death Valley while they were hiding from the cops. Maybe the locals just shrugged this kind of stuff off.

I was comfy in a light silk shirt and loose cotton pants I'd found in a suitcase by the bathroom, but I wasn't happy. I sat brooding over the latest note from myself—this one apparently deemed so important by my goddess-self that it became my first and only tattoo. "Did you see this shit?" I waved my arm at Pelham.

He squinted. "Do Better. It seems good enough advice."

"At least it doesn't say 'fail better.' That would be too pretentious for words. How long before we get to Vegas?"

"Three or four hours. The roads in this part of the valley are a bit primitive. There are some charms on the RV to help it negotiate the terrain, but even so, the start will be slow."

"Let's get rolling, then. Life in the country doesn't suit me."

"This isn't the sort of place I'd choose to settle, or even visit, under other circumstances," Pelham agreed. He moved to the driver's seat and began flipping switches and turning knobs. I dropped into the passenger seat—it felt like the captain's chair on a starship—and twiddled with the vents until a blessedly cold blast of air hit me full in the face. I sighed and slumped. "That's better."

Pelham deftly maneuvered the big camper around the tents the cultists had pitched, and a few of the black-robed figures waved at me solemnly as we pulled away. I pretended not to notice them, since that seemed the bitchy, goddess-like thing to do. Watching Pelly happily drive away from all that bad weirdness made my heart a little lighter. "I feel like we should talk, since I haven't seen you in a month," I said. "Except for me it doesn't *feel* like a month, it feels like a rough night's sleep, so you'll have to carry most of the conversation. What's new?"

On the long drive out of the national park and onto the highway, he filled me in on recent events. Pelham had mostly been dealing with pushy cultists. Rondeau had sold his property in Hawaii and invested in a hotel in Las Vegas, which was his new headquarters for debauchery. That made sense to me—Hawaii was beautiful, but Maui had been a little too laid-back and Zen for Rondeau. The flashing lights and ringing bells and vulgar glamours of Vegas were a better fit for his personality.

Pelham had heard from a couple of friendly acquaintances back home in my old city, Hamil and the Bay Witch, though for understandable reasons he'd been vague about what I was doing with my time—no reason to spread around word in the sorcerous community that I'd ascended (or descended, more accurately) to a position of part-time power. Sorcerers were pragmatic opportunists as a rule, and even the ones I considered allies would be tempted to find ways for my new status to help them.

Me, I never liked calling in favors that way, not if I could help it. I know a few beings of unimaginable power, sure. A psychic named Genevieve who can reshape reality at a whim, for one. My old apprentice Bradley, who'd become something as far beyond a mere god as gods are beyond humans, tasked with preserving the integrity of every possible universe. (I didn't envy him that gig, but talk about the student surpassing the master.) Hell, as far as it goes, I sometimes make out with the god of Death. I don't like leaning on people who are stronger than me, though. I didn't get where I am by letting other people save me. The best way to find out what you're really capable of is to get stuck in an impossible situation and fight or think your way out of it. (Then again, last time I got into an impossible situation, I ended up dead. Don't listen to me.)

We reached the outskirts of Las Vegas around dusk. I'd been there once before, in my mercenary days, but I was on a mission then, and hadn't exactly taken in the sights. The place had a dusty, worn-down vibe on the outskirts (I kind of liked that part, honestly), but became increasingly plasticized and flashy as we got closer to the Strip, every establishment trying to outdo the others and grab the attention of the walking cash machines—I mean, tourists.

Pelham pulled into some kind of gated VIP parking garage at a place just off the Strip called the Golden Light Hotel and Casino. Not one of the monster luxury resort hotels, like a city in miniature, but no little shithole motel, either.

"Rondeau's place?" I said.

"Half his," Pelham said. "But the other owner is retired and lives on a ranch in Montana, so it's mostly Rondeau's to run."

"I hope he has good pit bosses. Rondeau's not exactly management material."

"He did run a bar and nightclub for years," Pelham said.

"Sure. But a casino's not the same as a bar."

Pelham chuckled. "That's true. But it turns out, having a psychic running a casino is very cost-effective. *No one* gets away with cheating at the Golden Light." We climbed out of the RV and headed into the building through a side entrance that Pelham unlocked with a key card. I have always had an abiding interest in shortcuts and back ways and secret passages, so I enjoyed passing through the tunnels used by the employees and staff, those gray corridors with cinderblock walls and ugly metal doors. We wound our way through the non-public portions of the Golden Light, passing showgirls with feathers on their heads and blackjack dealers in red vests and hyperkinetic maids and serious-looking gorilla-shaped men in dark suits. Pelham knew and greeted every single person by name, and didn't even once try to introduce me to anybody, bless him.

Eventually we emerged from a door partly concealed behind an immense potted plant and stepped out into the lobby. "Why couldn't we just walk in the front door if this is where we were going?" I said.

"I thought you'd enjoy going the long way," he said. "Seeing potential escape routes." I couldn't argue with that. I wanted to resent the wasted time, but I couldn't, quite. In one sense, time was short: at the end of the month I'd be going back to the underworld for another thirty days of service. But since I didn't actually have any plans for what to *do* with my month on Earth beyond eating and taking showers, there was no harm in taking the scenic route.

The lobby was very golden, though of course none of it was actually gold. The floor was white marble, flecked with gold chips. The chandeliers gleamed a brassy yellow. The reception desk was black and gold. The ashtrays—because in Vegas, you can still smoke most places—were golden pillars so beautiful they could have passed as artifacts in a gaudy emperor's tomb. Pelham led me to the bank of elevators—even the doors were reflective and yellowish—and once inside, he swiped a keycard and hit the "P" button.

I have to say, after crawling up out of the dirt, it was nice to smoothly ascend through a beautiful gleaming tower. Even if the whole place did stink of cigarette smoke and gambler sweat.

The elevator doors opened at the top of the building. The hallway here had only three doors, the pricy penthouse apartments, and Pelham led me to the farthest one on the right. Before he could swipe a card, the door swung inward, and Rondeau was there, arms outstretched. He looked the same as always—tall, lean, grinning like he knows a secret I don't, which is *so* not the case—except that instead of some hideous vintage thrift-shop leisure suit or an Aloha shirt, he was wearing a yellow silk robe with the name of the casino embroidered over the chest.

I consented to the inevitability of a hug—I'm not much of a hugger—and then wriggled free and walked past him into the suite. The place had the kind of impersonal opulence you find in fancy hotel rooms, all overstuffed white furniture and golden lamps and deep pile carpet and floor-to-ceiling windows, with a view of the Strip and—farther out—the desert. There was a cute half-naked guy sprawled on the couch, deeply asleep and faintly snoring, and a table heaped with room service trays that held everything from bunches of grapes to shrimp. Good. I was still hungry.

Rondeau pulled up a chair by the table and dropped into it, while Pelham *tsked* and found a blanket to throw over the unconscious man. "Marla! So how was life in Hell?"

I didn't answer him, at least partly because my mouth was full.

"She doesn't remember anything." Pelham joined us, plucking a single grape and squeezing it mistrustfully between his fingers before popping it in his mouth.

"Ah, right, like the letter from beyond said." Rondeau shook his head. "Here I was, hoping for a few secrets of the afterlife. Not that I ever expect to actually *go* there, but I'm curious."

I glared, then swallowed. "Should we be talking about this stuff with your boy toy over there?"

"Oh, he only speaks Danish. Even if he was awake he wouldn't know what we were saying."

"You had sex with someone and you don't even speak his language?"

Rondeau shrugged. "The other guy speaks Danish *and* English, so there was a translator, it's all aboveboard."

"What other guy?"

Rondeau looked around vaguely. "Huh. He was here a minute ago. I think he went to buy some cocaine."

I rolled my eyes. "Cocaine? Seriously? I thought your psychic powers made you too delicate for drugs. Last I heard you couldn't even drink espresso without getting the shakes."

"Shakes, nightmares, the whole deal." He grimaced. "Not being able to do stimulants is a pretty brutal downside to having insight into the deeper workings of the universe. Nah, the cocaine's not for me, but the boys like to have their fun, and it sure does give them energy. I just told them I'm allergic to the stuff. At least I can still drink champagne. Speaking of, maybe we should crack open a bottle to celebrate your arrival before you head off on your mission, ha, *head off*, did you see what I did there—"

"Rondeau," Pelham said. "She doesn't remember *anything*. She doesn't remember the head."

Rondeau stared at him, then stared at me, then stared back at Pelham again. "Oh. Right. I didn't even think about that. I had all these puns ready for nothing."

I cut off a hunk of brie and smeared it on a hunk of bread. "All right. What's all this about a head?"

Rondeau started to rise. "Oh, I'll show you—"

"Rondeau!" Pelham said. "If you just show her, she might—well—it might not end well. It probably won't even begin well. We have to explain first."

"We have to explain to Marla something *she* told us to do?" Rondeau shook his head. "This amnesia crap is a pain in my ass."

"Yours and mine both, brother," I said.

Rondeau sat back down. "You sent me a vision. The ghostly skull of a dog."

"Pelham mentioned that."

He grunted. "But he didn't tell you what the skull said, huh? Decided to leave that to me."

Pelham sighed. "I thought perhaps you could simply show her the video, Rondeau. That way we could avoid any… miscommunications."

He snapped his fingers. "Yeah, that's right. Then she can just get mad at the TV!"

"You filmed it? I sent you a ghostly apparition from the underworld and you took a video? Is this shit up on YouTube?"

"Well, nobody uses film anymore, but yeah, I recorded the whole thing. Pelham suggested it, so we'd have a record, and wouldn't have to rely on remembering what you said. And, no, no YouTube, though that's a good idea."

"Huh. I thought supernatural stuff didn't tend to show up on film. Video. Whatever."

Rondeau shrugged. "This did. Maybe back in the old days supernatural creatures didn't let themselves be captured on film because of, whatever, magical self-preservation. But these days you can fake *anything* in a video. A high school kid with the right software can make a totally realistic movie about ghosts or demons. So what's the harm? Nobody'd believe it was real magic. If I showed the video I've got here to anybody, they'd assume it was from a low-budget horror movie, the fake-documentary kind. You know how adaptive magic can be."

He fumbled around for a while and then found a remote control buried under some magazines on the table. He pressed a button and the doors of a cabinet across the room slid open, revealing a television screen that had to be at least seventy inches from corner to corner. Pelham, meanwhile, carried a laptop across the room and hooked it up to a cord near the television. "To the couch!" Rondeau cried. He shoved the sleeping man's legs out of the way and flopped down facing the TV.

I took an armchair. "What if the Prince of Denmark there wakes up?"

"I'll tell him I'm producing a low-budget horror movie," Rondeau said. "And he won't understand a word I'm saying on account of *Danish*-ness. Now watch the show. You won't believe the shit you made us do."

Two Heads

I'M GETTING SICK OF WRITING "I I I me me me my my my" so I'm just going to tell you what was on the tape.

Rondeau, wearing a yellow silk robe, dimmed the lights in the suite's gargantuan bathroom, leaving the room to be illuminated by what seemed like a hundred candles—though maybe it was fewer, their light doubled and tripled and quadrupled by the bathroom's many mirrors. Rondeau glanced back through the door, toward the camera. "Are you rolling?"

The cameraman—presumably Pelham—must have given some non-verbal sign of assent, because Rondeau said, "Good. Probably best if you stay outside the room. Oracles can be… twitchy." He knelt down on the furry rug beside the shower (which was easily big enough for three people, or four if they got cozy), his back to the camera. "Okay, Marla, I'm here, at the appointed hour, in a room of fire and mirrors—being queen of the dead sure has brought out a poetic streak in you—and I'm opening up the doors of perception as wide as I can without recourse to chemical accelerants—"

An apparition began with a shimmer in the air, like an orange-red ribbon fluttering above Rondeau's head. Within a moment that flicker had solidified into the skull of a small dog, white bone with flames flickering in its eye sockets and nose holes and inside its toothy jaws.

Rondeau grunted and lifted up his head, seemingly with great effort. "A pale dog burning in the flames of hell. Well, okay. What's the word?"

The dog's voice was full of terrible echoes and clashing asynchronies, but I could understand its words. "My mistress has chosen a mission to fill her mortal days. She will seek to right wrongs and—"

"Help the helpless, right. Walking the Earth, going from place to place and uplifting the downtrodden. Sure. She mentioned something about that before she took the express elevator downstairs." Rondeau's voice was strained, like he was trying to stay casual and conversational in the middle of a firefight. "She's seeking some kind of redem—"

"We do not say the 'R' word," the skull said, managing to make its piping, shrieking voice sound stern. "She merely seeks to keep herself occupied and entertained during those regrettable intervals when she is not serving as co-regent of the underworld."

"Right," Rondeau said. "Me, I'd just watch porn and eat ice cream sundaes, but me and Marla have always had our differences. So what does she need us to do? Your mistress?" (He snickered, and I couldn't blame him. *"Mistress."* Gods.)

"My mis—the queen of the dead requires a guide to the dark places of the world. A seeker after chaos and disorder. A tracker to lead her to evil."

Rondeau's shoulders began to tremble. Summoning up oracles was always hard on him. "Apparently she also requires a ghost dog who says the same thing three times and still fails to provide any information. What is she asking me to *do*?"

"My mistress has withdrawn death from the chaos witch Nicolette. She has decided that a fitting punishment for Nicolette will be to live on, instead, and serve Marla's mortal vessel as a guide."

Rondeau laughed and slapped his hand against the floor. "Oh. Okay. Wow. And you say she's *not* seeking redem—I mean, the 'R' word? She's voluntarily going to travel with the zombified version of her worst surviving enemy. How is that not penance?"

"My mistress has *nothing* to atone for, she is a goddess, she is above—"

"Okay, okay, I get it. Boy, becoming a fundamental power of the universe sure went to her head. I'm still waiting for the call to action, though, Lassie. What. Do. I. *Do*."

"You must retrieve Nicolette's head, and bring it here, to await my mistress's return."

No laughter this time. "Um. When you said Marla was withdrawing death from Nicolette, I figured that meant she was going to be... re-capitated, or whatever. She's still a headless horseman in need of a horse?"

"Our mistress has no need for Nicolette's body, which has at any rate been eaten by creatures of the sea. Why retroactively deny such creatures their sustenance? Nicolette's head alone will be sufficient. It remains at the bottom of the fish pond in Maui, where it was tossed by her murderer. You will retrieve the head and bring it back here."

"Marla, if you're listening, you *so* owe me for this, I just *left* Maui, some of us can't travel instantaneously through magical doors that aren't really there—"

The head flared with a sudden flash of red light, so bright it overwhelmed the camera's ability to compensate, flashing the screen to pure white for a moment. When the light faded, the head was gone.

Rondeau turned his head and looked back over his shoulder, making it appear that he looked directly out of the screen, into my eyes. "Psychopomp and circumstance," he said, and fell over on the rug, beginning to convulse. The camera wavered wildly, fell over on its side, and then went black as Pelham rushed to help Rondeau.

As the TV screen went black, the pretty half-naked Danish guy on the couch said, "*Det er bare forkert*," and then went back to sleep.

"What do you think that meant?" Pelham said.

"Probably 'that's fucked up,'" Rondeau said. "If I had to guess."

"No," I said. "No no no no no. Nicolette? Why would I want Nicolette's head for a traveling companion? For that matter, where the hell am I meant to be traveling?"

"I thought that much was pretty clear," Rondeau said. "You needed a psychic bloodhound, and you're going to walk the earth do-gooding. I was more curious about why you sent a talking dog skull that was also on *fire* to deliver the message. The underworld has some pretty fucked-up pets."

I covered my face with both hands. "You didn't get her head. Tell me you didn't."

"Of course we did," Rondeau said. "The queen of the dead told us to. Via screaming-dog-o-gram. We took my private jet to Maui. Pelham and I put on snorkel gear and got a big fishing net. We went in the middle of the night, so the beach would be deserted. Nothing like mucking around in black water in the dark. Nicolette was awake and aware down there in the mud. By the time we got her out into the dry air she'd nearly bitten through the net. She's been here in Vegas for a week, and she's even bitchier as a talking severed head than she was as a whole person. She keeps demanding to know what she's doing here, but I figured you could tell her yourself."

Nicolette. She'd once been a gadfly, and had grown into something perilously close to an arch-enemy, though I'd never admit that to her in a million years—she didn't deserve the validation of her ambitions. And anyway, she fucked things up more often than bona fide supervillains usually do. "Why. Why would I do this to myself? It's like infesting myself with bedbugs. I don't get it."

"Rondeau's suggestion of penance has the ring of truth," Pelham said. "Perhaps, while in the land of the dead, you began to feel guilty for, ah, certain mistakes you made recently..."

Look, I'm not a monster. Sure, I feel guilt sometimes, and shame. I've done some bad things. Killed some people when there were maybe non-lethal ways to deal with the situation instead. I've often been willing to commit small evils in the service of greater goods. And, yes, I've done a couple of selfish things that threatened the basic integrity of the multiverse, nobody's *perfect*, and anyway, I fixed it all, more or less. But my intentions were always good—or at least neutral—so I refuse to accept that I need to do *penance*. I sure as shit don't need redemption.

But the goddess version of me—who seems more and more to me like an annoying older sister who thinks she knows better—obviously thought otherwise. Was I supposed to believe her, just because she possessed cosmic wisdom my puny human brain couldn't even process? The hell I was.

"Okay," I said. "Fine. At least Nicolette will be as miserable as I am. She hates me more than I hate her. Will she actually do the job, though? Lead me to... wherever the Bride of Death, that asshole, thinks I need to go?"

"You'd have to ask her," Rondeau said. "I try not to talk to Nicolette."

"Likewise," Pelham admitted.

"Where is she?"

"Closet in the second bedroom," Rondeau said. "In an aquarium, because she bites."

"Technically a terrarium, since there's no water in it," Pelham said.

"*Det er bare forkert*," the Danish guy said again, and then ran into the bathroom, where he noisily threw up.

Time Sucks

I HAD THIS CRAZY IDEA that I'd stay up late that second night back on Earth, write it all down, catch up to the present moment, and then find a little time to update this journal or diary or whatever every day or two after that as I went about my business.

But it didn't work out that way. I got busy. So here I am opening up this notebook again days later, and I'm way behind, and there's all kinds of crap brewing. I think I started a supernatural gang war, I've discovered some shit about my new situation that's either disturbing or awesome or both, and I've come to the attention of something or someone called the Eater. I think I need to kill him or her or it, if I can figure out what it *is*, but I'll get to all that.

For the sake of continuity I'm going to marathon through the night here and try to bring everything up to date, right up through stomping that monster to death. And if I make it through the days to come with my brain and writing hand intact, well, I'll write down what happens next after it's done.

So where was I? Right. I was about to see Nicolette again. Yeah. I can see why I stopped writing when I did last time.

Pale Horse

I WENT INTO THE SPARE BEDROOM, took a deep breath, and pulled open the closet door.

Nicolette grinned at me. "Hey, the bitch is back. It's about time. Give us a kiss." Her head—which is all of her, now—rested inside a smallish glass box, the kind of thing where you'd keep a pet turtle. Being dead and submerged in a fish pond for a month hadn't done her much harm in the looks department, actually—I assume "withdrawing death" worked some magical rejuvenation on her. She was still sharp-featured and pale, and still had white-blonde duck-fuzz for hair, her signature dreadlocks having been shorn off during her stay in a mental hospital not that long ago. I wondered if the hair would grow back. She might look a little less stupid then, anyway. She had just enough neck left to act as a pedestal for her skull.

"You look well," I said. "From the neck up, anyway."

"You look like crap in a bucket. And not even a nice bucket. What's the point of this, Marla? Why make me do an Orpheus impression?" She wiggled her tongue at me suggestively. I considered barfing in her terrarium. Maybe I should've. It might have set a better tone.

"I need a guide to help me track down problems I can solve, preferably by doing violent things to bad people." I shrugged. "You get to be my GPS for evil. We're going on the road together. You'll use your connection to chaos to sniff out bad magic, and I'll kick the shit out of whatever we find. What, you had better plans to pass the time?"

"Being dead passed the time just fine. I don't remember what it was like, but it was better than being with you. Why would you recruit your nemesis to be your partner?"

"Less my partner, and more my bloodhound." I leaned against the doorframe. "And anyway, you were never my nemesis. Once or twice you *worked* for people I might have called that, before I kicked their asses into fragments, but you were never more than irritating. Which you still are, so points for consistency."

"If I could shake my head at you right now, I would. Send me back to hell, Marla. I'm not helping you. You're wasting my time."

I sighed. "I'd get rid of you if I could, believe me. This wasn't actually *my* idea, not exactly—it's hard to explain. But suffice it to say, it's not in my power to kill you. Re-kill you. Whatever. I could chuck you in the ocean, but you'd just sink, and be conscious forever while fish nibbled your eyeballs, and that's pretty cruel even by my standards. Wouldn't you rather have some kind of useful occupation?"

Nicolette sighed. I wondered how the sighing and talking worked, considering her total lack of lungs pushing air through her throat. I mean, yes, it worked by magic, obviously, but I wasn't sure how I'd go about creating a spell to produce that effect—which was funny, since I obviously *had* cast such a spell, in my goddess form.

"You want me to find trouble for you?" Nicolette rolled her eyes up, as if trying to gaze at the ceiling. "Huh. I could do that. I can do that *easily*."

I nodded. "You're hoping to lead me into a situation where I'll get killed." Nicolette wasn't aware of my special relationship with Death—not the full extent of it, anyway. She knew I'd kicked the god of death out of my city once, but not that we'd gotten married afterward. It's not like we had an announcement in the newspaper.

"Ding ding ding. You got it in one." She gave me her usual stupid grin, the one like a dog baring its teeth, and I wondered if she'd ever actually been happy. I'd seen her be *merry*, and certainly manic, but actually happy? I thought happiness was probably beyond her.

To be fair, most of the time I think it's beyond me, too.

"Good luck with that." I sighed. "Is there any way we can make this arrangement less horrible than it seems likely to be based on current projections?"

I could tell Nicolette wanted to cock her head. That was one of her birdlike mannerisms, back when she had a body, but it was tricky with no shoulders and precious little neck to work with. "You could feed me regularly. Those assholes who work for you haven't given me anything to eat. That might make me a little less furiously horrible at you. Not enough to make any difference, probably, but it's worth a try. "

I made a face. "I'm not sure I want to watch chewed-up cheeseburgers ooze out of the bottom of your neck stump. Sure you don't want to take up smoking instead, deal with your oral fixation that way? It's not like you've got to worry about cancer."

"Idiot," she said, not at all fondly. "I don't need food. Don't even crave it. Now, more than ever, what I want to eat is *chaos*."

"Ah. Somehow I don't think we're going to have a shortage of chaos if we go traveling together."

"Good. Just increase entropy in my immediate vicinity ten or twelve times a day, let me slurp up some of that disastrous energy, and we'll get along fine. Oh, and get me the fuck out of this fish tank, I feel claustrophobic. I need to feel air on my skin. What little bit I have left."

"Right. Reasonable requests. See? I can be reasonable if you can be. We leave in the morning." I closed the closet doors. She started squawking and shouting immediately, but I ignored her. I figured it was good to start practicing ignoring her right away, so I could hurry up and get good at it.

"Nicolette's as charming as always. Rondeau, I'm going to need a birdcage. Big enough for her head to fit in, small enough for me to carry easily. And some kind of tight-fitting cover so I can hide her from prying eyes, at least until I have a minute to whip up a semi-permanent illusion. Can you manage that?"

He already had a phone in his hand. "That's why Vegas invented twenty-four-hour concierge service, boss. And since I pay the concierge's salary, he's willing to go above and beyond."

"Good. I'm going to need wheels, too, since apparently I'm going on a self-mandated road trip through the dark heart of America—"

"Ah," Pelham said from the couch. "If you'll come downstairs, we have something to show you."

Rondeau hung up the phone. "Birdcage is incoming. Wait up, I don't want to miss the unveiling."

"Unveiling?" They just grinned. "Never mind, I can see you're into suspense." I pointed at Rondeau's bare legs poking out of the bottom of his robe. "Put on pants. I'm not leaving this room with you doing a Hugh Hefner impression."

I know I said "Never mind," but once we started walking down the hallway I badgered them anyway about what they had to show me. They wouldn't give me any details, saying they'd been sworn to secrecy, and when I demanded to know who'd sworn them to secrecy, they said that was a secret, too. I like secrets, but in the same way an obsessive gun collector likes firearms: I want to *own* them, and keep them, and caress them in the night. Other people having secrets I don't either bores or annoys me.

We took the elevator down to some sub-basement, and Rondeau led me through dark corridors to a locked storage room. He undid a padlock and pulled open the doors, doing a full game show-host "ta da!" flourish, to reveal a pale motorcycle with a whole lot of gleaming engine tucked under the seat.

"That," Rondeau said, "is a Vincent White Shadow, from 1949."

"Okay," I said. "So it's an old motorcycle. Did Captain America ride it when he punched out Stalin or something?"

"It is a *rare* old motorcycle," Pelham said. "It is essentially the same model as the Vincent Black Shadow—there were only seventeen thousand of those made, all hand-assembled—but they were, as the name implies, painted entirely black, even the engine. Fewer than twenty of them were produced with the engine in an aluminum finish—hence, White Shadow, instead of Black."

Rondeau patted the handlebars. "These things sell for six figures, easy, when they come up for sale at all. This one's been customized—the seats are white leather, and the rest of it's finished in mother-of-pearl, or *something* like that, anyway. Pretty, whatever it is. I'm no gearhead, and I'd rather straddle a man than a machine anytime, but this thing even gets my motor running."

"That is excessive information," I said.

"It's a gift from your husband," Pelham said. "Or so the spectral face in the mirror told me, the day it was delivered."

I nodded. "Huh. Sweet of him, I guess, though I've never been all that heavily into bikes. I prefer the bus."

"She doesn't get the joke," Rondeau said.

"To be fair, it isn't a very good joke," Pelham said.

"Oh, I get the joke." I climbed onto the bike, settling onto the soft seat and gripping the handlebars. "I'm an avatar of death. In the immortal parlance of Bon Jovi, motorcycles are steel horses. So I get to ride a pale horse. 'White Shadow,' though, really. It sounds like the name of a racist ninja."

Pelham took a step back, as if worried I'd crank it up and run them down. "Do you know how to drive one of these?"

"Please," I said. "My ethnic heritage is white trash. Of course I can ride a motorcycle. I just haven't in a while. I'm good at lots of things I don't give a crap about."

"They're very dangerous. Motorcycle accidents result in a disproportionate number of fatalities." Pelham clearly thought he was giving me new and vital information.

I laughed. "My new job description is traveling the world *murdering monsters*. And you think riding a bike is dangerous?"

"It's an *additional* danger," he said primly.

"I'm not too worried about dying in a motorcycle accident. I mean, if I do, it would suck, but I don't think the death would be all that permanent—I know a guy who can fix stuff like that." It did make me wonder what would happen, though, if some monster caught me by surprise and tore my head off. Would I become a head in a jar like Nicolette? Would Pelly have to sew my head on my shoulders, Herbert West, Re-Animator style? Or would I just get whisked off the underworld, get a talking-to from my dear husband about taking better care of my mortal carcass, and then catch an elevator back to the surface? Might be good to figure that out.

I ran my finger along the pearlescent finish on the gas tank. I'm not made of stone. I can appreciate something beautiful and well-made, even if it's not necessarily my favorite kind of thing, and the bike was a beauty. "This is all right. I'd rather have my old Bentley back, though."

"The Bentley was a fine machine," Pelham said. Back when I was chief sorcerer of my own city, I'd had a company car, and Pelham had been my chauffeur. I'd never much liked driving under any circumstances, and hadn't spent much time on motorcycles, honestly. I remember feeling kind of unprotected whenever I got on a motorcycle—like an exposed nerve. But America was a big place. I couldn't exactly walk across it. Or, I could, but I wouldn't get too far, and apex predator monsters tend to be sort of spread-out.

Still. A motorcycle. Why? All for the "pale horse" pun? My Dead Husband has a weird sense of humor, but in his defense, he isn't human. "I understand my DH wanted to get me something rare and fancy, because romance, but he couldn't have sprung for, I don't know, a Rolls Royce Wraith? A Tucker Talisman? And maybe a golem driver who doesn't mind working weird hours?"

"Isn't your new gig riding into little towns and ridding them of hidden evil?" Rondeau said. "It's hard to imagine an avenging angel-type rolling up in a vintage luxury car."

I leaned forward and put my forehead against the handlebars. "What am I doing? Walking the Earth, doing good? Is that really my plan? What the fuck was I thinking? I mean that question seriously, because I don't *remember*."

"To be fair, you tried being idle and sitting on a beach for a while, and you were miserable," Rondeau said. "Politics isn't really good for you, either—I mean, you got exiled from your last city-running gig, so you probably aren't going to get hired to run another one. I guess you could assassinate the head of New York or something and seize power, but you're not usually that bloodthirsty."

"I'm plenty bloodthirsty," I muttered. "If they made blood-flavored Gatorade I'd be all over that shit."

He ignored me. "You weren't much good at being an occult detective, either." I glared at him. He shrugged. "What? You've got a lot of strengths, nobody admires you like I do, but Sherlock Holmes meets Carnacki the Ghost-Finder? Not your thing. You could be a mercenary again, you were the best ever at that kind of stuff, but you don't need the money—even if your best friend wasn't rich and didn't owe you his life, you're a sorcerer, you can always get money. Hell, you're a *goddess*, you can just tap your cultists for a loan. Plus, you hate working for other people. This way, you get to make your own hours, beat up monsters, leave any given town whenever you're bored, answer to no one, be your own boss… It's not how I'd choose to spend *my* six months on Earth every year, that would involve more cocktails and massage oil, but it seems like a good fit for you. Anyway, nobody's forcing you. If you find a nice ostrich farm or something on your travels you want to run, you can always settle down."

I lifted my head from the handlebars. "Ha. Sure. Well, whatever. It'll pass the time, anyway. You have my weapons?"

"Your dagger is safe, yes."

"And the axe?"

Pelham blinked. "The one that belonged to Nicolette?"

"It never belonged to her, except insofar as she looted it from a dead wizard's vault, but yeah, that's the one, it's got a blade that shines like a shard of moonlight."

"Yes, we have it," Pelham said. "Locked up, under heavy wards. We aren't even sure what it does, exactly."

I shrugged. "It's sharp enough to cut off somebody's arm, I know that much. As for its magical possibilities, maybe Nicolette knows. It's a powerful weapon, anyway, and I could use as many of those as I can lay my hands on. I don't have a lot of resources anymore."

Rondeau whistled. "Riding a motorcycle, with a dagger in one hand and a silver hatchet in the other? That's an image. Modern valkyrie stuff. You're going to make me hetero if you're not careful."

"If she had a hatchet in one hand and a dagger in the other, how would she *steer*?" Pelham objected.

"With her boobs," Rondeau said. "Or knees, I don't know, she's resourceful. He looked me up and down. You just need a trench coat. Cowboy boots, of course. Definitely a hat—"

"If I had a hat, I'd make you eat it," I said. "Be happy I don't have a hat."

"Perhaps we could get Nicolette a hat," Pelham said. "Since it's really the only accessory she's capable of wearing at the moment."

And then we all giggled. It was the first really nice moment I'd had since waking up.

Godsdamnit

Looking back over the pages I've written so far, this is turning into more than a "just the facts" primer for brain-damaged future versions of myself. I'm afraid it might be turning into *therapy* or something.

Turns out it's easier to figure out what I think about things when I write them down. It's pretty late in my life to realize something like that. I've been through some heavy shit in the past couple years—hell, even just since I woke up—and writing is clearing my head a little, helping me turn disorderly things into neat lines. It's probably a false sense of order, but I'll take it.

I know, I'm just as embarrassed as you are. At least I'm not actually talking to a psychiatrist. So if you're impatient with all the digressions and stuff, Future Me, I hope it makes you feel better to know that I'm impatient, too. I didn't mean to go on like this. But this is the way it's coming out, so I'm going to move out of the way and let the words roll on.

At least sitting here and writing keeps me from having to make small talk with Nicolette. She's not the most fun person in the world to share a shitty motel room with.

Gifts

After I checked out the motorcycle and Pelham and Rondeau trundled off to bed, I didn't want to sleep—in a sense I'd been sleeping *all month*—and as you know I stayed up for a while writing. I had this idea of waiting up to see the sun rise, but my body had other plans.

While there are many magics that can keep you going without rest indefinitely, they all have a wicked backlash eventually, and I figured I should save such measures for when I really needed them, in one of the life-or-death situations I was likely to encounter soon. I bunked down in the spare bedroom, half-expecting Nicolette to keep me awake all night just to be bitchy, but she kept remarkably quiet, apart from crowing like a cartoon rooster around seven a.m.

So my second day on Earth I showered—wake up buried in dirt and you'll find a new appreciation for showers—and went out into the living area of the suite, where Pelham was laying out a big room-service breakfast, full of bagels and lox and scrambled eggs and rashers of bacon and hash browns and waffles; I was surprised he didn't have a chef manning a portable omelet station. I grunted a good morning and ate, sticking with black coffee and a couple of doughnuts, because I am a simple woman, and anyway I was basically still full from the previous night's gorge-fest.

"You'll stay a few days and rest up, won't you?" Pelham asked.

I shook my head. "I've only got a month, and if I'm going to 'do better,' or whatever, I'd better get started soon. I'm planning to light out as I finish my coffee, basically. Maybe even kill a couple of monsters before they wake up and get ready for work." I had no idea how likely that was, really. In my city, when I was in charge, most of the monsters knew to behave themselves, or at least make themselves useful. But out here, in the Southwest—or the heartland or wherever I was going to end up—with all those empty spaces and little towns? Who knew what I'd find?

(I mean, now I kind of know. And it was worse than I'd expected.)

"Would you like me to accompany you? I could follow in the RV. I hate to think of you out on the road, alone with just Nicolette for company..."

I patted his hand. "I appreciate the concern, Pelly. But you'd be better off making sure the cultists leave me alone—I don't want to wake up one morning and find them camped in the parking lot outside the Motel 6, having backtraced my aura or something. Anyway, I'm going out to be a freelance monster hunter, and if you came along, I'd just worry about you." I held up my hands before he could object. "I know you can hold your own in a monster fight, I've seen it, that's not what I'm saying—I just don't have that many friends left, and I'd like to keep you out of harm's way. That's not a concern I have when it comes to the disembodied head of Nicolette. She can have all the harm the world's got in store for her. But you, stick to High Priesting. Consider that a goddess-given edict from on high. Or down low."

He scowled. "Technically you are not a goddess just now, but I will accede to your wishes. I ask only that you call us, occasionally, to let us know how you're faring, and let us know if you need any assistance."

"I'll see what I can do." To my astonishment, Rondeau came into the suite carrying a couple of shopping bags. "This can't be real. Rondeau. It's not even noon. How are you awake?"

"You make the mistake of assuming I went to sleep." He dropped the bags on the table and said, "I come bearing gifts."

"Weaponry?"

"Nah, I know better than to try and buy weapons for a woman. You always get the wrong thing. I took the safer route and bought you clothes." He drew a long sand-colored coat from the bag, and I wrinkled my nose.

"That's a little bit trench coat mafia, don't you think?"

Rondeau sniffed. "It's not like it's *black*. And, look, I know you used to go around wearing a cloak, and that was fine when you were chief sorcerer—when you're powerful that kind of fashion choice is just a fascinating eccentricity—but you'd get a lot of weird looks tooling around the highway with a hooded cape. Besides, a cloak would get stuck in the wheels of the motorcycle and strangle you to death, probably. Wearing a duster is way more normal, and you're so weird, disguising you as normal is a good idea. Besides, just for you, this coat has got about a zillion pockets on the inside, big enough to hold your knives and vials and charms and whatever. It'll provide some protection when you dump the bike and go sliding along the asphalt, too."

I rose and took the coat. It was pretty nice—pale leather, bronze buttons, slit up the back to hip-level to make riding easier, and with little hidden leg straps so you could secure the back flaps to your body when riding a horse (or motorcycle, in my case).

"It's made of buffalo leather," Rondeau said. "Because, who the fuck knows, we're in the West."

I tried on the coat, and it felt good—gave me the same armored-up feeling I used to get from wearing an enchanted cloak. "All right. This is an acceptable gift."

"Check these out." He lifted a pair of deep red cowboy boots from the bag, and I snorted.

"No way. Not my style. My old stomping boots are fine."

He shook his head. "I had a cobbler I know make these. Yes, I'm the kind of guy who knows cobblers now. This is some bespoke artisanal footwear here. You just… try them on. Seriously."

I've never been more dubious, but I slid my foot into one of the boots… and couldn't help letting out an involuntary sigh. They were the most comfortable things I'd ever had on my feet—warm and soft and solid all at once. Rondeau handed me the other boot. "Check out the detail work."

At first glance the leather was just stitched in swirling patterns… but when I looked closer I saw the shapes of scythes, skulls, wings, and swords embroidered in the leather. "Ha. They're custom, I'll give them that."

"I figure you can enchant them so you can kick your way through cinderblock walls, like you did with your steel-toed boots back in the day."

"All right. I'm officially touched. I look forward to scraping monster brains off the heels."

Pelham slipped away while I was trying on the boots, and returned carrying leather motorcycle saddlebags that contained my truly potent tools: my old dagger of office, a blade capable of cutting through just about anything (including ghosts and astral tethers), and the silver-bladed hatchet that Nicolette carried around back when she had arms. I had no idea what the little axe's powers were, particularly, but it had to be good for *something*. If nothing else, I could use it to chop firewood if I got stuck sleeping under the stars.

"This is great, Pelham. Both of you. I appreciate it." I'm not always about thanking people for things. Mostly because I don't like to admit that I ever need help from anybody with anything at all—but I was trying to do better. "Guess I'd better load up Nicolette and get on the road."

"There's a cell phone in the saddlebag too," Pelham said. "With two numbers programmed in it: mine and Rondeau's. If you need *anything*, call."

"You know me," I said. "I never hesitate to call for help."

Talk to the Head

"**I THOUGHT YOU'D FIGHT ME MORE** on this whole cage thing." I settled Nicolette into the old-fashioned bell-shaped birdcage Rondeau had acquired for me. The bars were bronzey-golden, and it looked more like a theater prop than something you'd actually use to house a tiny feathered dinosaur-descendant. Nicolette didn't even try to bite me as I lowered the cage down over her head and secured it to the base.

"Who doesn't want to live in a gilded cage?" She frowned as I flipped the latches that attached the base to the bars. "Anyway, I gave it some thought last night, and I've decided this is better than the alternative."

"Which is?"

"Being *dead*. You do know every other enemy you've ever had a beef with is worm food now, right?"

"Not true," I said. "Some of them just decided it wasn't worth the trouble of trying to fight me anymore."

"Then they were never really your enemies. They were just people you had disagreements with. That's just politics. All the real implacable hardcore foes you've faced, they've been shuffled right off this mortal coil, whether by your hand directly or as a roundabout consequence of something you did. I was pissed to wake up all disembodied in that fish pond, but I don't really want to join the roll call of the damned, so for now I'm playing nice. This is a lousy kind of quasi-life, but at least I can still have some fun—eat some chaos, annoy the shit out of you, watch monsters try to unspool your intestines."

I lifted the cage. An adult human head weighs ten or twelve pounds—don't ask me why I know that—and the cage added a bit more. Hardly an impossible weight, but I'd get tired lugging her around all the time. Maybe I could rig up some kind of backpack. "So you're going to be my loyal guide and just hope passively for entertaining misfortunes to befall me? Right. I don't trust you."

"That's sensible."

"I *can't* trust you, Nicolette. My old teacher Artie Mann, back when I was an apprentice, he warned me about entropic witches—warned me not to *become* one. He said you can't trust that kind of chaos witch to do anything, not even to act in her own best interests. When a chaos witch has a plan, and it works out exactly the way she wants, she gets *weaker*. When a chaos witch's plans fall apart, she gets *stronger*. He told me that kind of mindset makes practitioners of entropic magic a little bit crazy. I can't say I've seen anything to make me believe otherwise. That's why I never studied the kind of magic you do—I value the integrity of my mind too much."

"Also you're a control freak," Nicolette said. "And you're predictable. And a fascist. So that works against you."

I shook her head. Like, picked up the cage and shook it until she fell over and her face got smushed up against the bars. That shut her up. For about a second.

"How'd you get the juice to bring me back to life anyway?" she demanded, after I put the cage back down.

"I told you, I didn't bring you back. Someone did it for me, so you could help me with my work. You might say I'm on a mission from god."

"Okay, Elwood. Whatever you say."

I was kind of annoyed that she'd caught the *Blues Brothers* reference. I don't like to think of us having similar tastes in anything. I snorted anyway. "Please. *You're* Elwood. I'm Joliet Jake."

"Bullshit."

"Elwood was practically a sidekick. Joliet Jake was the heart of the film."

Nicolette rolled her eyes. It was one of the only ways she had to express disdain, and I suspected she was going to be using it a lot. "Doesn't matter. I'm still Jake. You don't think John Belushi was an avatar of *chaos*?"

I didn't answer for a moment. Then I said, "Touché."

Road Food

I SHOOK OFF PELHAM AND RONDEAU before they could turn everything into some kind of heinous long-goodbye type situation with hugs and parting advice and declarations of affection. I got into the freight elevator with Nicolette's birdcage dangling from my hand—with a black cloth cover on top, of course, and strict instructions to only make noises that could be attributable to a bird—and a leather messenger bag slung across my back.

In the elevator, Nicolette said, "Squawk. Polly wants a shotgun."

"Shush."

The garage was empty that morning—I guess Vegas isn't really a town for early risers, except for the slot-machine zombies, who would already be at their stations. My boots clicked pleasantly on the concrete as I walked toward my bike, which was all gassed-up and waiting courtesy of Rondeau's minions.

I settled Nicolette's birdcage onto the rear of the bike, lifting the cloth a bit and lashing the cage into place with bungee cords threaded through the bars and hooked to solid bits of motorcycle. "Don't I get a helmet?" she said. "I need to protect my head. It's all I've got. Squawk."

"The cage is enchanted." I tapped the bars with the wedding ring on my left hand, making them *clink*. "You're safe as long as you stay in there. Besides, the motorcycle is so wrapped in magics I doubt I could crash it if I wanted to." I didn't know exactly what kind of charms Death had put on my pale horse, but even my rudimentary psychic senses tingled in its presence, so I knew it was serious stuff.

I packed most of the contents of my bag—a few minor charms, along with ordinary odds and ends and spare clothes—into the motorcycle's saddlebags. After some thought, I put the silver hatchet in one of the bags, too. Since I wasn't sure what the weapon did, exactly, I didn't want to keep it in my coat, so close to my body. For all I know it had the power to give you bone cancer. I wasn't worried about dying, particularly, but I'm no big fan of pain. I shoved my dagger down in a boot sheath, tied the flapping ends of my coat around my ankles, and put on my helmet, with the smoked visor flipped up, for the moment. I was ready to go.

"So. You're my monster-detector, Nicolette. Where are we going?"

Nicolette, muffled by the dropcloth, said, "Out of the city would be good. I sniff out disorder and disaster and chaos, and in case you hadn't noticed, we're in *Vegas*. I'm like a bloodhound in an aromatherapy factory right now. There's nothing *but* random chance and bad decisions and malice aforethought in the air, plus lots of gambling and shifting probabilities muddying up the signal, so I can't find anything useful. Get us out on the open road and I'll try to find something for you to murder for no good reason."

I settled myself on the motorcycle, taking a moment to sit and hold the handlebars and get a sense of my balance. Riding a motorcycle's not exactly like riding a bicycle, and I hadn't been on one in ages. I turned the key and twisted the throttle, easing the bike forward, and the rumbling purr of the engine felt good. Powerful.

I rode slowly through the garage, spiraling up the ramp and out into the glaring sunlight of a desert morning, then proceeded down a side street, away from the casino, heading for the highway. I was thinking south, toward Arizona, for no particular reason at all, except I'd never been there, and Death had once told me the Painted Desert was beautiful.

Riding the motorcycle was… actually pleasant. Maybe that old exposed-nerve feeling had more to do with my state of mind at the time than the actual experience. I've never much liked driving cars. I always feel isolated, like I'm gliding around in a box, insulated from the wider world. But riding a motorcycle is so much more like being *in* the world. You can feel the wind, the motion, the friction of tires on asphalt, and the bike eventually starts to feel like an extension of yourself, as opposed to an unwieldy machine.

My boots were comfy, my coat was warm, the wind whipping by was loud enough that I couldn't have heard Nicolette talk even if she'd screamed, my belly was full, my bladder was empty, and all felt right with the world. I began to relax, feeling tensions I'd hadn't even realized I was holding melt away.

Freedom. The open road. Had I ever really experienced that? Oh, I'd been homeless on the road before, as a teen runaway, but that was different.

Now I had power. I had resources. I wasn't *afraid*. I was going looking for trouble, not trying to avoid it. There were no meetings to take, no allies to reassure, no enemies to outmaneuver. No politics, no assassins—ha, I'd *been* assassinated, I didn't have to worry about that anymore—no sacred place that I had to protect.

I had no responsibilities, except to myself. A month—well, thirty days, now—of walking the Earth, trying to do good. Or, at least, to do better.

Soon I left the city behind. It doesn't take long to go from the outskirts of Vegas to big empty. I realized later that I could have taken a slightly alternate route and gone along the shoreline of Las Vegas Bay, and gotten a last glimpse of big—well, biggish—water before delving deep into the land of dust and sand, but I didn't think about it at the time. I took Highway 93 southeast for a while, and soon there was nothing on either side but dusty hills and rocks and power line pylons. Big open spaces, and nature in general, have a tendency to unnerve me. I consider myself a creature of urban spaces, and I find the press of people and buildings more comforting than claustrophobic. The American Southwest is a big place, and apart from flying over it a few times, it's not a landscape where I've spent much time. I'd looked over some maps, though, and was thinking maybe I'd cut over toward Texas, pick up I-40 East, head toward the more tightly-packed population centers of the East Coast, see what kind of trouble I could find—

Somebody was screaming behind me, so I pulled the bike over to the shoulder and turned off the rumbling engine. "What are you yelling about, Nicolette?"

"How else am I supposed to get your attention? You could at least stick a bluetooth headset on me so I could *call* you."

I grunted. She had a point. It wasn't like I was in a camper van with her head on the passenger seat, where we could chat. It's hard to hear anything but the wind in your ears and the hum of the road on a motorcycle at highway speed. "I'm new to this traveling-avenger thing. I didn't think about it. I'll come up with something when we stop for the night, to let us communicate."

"None of that telepathy shit," came the muffled voice beneath the cage cover. "I don't want you in my head, and I don't want to be in *yours*."

"Likewise. I'd rather stick my head in a septic tank than take a dip in your stream of consciousness. Now, what were you screaming about?"

"I got a sense of something. A twinge of a twinge. There's a lot of big empty up here, but there's a thread of chaos twisting not far ahead. Look for human habitation, and I bet we'll find something."

I pulled out the smartphone Pelham had given me and fiddled with it for a moment, looking for local landmarks, such as they were. "There's a truck stop a few miles ahead, with a diner."

"I could use a bite to eat."

"You don't eat food."

"No, but I eat chaos, and there's definitely a scent in the air."

"All right, then. Can you be a little more specific about what I'm getting into?"

Nicolette tittered. "Afraid it'll be something you can't handle? You've got a dagger forged in Hell—that's the rumor, anyway—and an axe with a blade made of some kind of supernatural moonlight, and thirty years of experience as a mercenary sorcerer—"

"Thirty years? How old do you think I am? It's only sixteen or seventeen years since I became an apprentice!"

"—so I imagine you can cope. And if you can't, lady, you're in the wrong business."

I started the bike again, mostly because I wanted to drown Nicolette out if she kept talking. The motorcycle ate miles as quickly as Rondeau downs drinks, so before long I signaled and swooped down a freeway exit and pulled into an oasis of concrete, diesel fumes, and big rigs. I parked my bike in one of the spaces away from the gas pumps, next to the diner itself, where I could see my ride from the windows. Not that anyone would have much luck if they tried to steal it or rifle through my saddlebags—I'd made sure the bike was enchanted with some nice anti-theft spells in addition to whatever Death had done to it—but because it was pretty much the only thing I had in the world, and I wanted to keep my eye on it.

I stood up from the bike and stretched, my spine crackling. The seat was comfy, but I wasn't used to sitting for hours at a time, and my ass was numb. I started toward the diner door.

"You're leaving me here?" Nicolette said.

I sighed. "I was. But okay. You can come, if you behave. Not a word out of you in there."

"Squawk. Polly wants a patty melt."

I unhooked the bungees that held the cage to the bike. I really needed to rig up some kind of quick-release attachment, or maybe just a sticky spell I could turn on and off, or something with magnets. The handle of the birdcage protruded through a slit in the cloth, so I picked up the cage that way and carried it into the diner with me. I chose a booth along the windows and set the birdcage down on one side before sitting on the other, where I had a view of the door. I scanned the room, but didn't see much to worry me—certainly no obvious impending vectors for chaos. Just a few truckers at the counter, putting away slabs of pie and buckets of coffee, and a family, clearly on a road trip, with a mom and dad looking exhausted, and two disturbingly well-behaved children, one little girl and one little boy, aged somewhere between four and eight (I'm not great with kids), noshing on burgers and fries.

A waitress of the take-no-shit veteran variety came over and gave my covered birdcage the eye. "Is there a bird in there?"

"No," I said truthfully.

"Because birds aren't allowed. No pets, except service animals. Health regulations."

"No bird, I promise." I wondered what health regulations had to say about bringing severed human heads into a restaurant. Probably didn't come up often, and likely covered by other existing laws.

The waitress cocked her head at me. "You travel around with an empty birdcage?"

I wanted to say "I keep my guns and drugs in there," but instead I just nodded. "Some people like briefcases. Not me. I'm an eccentric. But I tip well."

She rolled her eyes and pointed her pencil at me. "If I hear any chirps or squawks, you'll have to take it outside, all right?"

"Understood."

"Water? Coffee?"

"Yes," I said.

The waitress slid a menu across the table and walked back around the counter. I flipped the menu open, and my stomach grumbled. Nicolette wanted to come here to eat chaos, but I could go for a plate of eggs and sausage.

The little boy in the booth next to mine was standing on the seat, staring at the birdcage. "Did you know parrots can live for a hundred years?"

"In captivity, maybe," I said. "If you call that living."

"Sea turtles can live even longer," the boy said. He had ketchup on his face. Cute? Disgusting? Who am I to judge?

I wondered how we'd gotten onto the topic of sea turtles. I figured I'd roll with it, though. I'd been off the surface of the earth for a month, so I could use some conversational practice. "I used to live in Hawaii. I saw lots of sea turtles there." I even met a turtle god, but I figured maybe I shouldn't mention that.

"Leave the lady alone," the mom said, and tugged the child back down to his seat.

So much for human interaction. Who needs it? My mission was inhuman interaction anyway.

The waitress came back with the drinks and took my order, and I warmed my hands on the porcelain coffee mug. I didn't get any sense of impending chaos, but then, if I had a good sense for that kind of thing, I could have avoided a lot of problems in the past, and I wouldn't have needed Nicolette.

A few minutes later, the waitress brought over a big plate of fluffy yellow scrambled eggs and crisped-black sausage and a little plate of light brown toast. I took a couple of bites as she refilled my coffee mug, right to the brim, with scalding rocket fuel. All good stuff, but I couldn't enjoy my meal, because I couldn't relax. Was anything even going to happen here? Had Nicolette actually sensed impending chaos, or was she just messing with me, asserting her independence, wasting my time?

I slid the wedding ring off my finger. I'd given Death a plain old ordinary gold band, but his ring for me was a little fancier. I held it up to my eyeball and looked through the hole, peering around the diner. Doing so doubtless made me look like a weirdo, but I was already the chick in a leather coat who'd brought a birdcage into a diner, so that ship had pretty much sailed.

Peering through the ring can give me a glimpse of the future. The immediate future of the immediate area and, if I focused on an individual, a deeper look at their *personal* future. Unfortunately—or maybe fortunately—the future isn't fixed, so the ring just shows me the most *likely* futures, and the view is more-or-less blurry depending on just how likely, or unlikely, a given future is. The layout of the diner itself didn't change much, which meant that, shockingly, it would still be standing for the next ten minutes or half-hour. I caught a glimpse of flashing lights outside, implying police cars or fire trucks in the future. Okay, that was something. I focused on a couple of the truckers, and saw nothing remarkable—them, driving trucks, eating beef jerky, watching TV in motels. The little boy popped up and stared at me again, so I gave him a long look, and was surprised—mostly I saw haze and blurs and school corridors and beaches, but I did get a brief, sharp image of him much older, probably in his twenties, in a jungle, his face and bare chest smeared with blood, his hair decorated with bright feathers, a halo of bluish magic crackling around his upraised hands. The kid had at least a chance of stumbling into the world of magic and becoming a sorcerer at some point. The future holds all kinds of weird possibilities.

His mom tugged him down again, so I swept my vision toward the approaching waitress—

—and saw her crumpled on the diner floor, a gash in her throat and a wound across her face, blood everywhere.

There we go.

The bell over the door rang as someone entered, and I slid the ring back onto my finger and watched as a twitchy, scruffy-looking guy in his thirties shuffled in. He wore a dirty red flannel jacket, and he kept wiping his nose with his crusty sleeves. The guy was on some kind of drugs, obviously, and from the look of him, I didn't want any of what he was having. "Lucille!" he shouted. "Lucille, I need to talk to you!"

The waitress who'd served me crossed her arms and scowled. "Lucy ain't here, Gary. Why don't you just go on home and wait for her."

"She worked today!" he shouted. "She works every Friday! Don't you lie to me, Arlene!"

"It's Thursday," Arlene said. "You look like a mess. Maybe you shouldn't be driving. You have a seat and let me get you a cup of coffee—"

"I don't need coffee, I need *Lucille*, it's payday and she needs to sign her check over so I can get my medicine, I can't wait no more—"

"It's not payday until tomorrow, anyway, and you can't be shouting like that, you'll scare the customers—"

"*Don't you tell me what to do!*" he shouted—screamed, really. "Lucille, get out here right *now*!"

"She told you Lucille ain't here, son," one of the truckers said. He was a big guy, probably ran two-eighty and only some of it fat, and he put his hand on Gary's arm, not even in a threatening way, more conciliatory.

Gary came out with a hunting knife and slashed at the trucker, who fell back, shouting. He slid off his stool, blood welling through a long tear in his sleeve. Gary had slashed his bicep, which probably hurt like hell, but he wasn't likely to die from it.

Gary started for the counter, knife raised high. Arlene was pretty clearly his next target. He around the counter, and Arlene surprised me by vaulting right over the counter before he could get to her, knocking salt shakers and coffee cups out of the way in the process. Gary wasn't impressed by her athletic prowess. He just changed course, came back around to our side of the counter, and lifted his blade. Arlene moved past me, toward the booth where the family was sitting, but there was nowhere for her to go after that, and Gary was advancing. Lucky for Arlene, he'd have to pass by me to get to her.

I've been trained by some of the best knife fighters in the world. I know about the advantages of the reverse grip, hammer grip, icepick grip, and fencer's grip. I know the uses of biomechanical cutting—slashing at your opponent's muscles to disable them—and I've been in my share of actual trying-to-kill-somebody fights. Plus, I've got a dagger so sharp it can cut through ghosts.

But I didn't pull my knife and tussle with Gary. The thing about knife fighting is, it's ugly. The only time you get to use fancy moves is in a formal duel or a demonstration bout between masters. If you want to win a knife fight in the real world, the best way is to strike before the other person even knows they're *in* a knife fight—just rush them and stab them as hard and fast as you can, prison-yard style. A surprise blitz attack is almost impossible for any knife fighter to defend against, no matter how well trained they are. Going at Gary, when he was jacked up on who knew what exciting substances and clearly had no particular concern for long-term consequences or self-preservation, would be a good way for me to get cut, and getting cut hurts.

So instead I picked up my full coffee cup, took aim, and threw it at Gary's head as hard as I could. The side of the heavy porcelain mug struck him right in the middle of the forehead, staggering him and splashing hot coffee across his face and scalp, and all down his front as the cup tumbled. He didn't fall down, but he wobbled, and the arm holding the knife hung loose at his side.

I knew he was seeing stars, but depending on what he was on, he wouldn't be staggered for long. I slid out of the booth, the plate in my hand, and took a few quick steps toward him. His eyes finally focused on me, but before he could bring the knife up, I smashed him across the face with my plate, getting scrambled eggs in his eyes. Too bad for him I like my eggs with lots of hot sauce.

He screamed and fell backwards, and when I saw my chance, I stomped on his wrist. I hadn't had the chance to work any nasty inertial charms into the boots yet, but a heel with all my weight on top of it was sufficient to make his hand fall open, releasing the knife. I kicked the blade away, knelt down, flipped him over on his belly, and jerked his hands up behind his back. I had zip ties in one of my coat pockets—among other useful things—so I bound his wrists, then grabbed the tie and used it as a handle to drag him across the floor. I don't *think* I dislocated his shoulders, but he hollered like I did. I left him in the entryway, shoved off to one side by the bubble gum machine and not blocking the door, on account of fire safety, and also because I knew I'd better be leaving soon.

Gary groaned, and I didn't even kick him, because I'm trying to Do Better.

I stood up, and the whole diner was staring at me. The cook, an old fat guy, had finally emerged, and was pressing a wad of paper towels against the trucker's bleeding bicep. Arlene's mouth hung open, and the other diners were all on their feet. One of the truckers clapped, and someone else cheered.

The only person not looking at me was the little boy, and his behavior went unnoticed by his parents, since they were focused on my selfless act of violence. He was crouched by my booth, lifting up the edge of the cover over Nicolette's bird cage. His eyes were wide, and he was nodding, as if agreeing with someone.

"I'd better be going," I said, and shoved through the crowd, which parted for me the way they usually do for someone who's shown a capacity for mayhem, only with more of an air of gratitude. The boy let the cover drop and backed away hurriedly, trying to look innocent and failing. I started to pick up the birdcage, then swore and reached into my pocket for some money.

"Honey, your meal is on the house," Arlene said.

"I should really be going." I said.

She chewed her lip. "The police will want to—"

"I'm not a big fan of the police."

Arlene nodded like she understood. "Which way are you headed?"

I hesitated. "South."

"Is that true, or what you want us to tell the cops?"

"It's true."

"Then if anybody asks me I'll say you headed north."

Despite myself, I smiled. "That'd be fine. Thanks, Arlene."

"Honey, thank *you*. Gary Singer's always had a mean streak, but he's never been mean *and* armed before."

"Yeah. People change." I picked up the bird cage.

"Now tell me the truth," Arlene said. "*Is* there a bird in that?"

"No," the little boy said.

"Squawk," Nicolette said, sounding pleased with herself.

I got out and got on my bike and got clear.

Small Rooms

I CAME OUT OF THE MOTEL BATHROOM, drying my hair. Like I said, I'd gotten a real taste for showers since dragging myself up out of the dirt. Plus beating up guys in diners makes you sweaty. Nicolette's uncovered cage rested on a little desk in the corner, where she was watching some horrible reality show.

I picked up the remote and turned off the TV, to her annoyance.

"What did you say to that little kid?" I asked.

"What little kid?"

"In the diner. I saw him talking to you."

"What can I say? I'm approachable. People love me."

I growled. "Unless you want to spend the night outside strapped to the motorcycle—"

"Oh, fine. I just told him that if he ate the heart of a parrot and drank the blood of a sea turtle he'd live more than a hundred years."

"You're sick." That explained the glimpse I'd had of the boy wreathed in magic, though—seeing Nicolette's living head, hearing her speak, had opened up a possible future path that led him toward the secret world.

"What? Those are legitimate components in a spell to increase longevity. Obviously I didn't have time to give him ritual instructions, but he seemed like a smart kid. He'll figure it out." She snickered.

I tossed my towel across a chair and got dressed, ignoring Nicolette's gagging sounds. She said, "I do not need to see you in all your naked glory. How many more scars are you planning to collect?"

"At least I've still got a body, Orpheus. What was that supposed to be this afternoon? You're supposed to find evil, and you lead me into the path of some meth-head with a knife?"

"You asked for chaos. I obliged."

"I was thinking something supernatural. Something a little better suited to my skills. Which you *know*."

"Sure, and when I smell something like that, I'll tell you. What, you want me to ignore ordinary people knifing other ordinary people? Okay, that's fine with me. It's not like I give a shit."

"You are a very frustrating traveling companion," I said, showing off the gift with understatement for which I'm so widely known.

"*You're* frustrated? I'm a head, in a cage, draped in darkness at your whim, strapped on the back of a motorcycle, only given a glimpse of daylight when it suits *you*. If I had hands, I'd strangle you."

"If you had a neck, I'd strangle *you*. So we're both out of luck."

"This is some Gift of the Magi type shit right here."

I couldn't help it. I started laughing, then turned the TV back on to keep Nicolette entertained. I retreated back into the bathroom for some relative privacy and fiddled with my phone until I figured out how to call Pelham.

He picked up before the first ring even finished. "Mrs. Mason? Are you all right?"

"Sure, I'm fine."

"Are you still on the road?"

I sat down on the toilet and propped my feet up on the edge of the predictably water-stained tub. "Nah, decided to stop early today. I'm in a motel. I smashed a guy in the face with a cup and a plate earlier, which was fun, but I figured I'd rest up after all the excitement."

"I am pleased to hear you're finding a pleasant routine. How may I assist you?"

"I brought some of my basic tools with me, but I'm in need of a couple of specialty items. I could use a handful of *bombyx mori*—alive or dead, doesn't matter—and a noctuid moth. A tiger moth would work in a pinch, though."

"I will get in touch with one of our entomological suppliers," Pelham said. "Silkworms and moths? May I ask what sort of enchantment you're planning?"

"I'm tired of Nicolette screaming at me from the back of my motorcycle, so we need a better way to communicate. You can probably get the stuff without much trouble, but the problem is getting it to *me*. You could make a reservation for me at some motel along tomorrow's route and overnight the package there, so it'll be waiting for me—"

"I think I can do better than that. Where are you now?"

I told him the name of the motel, then said, "Any other news of note?"

"I haven't heard anything from the cultists. But they're deep in the caves below Death Valley by now, where, I imagine, phone reception is unreliable." He sighed. "I do hope they emerge safely from their explorations."

"We might be better off if they just stay down there. They can form a new society, eat blind lizards, stuff like that."

"Hmm. More likely they'll die. And if that happens, won't they just show up in the underworld, and pursue their devotions for you there instead?"

I grunted. "I hadn't thought about that. My memory of the afterlife is too messed up for me to know if that's going to be an issue. But my suspicion is that the underworld is a big place, and I can probably avoid them." I sighed. "I don't want to be responsible for them, Pelham, I didn't *ask* them to worship me—"

"And yet, they do," he said gently.

"Fine. If they don't crawl out in few days, maybe send somebody with subterranean magic experience down to look for them?" Then I winced. "Shit. It's like somewhere in the back of my head I still think I'm running a city, with all kinds of specialists at my disposal—"

"We can hire someone appropriate, Mrs. Mason. Rondeau's funds are not literally inexhaustible, but they might as well be, and he assures me it is difficult to lose money operating a casino—at least when you're a psychic. In any case, you're running something much more *important* than a city, now. Co-regent of the underworld..."

"I'm glad you're so proud, Pelly, but it's just a part-time seasonal gig, really. I'm basically like an apple-picker. Talk to you soon."

I put a couple of protective wards on the door—a few more scratches in the doorframe would hardly be noticeable—and went out to get some dinner, leaving Nicolette behind. My options were a Waffle House or an International House of Pancakes or gas station hot dogs or a local diner, and I picked the latter. I wondered if diners were going to be bad luck for me, but I got through a chicken-fried steak and mashed potatoes without having to bust any heads.

There wasn't a lot of nightlife to be had around that particular freeway exit, but I stopped by the gas station/convenience store to rifle through their cheap jewelry rack, finding most of what I needed. I checked my phone and discovered there was a tattoo parlor just a few miles away, in what passed for the outskirts of what passed for this town. I drove there, went inside, made some demands that confused the owner, then dispelled his confusion with a large wad of cash, part of the riding-around money Rondeau had given me. I got the owner to give me a demonstration—luckily someone had an appointment for the right procedure around that time anyway—then bought some tools and went on my merry way.

When I returned to the motel, Nicolette ignored me, staring at the television. I didn't mind.

Eventually the drone of the TV turned to white noise in my ears, and I tried reading a copy of *Zen and the Art of Motorcycle Maintenance* that Rondeau had slipped into my saddlebags. Of course, once she saw me trying to read, Nicolette interrupted me.

"Is that any good?"

I shrugged. "I could live without the Zen bits. The motorcycle maintenance parts are okay."

Someone knocked at the door. I frowned, tossed the cover over Nicolette's cage, and drew my dagger. The motel door didn't have a peephole, which was fine. I've never trusted those, anyway. I knew a guy who got stabbed in the eye right through a peephole once, with a metal shish kebab skewer. I twitched aside the curtain, and saw a young man in black motorcycle leathers, holding a cooler marked with a caduceus symbol.

I opened the door. "Can I help you?"

"Marla Mason?"

"I am."

"I've got a delivery for you."

I looked at him blankly, then laughed. "That was quick."

"I usually deliver organs to hospitals. I drive fast. But you're not far from Phoenix anyway."

Ah. That explained how Pelham had organized things this neatly without bending time. He hadn't sourced my bugs from Las Vegas, but from a city closer to my position. I took the cooler. "Do I, like, tip you, or—"

"I'm not the *pizza guy*," he said, affronted, and put his helmet on before striding away.

"Okay then." I shut the door, put the cooler on the table, and opened it up.

"Do you *mind*," Nicolette said.

I took the cover off her cage and tossed it aside.

She looked at the cooler. "What's in there? Human heart? Fried up with a little butter, those are delicious—"

"Silkworms." I reached in and removing a little baggie full of dead bugs. "And a tiger moth." Vividly striped, in another plastic bag. I retrieved my sack from the convenience store and pulled out some ugly Southwestern-style earrings, all turquoise and fake silver, and a simple black leather necklace with a dangling turquoise pendant. I got my tool bag and took out a mortar and pestle and a small pair of scissors and some assorted tinctures and essences in little glass bottles. Nicolette watched with interest as I crushed up the tiger moth with various other substances, said the right words, and then applied the resulting clear fluid to the earrings. The stones sucked in the fluid like they were made of sponge instead of turquoise.

"You're a decent enchanter," Nicolette said, with grudging appreciation. "Why tiger moth?"

"They have some of the best hearing of any animal. Bat ears, or the lower jaw of a dolphin—those pick up sound transmitted through the water—would work, too, but they're less portable and harder to find."

"Huh. I thought you were crap at all the kinds of magic that didn't involve beating people up."

"I am a woman of many talents." Actually, not that many. I'm not even that great at magic—or, to be fair to myself, magic didn't come naturally to me. But enchanting is something anyone can do, if they learn how, and if they do it *exactly right*. It's no harder than neurosurgery, I'm told. I fucked up a lot in the learning process, but I seldom made the same mistake twice, and an enchantment of hearing-and-listening isn't that hard. Most sorcerers don't bother learning to do this kind of enchantment—because we have these little things called *phones* now—but they're useful in places where there's no phone service, or, for instance, when you need to communicate with someone who doesn't have the appendages necessary to operate a phone.

She said, "So that's the listening. How are you going to handle the talking?"

I showed Nicolette the silkworms. "They can communicate over incredible distances. I'm not convinced they have anything all that interesting to *say*, but they can say it to other worms a long ways away." I prepared the specimens, working meticulously and slowly, and applied the resulting shimmering oil to the necklace's pendant, where the stone soaked up the fluid, just like the earrings had.

"So, a necklace for you to talk through. What about me? We've already discussed my lack of a neck."

I opened the bag of things I'd gotten at the tattoo parlor: forceps, a 14 gauge tongue stud, and a 14 gauge needle. I hadn't bothered with getting any ointment. Infection wasn't a concern.

"What's all that for?" Nicolette said.

"To improve our communication." I lifted off the cage lid. "Stick out your tongue."

She eyed the tools on the table. "Oh, hell, no."

"Like you've never had a piercing. You've got like eight holes in each ear."

"I've never had my tongue pierced. Or anything pierced by someone I *hate*."

"There's a first time for everything. Look, I can get some dental tools, and some c-clamps, and fix your head to the table, and force your mouth open—"

"Kinky," Nicolette said.

"—or we can skip all the trouble and you can just stick out your damn tongue."

"Marla. If I could shake my head right now, I would. When have you ever known me to *avoid* trouble? Bring it on. I bet I can bite off one of your fingers at least."

I rubbed my eyes. I'd been enchanting for two hours, and it takes a lot out of you. "Look. Can I bribe you instead?"

"I am always open to bribes."

We haggled, and I finally got her to agree to something I was willing to give, so she stuck out her tongue, and I grabbed it with the forceps. After lifting up her tongue and looking to make sure I wouldn't tear the webbing underneath, or hit the big vein running through the tongue—which probably wouldn't hurt her, but I was following the procedure the guy at the tattoo shop showed me—I jabbed down with the needle, piercing straight through. "You're drooling," I said.

"Uck oo," Nicolette replied.

"Here comes the stud." I positioned the barbell tongue stud, pushing it into the new hole as I slid the needle down and out. Then I twisted the ball onto the underside of the stud, making it secure. "Voila," I said.

Nicolette wiggled her tongue, frowning.

I snapped my fingers. "Crap, I forgot to apply the silkworm oil. I'll have to do it now." I *had* forgotten, but I didn't feel bad about it as I dabbed essence of squished silkworm and other foul substances into Nicolette's mouth, coating the stud and a good swath of her taste buds in the process.

She spat and gagged and cursed when I was done, which put me in a pretty good mood.

I slipped the uglier pair of earrings, big dangly ones, into her ears, then put the smaller and slightly less hideous earrings in my own lobes, and slipped on my necklace. "Okay. The earrings are always on—the hearing is a passive spell. Speaking is active. If you want to talk to me, click the stud against your teeth, and speak. Click the stud again to deactivate communication. Let's test it."

I went into the bathroom, shut the door, tapped the pendant on my chest, and said, "Watson, come here, I need you."

"Suck my balls," Nicolette replied, her voice clear in my ears.

"Even if you'd started life with balls, you wouldn't have them anymore." I tapped the necklace again to turn it off. Now I'd be able to hear Nicolette even at great distance, or over the roar of the motorcycle on the freeway.

Oh, joy. I'd rather listen to a gossipy silkworm.

Sunlight Shores

I cruised into Phoenix early the next day, driving slowly up and down assorted streets and hoping Nicolette would get a whiff of something tragic and treacherous within the city limits. Sure, the sky's still too big and the ground's too dusty, but at least there are buildings more than two stories high, and the intangible pressure of a million and a half other souls in the immediate vicinity was pretty comforting. "Anything?" I said, rolling through downtown, past palm trees and glass buildings.

"Just the ordinary sorts of chaos. Collapsing marriages, botched business deals, interpersonal catastrophes. No problems that can be solved by kicking, punching, or stabbing, so you're useless. Certainly nothing supernatural. Phoenix *does* have sorcerers, you know, to take care of things like that. You probably think Canadians live in igloos."

"Damn it. I'd settle for a serial killer at this point."

"I could probably find a mugger for you to beat up, if you hang around until twilight."

"Fine. Let's keep going." I worked my way back to a highway, and in too short a time I'd left the comfort of the city—such as it was—behind, and it was back to two-lane blacktop, cacti, and scrub. The miles disappeared underneath my wheels. I figured we'd hit New Mexico by afternoon, unless we found a good reason to stop first. At least I could get some decent tacos for dinner.

About an hour past Tucson, Nicolette was annoying the shit out of me by singing to herself, a wordless collection of high-pitched wails and vibratos. "What the hell is that noise you're making?"

"I'm not fifty-two string instruments, so I can't do it justice, but I'm doing my best to sing 'Threnody for the Victims of Hiroshima' by Penderecki. It's a great piece, full of required improvisations, so no performance is ever the same twice." She paused. "You goddamn uncultured savage."

"Great. Consider me enlightened. Can you keep it down?"

"I'm in a cage in the *dark*. I'm just trying to keep myself sane here."

"You weren't sane to start with. You could at least deactivate your tongue stud so I don't have to hear it."

"Yes, but then I wouldn't *annoy* you—wait, hold on, stop."

I pulled over to the shoulder, but didn't cut the engine. "Yeah?"

"Uncover me, would you?"

I looked around. We had the road to ourselves for the moment, so I lifted the cage cover. Nicolette was facing roughly north. "There's something in that direction..." She squinted. "Lines of force, converging, but looping back in on themselves, contained, but I can't tell *what* they're containing, but it's something bad and disruptive..."

"Hmm. Let's get a little closer, then." I pulled up the map on my phone and found a road that cut toward the north, more or less. I re-covered Nicolette and made my way along the winding road, while she muttered unhelpful comments through my earrings: "Spatial distortions," "Ghost traces," "Blood and charcoal," and things like that.

Finally she shouted, "*There*!" and nearly startled me into running off the road.

"There *where*?"

"West, west, west—"

"Hold on, I see a sign." I pulled the cover off her cage, and we both looked at a dusty, faded sign that said "Come Home to Sunlight Shores!" and depicted a row of neat houses beneath a warm yellow cartoon sun, nothing at all like the baleful hellstar beating down on us from the endless pale blue sky above.

"Looks like there was going to be a housing development here." I squinted, and saw a few houses clustered off in the distance, like herd animals huddling together for warmth.

"Lots of abandoned places, since the economy started nose-diving," Nicolette said. "I do love a good financial collapse. There are whole ghost suburbs all over the Southwest, with abandoned half-built houses or model homes standing in the middle of a sea of sand. But there's something different about this one... I think something's *living* there. And I don't mean an off-the-grid squatter. Something that's not human."

"Huh. Not everything inhuman automatically deserves to get knifed-up."

"True," Nicolette says. "I'm pretty sure this one's been feeding on humans, though. I'm sensing a lot of death, and fairly recent."

"Cool," I said. "Let's kill it." I covered the cage and aimed the motorcycle at the nearest sand-drifted street that led into the vestigial neighborhood of Sunlight Shores.

If I'm honest, I've done a lot of stupid things in my life, and that was definitely one of them.

The streets were laid out in neat grids, but they were almost all bordering empty lots, spaces bulldozed and then left bare. I parked the bike a couple of streets away from the cluster of houses, preferring to approach potentially dangerous locales on foot. "Bring me with you," Nicolette said. "I smell disaster."

I sighed and picked up the covered cage in my left hand, keeping my right free to grab for my dagger if the need arose. I had the silver hatchet hanging from a loop inside my coat, too, because why not.

The streets were mostly unpaved, and the churned-up dirt in the lots hadn't all been graded flat, so there were heaps of spoil and gouged-out, dusty pits full of stony fragments. I knelt when a flash of something pale and sharp caught my eye, and picked up a fossilized tooth, probably from a shark, half as long as my little finger.

I smiled a little, thinking of a shark god I'd met during my time in Hawaii, who'd had tooth problems of his own until I helped him out. Bits of ancient monsters can be magically potent, and utility aside, fossils are cool, so I slipped the tooth into one of my pockets. After that I divided my attention between watching the ground for more treasures and watching the cluster of seemingly-empty houses, and collected two more fossil teeth, though both were smaller than the first. The desert is full of wonders, even if most of them are dead.

I paused a block away from the nearest house. There were half a dozen homes completed, clustered around a cul-de-sac with a circular driveway, all the buildings variations on the single-story ranch house with two-car garage. No lawns, though a couple of the houses sported the remnants of vegetation, clinging on in the absence of irrigation. Nice, boring little houses, gradually being eaten by the desert.

"Well?" I said. "Care to give me some guidance to the source of the chaos?"

"It's all around us," Nicolette said. "It's… this whole area. I can't narrow it down any more. It's like we're standing in the middle of Times Square and you're asking me where Manhattan is."

I hate to use magic when simple observation will do, but going door-to-door and searching for signs of life struck me as way too tedious, especially since a thorough search of each house would give any persons (or creatures) of interest ample opportunity to notice me and escape, or lay an ambush. I fished in one of my coat pockets for a vial containing a potion made of various things, the most repulsive ingredient being bed bug antennae, and swigged it down. The taste was sugary in the extreme—Pelham always tries to mask the nastiness of the potions he prepares for me with non-reactive flavorings.

I waited a moment for my eyes to adjust, and my visual spectrum expanded into the infrared. (Bed bugs are equipped by nature to be heat-seeking bloodsuckers.) I glanced at the cage in my hand, and was surprised to see that Nicolette's head glowed with body heat. I'd expected her to be cold, since she didn't exactly have blood circulating through her, but whatever magic animated her produced heat of some kind. I scanned the houses, and saw only one heat source of significance, human-sized. The other houses had a few rodents and birds, but nothing worth worrying about. Probably. The houses could have been filled with things that don't give off heat, of course—animated skeletons or liches or golems or ice elementals—but I wasn't too worried about stuff like that. They were unlikely, for one thing, and for another, unambiguous monsters are way less tricky to deal with than people, anyway. Monsters mostly want to kill you, eat you, or use you. People can go either way, but sometimes they know stuff.

"Hello the house!" I shouted as I approached, striding up a flagstone walk to the front door.

"Way to exploit the element of surprise," Nicolette muttered.

The door banged open, and a man lurched out. He was a big guy, reddish hair too long, big bird-nest sort of a beard, wide eyes, generally sloppy-looking, with his shirt half untucked. If I hadn't seen him literally emerge from a home, I would have assumed he was homeless. "You shouldn't be here!" he said, his voice cracking with anguish. "Now it'll get you too!"

"See, that was an unclear antecedent right there." I strolled toward him, checking him out for any possible weapons, but if he had a gun or a machete or something he'd concealed it well. "When you say 'it' will get me, what do you mean by 'it'?"

He shook his head, waved his arms around, then took a deep gulping breath, obviously trying to get himself under control. When he let out a long exhalation, he seemed to deflate a little bit, but he also lost some of his manic over-the-edge energy. "You should come in. I'll tell you. You… you deserve to know what's going to happen to you, I guess, though it might be kinder to just let it take you, so you don't have to worry, or be afraid…" He frowned. "Is that a bird?"

"No," I said. "Got anything to drink?"

Ancient Oceans

The guy—his name was Andrew Lin—didn't have anything to offer but water, warm and stale, in those big square stackable bottles people buy in bulk in case there's an earthquake or civilization collapses, so they won't get dehydrated while they cower in their homes and wait for the skin-eating mutants to come devour them. The house was fairly clean but not really furnished—his décor was camping gear, pretty much. He sat in a folding chair while I sat on the floor, my back against a wall, where I could see the front door and the windows. Nicolette was beside me, silent so far, but watchful. Living heads in cages are even creepier when they just silently stare, it turns out.

"There are these deserted housing developments all over now," Andrew explained. "Arizona was one of the fastest-growing places in the country during the housing boom, and when the economy flatlined, a bunch of projects got abandoned. The banks seized them, mostly, but banks aren't construction companies or realtors, they can't *do* anything with all the property, so the houses mostly just… sit here. I used to work in construction—I helped build this place, right here, where we're sitting—but then the work dried up, and I had lots of medical bills because my wife was sick, and I lost my house. That's bullshit, the bank taking a house when there are so many houses sitting empty, but that's how it goes. I had the bright idea to come move into one of these empty places. Seemed fair, to take something back from the job that dropped me. My wife didn't like it, but my kid, he's—he was—ten, he thought it was a big adventure. We stocked up on canned goods and water and stuff before our Costco membership ran out, brought the generator, and moved in." He stared down at the metal cup in his hands, quiet, for a little longer than I was willing to wait.

"So what happened?"

He laughed, hollowly. "Well, we weren't the first ones to have my bright idea. There was another family living in one of the houses here, nice folks—the wife still had a job, part-time, at a coffee shop, and she actually commuted into town every day, and had two little daughters who played with my son, even though they were younger than him. And there was a survivalist-type guy, a little paranoid, an off-the-grid kind of person, but we gave him a bunch of our canned goods and he decided we were part of his 'tribe,' so that was fine. We had… sort of a little community, almost, for a few weeks. I can't say we ever *relaxed*, you're always afraid the cops will come or the bank will send someone to look at the property and they'll find you, but it's not like we're bothering people out here, so sometimes we could even convince ourselves life was normal, apart from cooking over a camp stove and taking baths with a washcloth and a bucket of cold water. My wife and kid and me, we didn't leave much. It was summer, so there was no school. We were trying to figure out what to do in the fall, whether our son would be able to keep where we lived a secret, if we could pretend we still had our old address, send him to his same school…" He fell silent again. "But it didn't matter. My son… he was taken. The thing, it took the kids first, because it wasn't strong enough to take grown-ups, not when it first woke up, I think. Then Pete, the survival guy, he went out hunting the thing, armed with every kind of gun you can imagine, and he never came back, though we heard some shots in the night. Anyway. Next it took the women. Then it took Harry, my neighbor, but he would have killed himself anyway, I think. I'm the only one left… until you got here." His mouth quirked in something almost like a smile. "Maybe it'll take you first, and I'll get to live another couple of weeks. I can't decide if that makes me happy or not."

"Just a couple of questions, Andrew," I said. "After the first person got taken, why didn't you call the cops, or at least *leave*?" Then I caught a glimpse of the tattoo on my inner arm, "Do Better," and hurriedly added, "Uh, and I'm sorry for your loss."

He shook his head. "We can't leave. You haven't figured it out yet. Sunlight Shores is like… a tiger pit. A pitcher plant. People can come in—the bank *did* send a guy, a couple of weeks ago, and he was taken, too, that's why I'm still alive, I guess the thing hasn't gotten hungry again yet—but nobody can get *out* again."

"Huh." That might explain the spatial distortions Nicolette had noticed. "What happens when you try to leave? Do you hit an invisible wall? Or is it like a treadmill, and you never get any farther away from the development, no matter how much you walk? Or do you get confused and lose your train of thought when you walk too far away? Or—"

"It's like a *loop*," he interrupted. "You start walking in one direction, out the front door, and before long, you see the *back* door in front of you."

"Mobius loop," I said. "Space folded back on itself. Well, that's a nasty trick, but nothing I can't fix. We'll get you out of here. I guess I'll have to kill this 'thing' of yours, though, whatever the fuck it is. Did you want to help me, to, whatever, avenge your family?"

"What are you talking about?" It was hard to read his expression underneath all that beard, but he seemed... anxious, maybe. Not incredulous, or hopeful, or surprised, or any of the other emotions I would have expected.

"I didn't just happen to wander by here, Andrew. I'm sort of a hunter. But stalking deer and bears and man-eating tigers is a little too dull, so I hunt bigger game. Monsters, mainly. Sounds like you've got a monster problem. And I'm a monster solution. Match made in heaven."

"You're insane. You haven't seen it. It's not... it's not something you can *fight*."

"What is it? Chupacabra that developed a taste for human blood? Some kind of subterranean sand-worm? Feral scorpion god? Give me something to go on here."

"We knew we'd uncovered something," Andrew said, gazing toward one of the windows. "When we broke ground, it was mostly normal, except for a lot of fossils, teeth and stuff, more than we usually found. I picked up a few for my son, he was so excited. But in one of the lots, we dug down, and we uncovered this... I don't know. Some kind of a seal. Or a lid to a tomb. A big flat stone, almost round, marked with strange designs, these spirals, they hurt your eyes if you looked at them. The backhoe cracked the lid right in half, and underneath there was this cavern. We got a couple of lights, shone them down in the hole, but didn't see anything, just rock and darkness. We didn't know how big the cavern was, and the foreman said we should just mark it off with caution tape and leave it for the night, and get the developer out here the next day, let him know we had a potential subsidence situation, that we couldn't build on that spot unless he wanted to fill the hole with concrete or something."

Spirals. They're often used in order magic, to contain forces of chaos and disorder. "You found some kind of ancient artifact and you didn't tell anybody?"

He grimaced. "Archaeologists and housing developments don't mix. We didn't want anyone to find out about it, and risk shutting down the whole job site. The boss, he said it was better just to fill it in. So the next day, that's what we did, dumped in a bunch of dirt and rocks and junk. Honestly, it didn't take that much, a couple of dump trucks worth. But before we filled it in... something must have gotten away. Maybe it was weak at first, and fed on mice and birds and stuff it found in the desert, but then it got stronger, and after I moved in here, it trapped us, and..." He began to weep.

I always get uncomfortable when people cry at me. "Okay. But what *is* it? You didn't see it when you found the cavern, maybe it was small or intangible or something then, but you've seen it since, yeah?"

He shrugged, still weeping. "It's hard to describe. Your eyes slide away from it, and it comes in the night, but... it's like stilts, bird legs, scissors, tent poles... sharp and pointy and long and bony, but made of shadows, always folding and unfolding. It goes from something compact, the size of a horse, to sprawled-out as big as a house, all claws and angles, coming at you from every direction..."

It didn't sound like any kind of monster I'd ever heard of. But, hell, there are half-a-million different species of beetle on Earth. Biodiversity has never been a problem for our planet, and that applies to things that live partially in other dimensions or come from deep time or eat fear or have parasitic relationships with dreams or whatever, too. Shit gets weird. "I wonder if it really eats people. I mean the way *we* eat. Or if it feeds in some other way. Have you found any body parts? Or blood?"

He shook his head. "It comes, and reaches out, and wraps someone up, and drags them away. I've looked—we all looked, when there were more of us—but we couldn't find any remains. We couldn't find any... sort of a lair, or anything, either. Do you think the people who were taken might still be alive?"

I shrugged. There was Doing Better, and there was giving a grieving man false hope, and I wasn't comfortable with the latter. "I wouldn't expect it, no. I'm sorry. Even if it's not literally eating their flesh, it could be feeding on them in some other way, using them up just as effectively. There are monsters that drink serotonin, monsters that feed on auras, monsters that eat memories, or suffering, or breath... none of them leave their victims better off than they were to start with."

"That's... almost worse than thinking they were just devoured."

"No argument here. Okay. It comes at night, you say? And goes a couple of weeks between appearances? When is it due to come again?"

"Any time now." He frowned. "You're actually going to try and fight it? I told you, Pete—"

"My weapons aren't the same ones Pete used. I'm not into guns. Hmm. I think you've got to wait it out, Andrew. You should hole up in here, I can set some protective wards."

"You said you could break the spell, make it possible for us to escape, let's just *run*—"

I shook my head. "Bad plan. Breaking the Mobius loop—the spatial distortion that's trapping you here—is going to take some effort, and once I start trying, it's going to notice, and attack me, probably—I won't be able to finish breaking your jail cell open anyway. I'd rather save my energy for fighting. After I kill the thing, I'll set you free. There's a good chance its death will break the spell anyway, and spare me the effort."

"But… what if you die first? How will I get away then?"

"I don't expect to get killed, Andrew, but if I do, you're no worse off than you were before. I don't want it to know I'm more formidable than your average drifter wandering through the desert, anyway. Let it think I'm another helpless little morsel. The element of surprise will help."

"You really think you can fight it?" He still read as anxious to me, not hopeful, or even curious. Maybe he was just a nervous guy.

I stood up. "I've killed gods, Andy. I'm not worried about a collapsible shadow monster. I'm going to scout around, though, while there's still a little daylight. See about setting up some traps and wards around the houses, so I can at least get a warning if something nasty comes close. You hang out here."

He nodded, staring at me like he didn't quite know what to make of me, which is a look I'm pretty familiar with.

I carried Nicolette out with me, through the kitchen and its dwindling stockpile of canned goods, into the backyard. "What do you think?" I said.

"I think there's a chance you might get eaten by a monster—so, hurray!"

"If I get eaten, you'll be a head in a cage stuck in a Mobius loop with a grief-stricken bearded guy for very temporary company."

"I never said there I didn't see a downside," Nicolette said.

The backyard had clearly been a sort of communal outdoor kitchen/ dining area. There were a couple of barbecue grills, now very dusty, lots of lawn chairs, a patio table, a long redwood picnic table flanked by a couple of benches, and the remains of one of those squarish folding canopies you see at farmer's markets and outdoor weddings, one of its four supports bent and the whole structure leaning.

"Huh," Nicolette said. "Something *bad* happened out here."

"Well, duh. We're in a monster's pantry."

"No, I mean, right *here*—screaming, suffering. Not just once, and not quickly, something drawn-out… Shit, it's pretty overpowering, it's all a mishmash, I can't get anything specific out of the general mess."

"Hmm." I put Nicolette's cage down on the patio table, then walked around the grills and chairs, and toward the picnic table.

The wood was red, but there were splotches of darker color, deep stains, reddish-brown and crusty. I've seen enough old blood in my time to recognize it instantly. The table had holes drilled in it, too, each about the diameter of a quarter: a pair of holes spaced six inches apart in the middle plank at one end of the table, and at the other end, two sets, one close to the table's left edge, one close to the right. I crouched down to look under the table, where the dirt was stained with various leakages, and saw three of those u-shaped bicycle locks tucked under one of the benches, all with keys sticking out of their holes.

The underside of the table was carved with designs. I didn't recognize them, specifically, but I recognized them generally: magical runes and sigils. Messages—or, more likely, commands, or possibly pleadings—written in an inhuman language.

"Oh, fuck," I said, but didn't have time to elaborate on my revelation, because that's when Andrew buried the blade of an axe right between my shoulder blades.

Then he wrenched it out, and as I fell, he brought the axe blade down on the back of my skull.

No Picnic

I CAN'T SAY IT DIDN'T *HURT*. I'd never had an axe in the head before, obviously, and I don't recommend the experience. I'm not sure what parts of my brain it chopped up—I'm not a neurosurgeon, in case you hadn't noticed—but I can tell you I saw bright colors, tasted hot metal and chili peppers, smelled rubbing alcohol, and puked a bit.

Fortunately he wrenched the axe out, which saved me the trouble of trying to lever an axe out of my own skull. As soon as the blade left my brain, my devastated tissues began to heal.

That's how I found out that not dying when you're supposed to is one of the perks of being the Bride of Death. According to our deal I was supposed to spend half the year alive on Earth, and that meant I had to *stay* alive, and apparently my DH had chosen to just… cancel dying, in my case. As far as solutions go, it's pretty elegant. Technically I was in my mortal body, I was flesh and blood and bone and lymph and so on… but just as death was withdrawn from Nicolette, it was also withdrawn from me.

So the axe-blow knocked me down, but not out. Still hurt like a bastard, though. Then again, pain is a great motivator.

I stared at my puddle of puke for a minute, my head resting against the edge of the table, letting Andrew assume I was dead. Nicolette, obligingly, started yelling from beneath her cover: "What the fuck was that? Who's puking? What's going on?"

Hearing a human voice emerge from a birdcage distracted Andrew—a parrot would have probably been just as effective—so I rolled to one side, drew my dagger from my pocket, and slashed out at his Achilles tendon. He dropped the bloody axe and fell over, screaming and clutching his ankle. I kicked the red-bladed fire axe aside—not very far, since I was still a little wobbly as my skull knit itself back together—and stood over Andrew.

He stared at me, whimpering. "I *killed* you!"

"You've got lousy aim," I said. Nicolette didn't know I was married to Death, and I didn't especially want her to know I was immune to axe-in-head syndrome either. She was my ally now, but she was also my enemy, and I don't like giving enemies any more intelligence than I have to. Besides, knowing I wasn't likely to die in an accident of Nicolette's devising would only depress her, and she was hard enough to deal with when she was cheerful.

I tore the cover off the cage. "Will you stop squawking?" I moved the cage to the edge of the table so Nicolette could see Andrew. "He just tried to murder me, but he did a terrible job."

Andrew looked up at the severed head in the cage grinning down at him, then shrieked like a little kid in a haunted house.

"Ahhh," Nicolette said. "Delicious screaming. There's a lot of blood on that axe. You sure he didn't hit you, Marla?"

"He might have nicked me on the back," I said, reaching around and touching the tear in my coat. Damn it. I liked that coat. I hoped the hole wasn't too big. "Okay, big boy, up on the table."

I grabbed him by the hair and one arm and dragged him upright. He hopped on his good foot as I shoved him onto the picnic table on his back. "Nice altar you've got here." I knelt and picked up one of the bicycle locks, opening it up. Andrew tried to roll away, but I smacked him in the forehead with the heavy end of the lock and he groaned and lay still. I slid the prongs of the lock over his throat, and as I'd expected, the sides of the U-bold slid easily into the holes drilled into the table. "Guess you knocked them out before you put them on the table, huh? You don't seem like you're tough enough to lock down a victim who's struggling." I ducked under the table, fitted the bottom of the lock over the ends of the U protruding from the underside of the table, and turned the key. Now Andrew was fastened to the table by his neck, and he wouldn't be going anywhere. I didn't bother locking his legs, as he'd done with his victims—I wasn't all that worried about getting kicked.

Andrew stared at me, eyes slit, the black bar of the lock pressing against his meaty throat, but not tight enough to cut off his air, unless he struggled. "So," I said. "What's the deal? Human sacrifice is fuel for big magic, especially if you sacrifice the ones you love—or was that stuff about your wife and kid bullshit? Somebody sure died on this table, though. What's the sorcery you're working? Immortality?"

He laughed, and it was a horrible sound. "Immortality? I'm just trying to say *alive*. There is a monster, and it *did* eat my family, and the others who lived here. Or… I don't know if it ate them, it tore them apart, it seemed to get something out of that, from their pain, or maybe it sucked out their souls or something, I don't *know*, but I had to bury the pieces, bury what was left of them—can you imagine how hard that was for me?"

"Harder than strapping your friends and family down on this table as sacrifices?"

He squeezed his eyes shut and shook his head, as well as he could with the lock pressing against his throat.

"Open your eyes, Andrew. We're not done talking." I sat on the redwood bench and put my dagger on the table, spinning it around. When it stopped, the point aimed at his cheek. "Did you really crack open a seal and let something out, or was that bullshit?"

"After we found the pit, I… started having these *dreams*. I saw shapes, the shapes I carved into the table later. And I dreamed about coming back here, to this place. I resisted, for a long time, but I came anyway, I'd go to sleep and wake up hours later in my car, parked here. So when I lost my job, I just… gave in. I listened. I came. And the thing, the taker, *it*, spoke to me, and told me it had marked me when I looked down into its pit, when I pointed a light into its darkness, and made it hide. The thing said it was going to consume me… unless I made myself useful, instead. It promised…" He closed his eyes, and tears leaked down his face.

"Fed his wife and kid to a monster to save himself," Nicolette said. "That's low."

"It was in my *mind*," Andrew whispered. "The… beast. And I was in *its* mind, sometimes, and I knew I couldn't fight it. The beast is old, older than almost anything, it lived here when this was all underwater, when this desert was an ocean, and it hunted, and it fed. Some people managed to trap it for a while in the cavern, under the stone, but… I don't know what those people knew! I couldn't stop it, I could only—"

"Collaborate?" I said. "Shit, Andrew. You sacrificed your family so you could live. But what are you living *for*? You killed the reason you had to stay alive. I will say this, though. Meeting a piece of shit like you makes me feel better about my own horrible mistakes. I've done some bad things, but you've got me beat."

"It will be dark soon," Andrew said, winning the Stating the Obvious challenge. "There's fresh blood on the table—*my* blood. That's what calls it. The beast will come. For me."

"Couldn't happen to a nicer asshole."

"Are you going to let this beast eat him, Marla?" Nicolette asked.

I sighed. "Of course not. I'll kill the monster, then call the cops and let them know there's a guy locked to a table, and they might want to inquire about what happened to his wife and kid, and maybe check the table for lots and lots of DNA."

"He'd let *you* get eaten," Nicolette said, joining the state-the-obvious party. "That was the whole point."

"Yes, Nicolette, but *my* whole point is that I'm better than him."

"Aw, I wouldn't go that far," Nicolette said. "You're just horrible in a different way."

"You have to let me go," Andrew said. "You can't possibly fight it, you have no idea what—"

A shadow passed over the sun. I looked up as Andrew whimpered. There were no clouds, no birds, no airplanes—the sky was just *dimming*, as if we'd been placed under a smoked glass dome.

I drew my dagger, and after some thought, reached into my coat for the silvery axe. The blade glimmered, like a fragment of moonlight, something I'd noticed it doing before, though I hadn't yet figured out what it meant.

"Is that an eclipse?" Nicolette demanded. "Damn it, not having a neck sucks, I can't even tilt my head back."

I rolled my neck around on my shoulders. "No eclipse, but something's coming. I guess the beast didn't want to wait for natural nightfall, so it brought its own."

Andrew was openly sobbing, but I didn't have much sympathy for him. He'd made his bloody altar, and now he had to lie on it.

Something approached from the north. I squinted, but that didn't help my vision much, especially with the still-diminishing brightness. The vestiges of bedbug-potion were no help, either, since it didn't give off any heat I could detect. The thing seemed to be a bodiless ball of writhing wires or tentacles, limbs crossing and recrossing, the whole moving by some form of locomotion that defied analysis.

I grunted. "Your beast is only a little bit in this world, Andrew. It's operating in dimensions we can't see. That explains its ability to turn this neighborhood into a Mobius strip—it's some kind of dimensional manipulator. Sure makes it hard to tell what we're dealing with, though. We might as well be in Flatland here, perceiving a bouncing ball as an expanding and contracting circle."

"Nerd," Nicolette muttered.

Still, there were parts of the beast projecting into this reality, and I didn't see any reason I couldn't chop all those parts off and hope some of them were vital. I rushed around the table and ran toward the thing, silver hatchet in one hand, knife in the other. Within seconds one of the—tentacles? Bones? Appendages?—was in reach, so I lashed out with my dagger.

The supernatural blade sliced cleanly, and the limb—a glossy black thing segmented like a scorpion's tail—snapped like a wire under tension, one end falling to the dirt, the other recoiling and vanishing into thin air. The creature *did* seem to have a central mass from which the writhing appendages radiated, but that body shifted in and out of sight, as if obscured by a moving curtain.

I did catch a glimpse of its mouth, though. It had a six-foot-long tooth whorl, a lower jaw full of serrated teeth that spiraled inward like the head of a fiddlehead fern crossed with a circular saw. I'd seen tooth whorls in artists' renditions of the prehistoric sea monster helicoprion, the only creature known to possess such weird-ass mouthparts , but this beast was no deep-sea prehistoric predator that had survived into the modern day. For one thing, helicoprion didn't have tentacles or the ability to shift through dimensions and manipulate space-time (presumably). But the beast's curled-up jaw full of fangs did make me wonder if some of the fossilized teeth whorls attributed to helicoprions had belonged to things like this instead. There really *were* giants in the earth in those days, is the thing.

I lashed out at every appendage that whipped or twisted its way into my sphere of destruction, and hissed when one wrapped around my wrist—it didn't hurt or burn or anything, but its touch was *foul*, carrying some fundamental contagion that revolted me instantly, broadcasting horror right at my reptile backbrain. When I cut that tentacle loose, and the limb unwrapped from my arm, it left behind an ugly smear that stank like a skunk carcass.

Still the thing advanced, and its appendages didn't seem to dwindle in number, fresh ones appearing faster than I could sever them. Soon I was slashing with axe and knife both, and managing to hold my own—until its tooth whorl unfurled out of thin air, a muscular curl of jaw studded with triangular fangs, lashing out for my face. I ducked and cursed and fell back behind the picnic table.

"Tactical error, huh, Marla?" Nicolette said.

Truer words. I'd assumed I could kill the thing—I have a lot of experience backing up that assumption—but for all I knew I was just trimming its fingernails and cutting its hair.

"Sorry, Andrew." I tucked the hatchet back into my coat and grabbed Nicolette's cage. I headed back to the house, turning for a moment to watch as the creature loomed over the picnic table, appendages scrabbling across the yard toward the man on the makeshift altar. The beast's tooth whorl unspooled from the dark, and something that might have been a tongue—or rather a cluster of tongues, like a cat-o-nine-tails—appeared and drooped down toward Andrew's screaming face.

Ah, well, fuck him, the kid-murdering piece of filth.

I got inside and slammed the door, then dove for my bag. I dug out a bag of salt—well, mostly salt—and poured it on the floor in a big circle, enclosing Nicolette and myself.

"Cowering in a warded circle," Nicolette said. "You're a strategic *genius*."

"I just need a minute to try something else," I said, and that's when the creature tore the roof off the house.

Ghosts with Sharp Teeth

It was really quite impressive. A crack, a ripping sound, and then the roof was just *gone*, ripped cleanly away as if by a tornado. The creature's limbs came over the top of the walls and began to tear those too, too, and in a moment we were sitting in an exposed ruin, with a full view of the backyard, and Andrew's bloody remnants cooling on the picnic table. The appendages probed toward us, but stopped when they reached the salt, questing blindly off in other directions. We were invisible, inaudible, and invincible, more or less, while we were in the circle, but it was a temporary magic. A strong wind breaking the line could undo it.

"What *now*?" Nicolette said.

I reached into my coat and touched the shark's teeth I'd found. I think I might have smiled. "Now, I do a little necromancy."

"What, are you going to resurrect Andrew to fight for us? That might work if his legs or arms were still attached. He's not even intact enough to head butt the beast. Besides, I thought you hated necromancers"

"A compulsion to play with dead things for a living tends to indicate a pretty fucked-up personality," I said. "But I'm a pragmatist." I put the teeth on the ground in front of me, and dug through my bag for the standard components I'd need—a little cup made of bone, a silver dish, a bit of graveyard earth. I cut my palm with my dagger and dripped a little blood into the cup, then poured it into the dish and mixed it with the soil. Necromancy is powered by death. The bigger the effect you're trying to achieve, the bigger the sacrifice you need—but there was a human sacrifice right in the back yard. I hadn't killed him, but I'd *bound* him, which meant I bore some responsibility—and that meant I could use his death to fuel my magic. It seemed a shame to let his sacrifice be for nothing.

I smeared my blood on the fossilized shark teeth, watching the blurry tangle of the beast sniff and quest its way all around us.

"That's ballsy," Nicolette said. "They're *sharks*. I've never heard of anyone calling up the ghost of a shark."

"I did a favor for a shark god not that long ago. He taught me a few things. Sacred words in a language older than humankind." I muttered those words, and then I hurled the shark teeth toward the blurry mass at the center of the forest of writhing limbs.

I'd hoped for a megalodon, the apex predators of the ancient oceans, sixty feet long with jaws that opened as wide as a garage door. But I didn't get anything *quite* that good. Later on I did a little research, and I'm pretty sure the biggest shark that appeared was a *Kaibabvenator swiftae*, a good twenty feet long, lashing its spectral fins. Two other, smaller sharks were probably *Neosaivodus flagstaffensis*, not so big but vicious little killers all the same. The ghost sharks looked just like living sharks, except they were silvery-gray, and they swam through the waters of an ancient ocean that had receded long ago, gliding with surreal ease through the air above our heads.

I don't know how ghost sharks see the world, but when they saw the beast they saw *lunch*. Even though I'd only thrown three teeth, other ghosts began to precipitate out of the air, called by the feeding frenzy and their bone and tooth fragments in the soil. Soon there were a dozen prehistoric sharks converging on the monster, and they *dragged* it out of the dimensions where it was mostly hiding. The lower jaw curled and uncurled like a party noisemaker being blown on New Year's Eve, and the whips of its arms contracted before the sharks tore it to pieces.

The sky brightened again, and in the late afternoon light, the ghost sharks first became translucent, then invisible, and at some point I realized they were gone. The ground was littered with bits of scale and armor and greenish blood—don't squids have green blood, because their blood is copper-based, not iron-based like humans?—and unidentifiable fragments of the beast. The mouth-parts were still more-or-less intact, connected to a twitching mass that might have been a head. Either it wasn't quite dead yet, or it was experiencing random nerve-twitchings, the way a freshly dead octopus on a plate will wriggle its tentacles if you pour salty soy sauce over it—

A voice spoke in my head. The voice was cold, killingly so, vacuum-of-space cold: *I will be avenged*, it whispered. *The Eater will get you.*

I had no idea if the creature could hear my thoughts, but I gave it a try anyway: *With a name like 'the Eater' don't you mean he'll eat me? I mean, he's not called 'the Getter,' right? But okay. Who or what is the Eater?*

The death of your future, it mind-whispered, pretty articulately for an ancient chthonic horror with a rolled-up buzz saw for a lower lip, but it had a history of manipulating humans, so maybe I shouldn't have been surprised.

The twitching stopped. *Hello?* I thought. *You still there, Squidward?* There was no response.

"That's one big mess of ugly," Nicolette said. "What do you think that thing even was?"

I had no idea. Ancient predator from prehistory, slumbering into modern times, or an alien astronaut stranded on a hostile planet, or an Outsider from another reality who'd wandered into our bubble of the multiverse and just tried to survive. Whatever it was, the beast had made at least one friend: something or someone called the Eater. Or maybe that was its deity or something, and threatening me with the Eater was the equivalent of a dying person telling his murderer that "God will judge you."

"Whatever it was, now it's a dead one of whatever it is," I said.

I stood up, kicked the salt circle open, and picked up Nicolette's cage again. "How about we try to get the fuck out of here?" I said. "I don't much feel like bedding down in what's left of Andrew's place."

"Do whatever you like." Nicolette belched, though the exact mechanics of *how* she belched, lacking pretty much all anatomy from the chin down, still escapes me. "I'm *stuffed* with chaos. I just want to nap."

We went back to the motorcycle and I got everything loaded, including strapping her cage down. Then I stopped. "Damn it," I said.

"What?"

"Just wait here. Sleep. I'll be back in a while."

"Where are you—" she began, but I covered up her cage and walked away.

There was a shovel in a little shed in back of the house, and gloves. I found the place where Andrew had buried his family and neighbors, a little ways to the south—there were no grave markers, of course, but he'd piled up stones. I dug a hole in the hard earth, and put what was left of Andrew's body in it, and covered it up again.

I stood by his graveside and tried to decide if I was responsible for his death or not. I hadn't killed him, but I'd *caused* him to be killed, thinking I could keep him alive, and failing. Hubris, again. Me and hubris are old friends.

A door opened in the wall of the nearest house. It was a door that hadn't been there a moment before, and after a man stepped out, and the door closed, the door went away without calling any attention to its departure. The man was tall, long-faced but handsome, with dark hair that fell past his shoulders, and he wore a dark blue sharkskin suit in what I assumed was a stylish cut. He was wearing rings on nine of his ten fingers. He used to have ten rings, but one of them was on the ring finger of my left hand, now.

"Hello, dear," he said mildly, standing beside the grave, not quite close enough to touch me. "I sensed a death in your proximity, and I thought I'd come see how you were doing."

I shrugged. "I've been better. I killed a monster, which is always nice, but there were drawbacks." I gestured at the churned-up earth.

He nodded. "If you want me to leave, I can. I don't mean to intrude on your, ah, mortal time."

"No, it's fine." Talking to someone other than Nicolette had its appeal. "It's not like I'm sick of you or anything. We spent a month together in the underworld, but..." I tapped the side of my head. "Somebody poured the memories out of my head like a bucket full of dirty mop water."

He winced. "Quite. Not my idea, in case you were wondering."

"So it was my idea, then." I wasn't sure if I believed him. Not that Death is a notorious liar, but you can't trust gods, and I say that as someone who's a part-time god herself.

He spread his hands. "I'm trying to stay out of it, honestly. True, leaving your memory totally intact would have been... disorienting... for you. There are things you knew as a goddess that a human brain and the associated sensory apparatus aren't capable of processing, and you—goddess you, I mean—had some legitimate concerns about your health and well-being if you retained all the memories. It's entirely possible that you'd spend your month on Earth in a state of essential schizophrenia, beset by visions and voices not your own. I argued for a more selective redaction of memories, but you felt strongly that your personal development as a mortal would benefit from a clean-slate approach."

I snorted. "My personal development. Right. I feel like I'm being nagged by a court-appointed therapist. Am I really such a mess, that I had to get 'Do Better' tattooed on my skin?"

He stepped closer to me then, and wrapped his arms around me, and though I didn't exactly melt in his arms, I didn't pull away, either. I've never been a big fan of human contact, but screw it, he wasn't really human. "I would argue that you aren't so bad," Death murmured into my hair. He drew back and took my face in his hands. "You aren't exactly tactful, it's true. And you're stubborn, and impulsive, and arrogant, and you can be selfish, and you always think you know best—"

"Stop, you'll make me blush."

"—but you're not *bad*. No one can call you that, not really. You're the sort of person who would literally tear holes in the fabric of reality to help a friend. Perhaps not the best idea in the world, and I admit the consequences were fairly dire, but it was hardly born from an evil impulse."

"I never claimed to be a demonic sociopath. I've got my good points. But intentions don't count for shit—just results, and consequences. If I'm honest… I know I've got a lot to make up for. I can't really make amends, or reparations, for the damage I've caused, and the people I've hurt, but I can try to balance some of the bad things I've done, and save others."

"I am pleased you have a purpose. If I can aid you at all in your work…"

I shook my head. "It's not really riding a bike if you use training wheels, hubs. I can't stand on my own feet if I've got you propping me up. I've already got one unfair advantage. I got an axe to the head today—it should have been me showing up on your stygian shores in the sunless lands today, not Andrew Lin."

"We have an arrangement. You bargained hard, and as a result, you get to spend half the year alive in the mortal world and half in the underworld with me. Letting you *die* would break our arrangement—and I'm not about to renege a deal I made with you. I'd never live it down."

"I guess adding a 'no pain' rider to the deal would be asking too much?"

He kissed my forehead. "Life is pain. Isn't that what you told me once?"

I pushed him away. Nobody kisses me on the forehead. "Are you getting along okay down there without me? I can only assume I'm the one who keeps the infernal trains running on time."

"We're muddling along. There will be messes for you to clean up when you return in a few weeks, of course."

"Why am I not surprised? Okay, Mr. Mason. I've got wrongs to right and dragons to slay. I don't much want to hang around Sunlight Shores here, so I'd better get on the road. And hey. Thanks for the motorcycle. It's a pretty sweet ride."

"Only the best for my blushing bride."

"Ha. I can't remember the last time I blushed."

"True enough. I do most of the blushing in our relationship. Give my best to Nicolette."

"Although it would be funny to look her straight in the eyes and say, 'Death says hello,' I think I'll pass. In case you forget, we didn't invite her to the wedding. She doesn't know about our relationship."

"Consider my greeting rescinded, then. I never liked her anyway."

"See, that's why our relationship works. We hate the same people."

Death strolled away, passing through another nonexistent door that vanished when it closed behind him, and I returned to my motorcycle and thumped the top of Nicolette's cage. "Ready to go? Need a pee break first? Oh, that's right, you don't have a bladder. Or a urinary tract."

She belched again, loud and long. "I've got the metaphysical equivalent of a full belly, though. That was a chaos buffet. We literally brought down the house."

"'We.' What we? You're just a dowsing rod. I'm the one who dug the well."

"You can't annoy me," she said, eyes half-closed, a sickeningly satisfied expression on her face. "You have no idea how good this feels. I'm talking heroin orgasms here."

"I could have done without that mental image." I covered her up, then drove away from Sunlight Shores as night began to fall, trying to decide if I should head for a freeway and look for a motel, or find a spot to camp out under the stars (which didn't sound all that appealing). After riding for a few miles on dark country lanes, I saw the lights of a roadhouse, with a gravel parking lot jammed full of pickups and motorcycles.

My stomach started grumbling instantly, and I realized I hadn't had anything to eat in ages—chaos doesn't do much to fill *me* up. I figured any decent beer-and-juke joint would probably offer up some burgers or onion rings or sausages or something, so I pulled into the lot. My plan was, get a meal, and if I was lucky, maybe some asshole would try to grope me, and then I'd get to have a bar fight. The ghost sharks had done the killing for me back there, and I was itching for more direct action.

I got something so much more interesting than a fight, though. I got myself a war.

Honkly Tonk

The place was called Danooli's, and it was a seriously old-school roadhouse. Lots of exposed wood, not in a fancy reclaimed renovated antique lumber way, but just because nobody'd ever bothered to cover it up in the first place. Sawdust on the floor. Jukebox about the size of the refrigerator in my last apartment. Guy with scraggly gray hair in a tight-fitting muscle T-shirt drawing foamy beers at the bar for an assortment of bikers, farmhands, and miscellaneous drunks. Quite an array, apart from every one of them being white. I guess the Hispanic population got drunk elsewhere. I projected my best "Don't hit on me unless you want to *get* hit" attitude and sauntered up to the bar, Nicolette's cage dangling from my fingers. She seemed asleep—who knows if she really sleeps, maybe she just zones out—and I had hopes for a quiet meal and a drink. I'm not a drinker as a rule, since I like my reflexes fast and my inhibitions don't need to be any weaker, but in a place like this, if you don't get at least a beer, you draw too much attention.

"You serve anything edible in this place?" I called to the bartender over the blare of trumpets. (You'd expect the juke to be playing some country shit, right, or classic rock at best? But it was some '90s pop-ska instead, at least at that moment.)

The bartender smiled wide, and if he hadn't been missing a bicuspid on the left side it would've been a really enchanting smile—it kind of was, anyway. I like people who don't give a fuck how they look. "The pickled eggs are all right," he said. "Burgers are hit or miss. Everything else comes so deep fried it don't much matter how it started out."

"Give me a basket of the finest of whatever you dip in beer batter, then."

"Eating light, got it. Jalapeños and mushrooms coming up."

"Anything on tap that doesn't taste like piss and rice water?"

He raised an eyebrow at that. "An import or two, but you're better off going with one of the local microbrews, if you're picky—"

Even in the dusty roadhouse department, things were getting fancy. "I'll trust your judgment. Something light, though, I've been riding all day and I'm hot as Hell."

"Oh, you don't have to tell me that. I noticed." He drew me a beer and slid it over. "You can grab a stool or take it to a booth if you'd rather. I'll bring your food over."

"Much obliged." I picked up my beer in one hand and the birdcage in the other and found the darkest, deepest, most distant booth available. I'm not normally so chatty with bartenders. Maybe I was starved for human contact of the non-headless, non-attempting-to-sacrifice-me-to-monsters variety. I folded my coat and draped it over Nicolette's birdcage in the seat beside me, then pulled out the paperback I was reading and squinted at the pages in the dimness. The bartender appeared a bit later and slid a plastic basket full of unidentifiable deep-fried blobs and a dish of ranch dressing across to me, and I grunted thanks without looking up from my book. I know, so suddenly antisocial. A little human contact goes a long way for me.

A young guy came bursting in through the front door, dressed in dusty, broken-in riding leathers, but he didn't have a hardass biker look, more the excitable demeanor of a kid who's just discovered drinking and sex and can't believe life is so amazingly good. There was a lull in the jukebox music and he shouted, "Hey! Who's driving that sweet fuckin' Vincent White Shadow out in the parking lot?"

I winced, and a couple of the other bikers walked over to the guy, then went outside with him, presumably to look over the vehicle in question. I tried not to worry about it. As long as they didn't try to touch it—or gods forbid *sit* on it—they'd be fine, and bikers by and large are extremely respectful of personal property. They came back in later, and now all *three* of them were excited. I'm not much of a gearhead myself, but I should have realized a bike that rare would excite comment among those who give more of a shit. Trust my boy Death to give me a gift as impractical as it was awesome. He was clearly a guy who'd never had to live in the world. There's privilege and then there's *privilege*.

The guys shouted some more, and general inquiries about the possessor of said *sweet-ass-ride* were addressed to the room, and finally someone who must have seen me arrive pointed me out. The young guy ran over like I was his long-lost first love and slid into the booth across from me. "Hey, I'm sorry to bother you, but lady, I think I *love* you."

I had no idea how long it had been since I'd had sex, not definitely—Death and I had gone on a honeymoon (which is a story for another time) the week before I descended to the underworld for my first month of indentured godhood, but it was possible I'd had some kind of crazy rarefied god-sex while I was down there, too, and just couldn't remember. Not that it mattered. I wasn't so hard up I'd go for the slobbering puppy-dog enthusiastic type, so I didn't give him even an iota of warmth in response. "Great. Get the fuck out of my booth. I'm eating."

"Okay, okay, I just wanted to say, that bike out there, I've never even *seen* one, I saw a Black Shadow once in a parade, but—"

"It's a nice bike," I said. "But I'm not a nice woman. Beat it."

"Any woman who rides a machine like that is plenty nice enough for *me*," he said, in a tone like he was doing me a favor. "I'd sure love to ride on that thing, I'd even ride bitch. Or if I can't ride the *bike*—"

I saw clear enough where that was going, so I tapped my wedding ring on the beer glass. "See this, kid? Means I'm taken." It didn't mean that at all, necessarily—Death and I are pragmatists—but I could suddenly see the usefulness of wearing a wedding band to fend off unwelcome admirers without resorting to physical violence or magical mind-fuckery.

For a moment the kid looked crestfallen, but then he rallied and said, "What makes you think I wouldn't love you better than he can? What's your husband got that *I* don't?"

I could've given lots of honest answers. The powers of a god. Dominion over the land of the dead. Better reasons for similar levels of cockiness. Instead I said, "For one thing, he gave me that motorcycle."

The kid sat back in the booth. "Sheee-it," he said, drawing it out low and slow.

"Yup."

He slapped his hand on the table nodded. "Can't see how I can argue with that. You have a good night, ma'am."

"You too, kid." He went across the bar to the other bikers, shaking his head, and I watched out of the corner of my eye to see if any of them were going to try their luck, but apparently he'd conveyed my utter unattainability adequately, because they kept to their end of the room.

The jukebox was blaring something by The Eagles—good, the cognitive dissonance from the ska music was starting to bug me—when suddenly the room went silent. I don't just mean the music stopped: I mean the music stopped, the talking stopped, the clink of glasses stopped, the pounding of feet stopped, *everything* stopped.

I took in the room at a glance. Everyone was standing still, but time itself hadn't stopped, which was good—that kind of thing was major magic. This was more like actors in an improv class told to "*freeze*!" I could see they were still breathing, and the ones who'd gotten stuck in particularly awkward positions were trembling a little from the effort of holding their poses, but their eyes were blank and empty. As far as everyone else here was concerned, this was lost time blackout territory.

I sighed, tore a piece off the napkin in my lap, and used it to mark my place before closing my book. Then I pulled my coat into my lap, so I could reach into the pockets if need be.

"Well?" I called. "Come on if you're coming."

The bathroom door swung open, and something mostly man-shaped stepped out. He was dressed in flannel and denim and work boots, but his skin was a curdled-cheese color not generally found in nature, his eyes were set too far apart and not quite level on the horizontal, and his hair appeared literally made of dirty steel wool. His footsteps made squishing sounds when he walked, even though the floor was dry, so that was pretty nasty.

"Hello." He slid into the booth across from me, then laced his hands together on the table. He only had four fingers on each hand, like a cartoon character. "You've made quite an impression with… certain people… since you came to town."

I sipped my beer. "Ha. I bet calling them 'people' is stretching it. What do you want?"

"I represent some prominent local interests. We noticed an act of mayhem you committed. Now we're curious about your intentions going forward."

"Intentions don't matter for shit," I said, echoing my conversation with Death earlier that day.

"Nonsense." He smiled, like we were old friends having a familiar argument. "Intentions matter a great deal. They're the difference between first and second degree murder, among other things. Intentions are the reason some things are tragic accidents and some things are crimes against humanity. There's a Latin expression, *'actus non facit reum nisi mens sit rea'*—"

"The act's not a crime if the mind isn't guilty," I interrupted.

"A biker, a monster-slayer, and a Latin scholar, too," he said.

I shrugged. "From time to time I've been called upon to be judge and jury and, as you've already noticed, executioner."

"Then you understand that the state of mind of the criminal does matter. You're the criminal here, in case that wasn't clear. Did you act with intent? With reckless disregard for foreseeable consequences? Did you *mean* to kill the creature you encountered today? Was it something you planned, or a murder of opportunity, or even self-defense? Do you intend to commit similar crimes in the immediate vicinity in the near future? These questions matter *very* much to those I represent."

I don't actually hate lawyers, as a class. I've met a few I got along with fine, both of the crusading paladin and conniving pragmatist types. But if this thing was some kind of lawyer for *monsters*, I had two reactions. One: "That's interesting." And two: "Fuck him."

"You know who doesn't give a shit about intentions?" I said. "The ones who suffer the consequences. The guy who gets smeared into nothingness by a truck doesn't care if it was premeditated, or an act of negligence, or recklessness, or catastrophic unavoidable unpredictable brake failure. He's just as dead."

"Mmm." The thing fixed me with his glossy eyes. "You're saying the creature you killed was a killer, and it doesn't matter *why* it killed—the killings were crimes, which had to be avenged. And you have chosen to be the avenger."

That wasn't what I was saying at all. I was thinking about some of my own acts, born of good intentions, and the deaths that had followed as naturally as rot follows slaughter. There wasn't even anyone around to avenge those deaths, not in a way that mattered... but I could pay penance. "What I'm saying is, fuck intentions. Actions are what matter."

"Really?" His rudimentary face looked incredulous. "What about homicidal somnambulism? People who commit murder while sleepwalking, without any input from their conscious minds? Or take the classic monster-movie version of the werewolf, an ordinary man, transformed by the moon, who commits terrible acts, but not willingly? How is that different from, say, someone being mind-controlled by a psychic parasite and steered toward murder? Are they to be judged exactly the same as one who murders for profit or sexual release?"

"You seem to think I'm talking about *blame*," I said. "But blame is irrelevant here. I wouldn't *blame* a guy who committed a murder while sleepwalking—but I'd make sure he slept in restraints, under supervision. I wouldn't *blame* Lon Chaney for wolfing out and eating somebody, but I'd make sure he got locked in a cell during the full moon. And if the sleepwalker slipped his restraints, and the wolfman killed his jailer and escaped, and I knew containment wasn't a feasible action? You bet I'd kill them, for the greater good. If there's a guy who kills strangers, it doesn't matter if he did it because he was possessed by a demon, or because he had a combination of bad genes and a shitty upbringing and a psychological stressor that made him snap, or because a brain tumor pressed on his amygdala and convinced him the strangers were ghosts from Hell—reasons aside, you stop him from doing the killing. I'm a pragmatist."

"Yet you say this as someone who *does* kill strangers," the lawyer mused. "You see no contradiction?"

"I guess I should've said 'innocent strangers.'"

"No one is innocent. From the point of view of those I represent, *you* could be seen as a mad-dog killer."

"More like a killer of mad dogs. But, if you feel that way—you're free to try to stop me."

"Mmm. We might have to. We're pragmatists as well, you see, and our future actions depend largely on whether we judge you liable to be a… repeat offender."

I nodded. "Okay. I can help you with that. Yeah, I killed a monster. There's every reason to think I'll do it again. At least until I run out of monsters."

"I see. Well, then." He drummed his fingers on the tabletop. Nasty brown water leaked out of one of his sleeves and puddled around his hands. "Do you know why World War I started?"

"Germans behaving badly?"

He smiled, and as far as I could tell his teeth were made of chipped bits of tile. "The Archduke Franz Ferdinand of Austro-Hungary was assassinated by a Serbian nationalist group called the Black Hand."

I put a deep-fried jalapeño (probably) in my mouth, chewed, swallowed, and said, "I hate them already. They've got a name like a comic book super villain team."

"Mmm. As a result of that assassination, Austro-Hungary declared war on Serbia. Then Russia, which had an alliance with Serbia, stepped in to honor their mutual-defense agreement and declared war on Austro-Hungary. Germany had an alliance with Austro-Hungary, and since the Russians were making threats, the Germans stepped in to defend *their* allies. The French were allied with the Russians, so of course they had to help out, too. The Germans struck at France through Belgium—which triggered the Belgian alliance with Great Britain, bringing the English into the war. Italy and Japan and the U. S. felt left out, so they all joined in, too."

"Who doesn't love a party?" I said.

"The *point* is, striking at one individual isn't a self-contained act. One small murder can trigger consequences, which trigger other consequences, and soon..." He spread his dripping hands before him. "You've got a war."

"Huh. So you're saying the beast I killed had friends, and now those friends are going to try to start some shit? And are *you* one of those friends?"

He shook his head. "Quite the opposite. I am a member of what might be described as an *opposing* faction to the beast's cohort. Personally, I'm delighted you killed that refugee from deep time with the buzz saw face. But the beast had allies, who now suspect that my friends *hired* you to kill the beast, in order to weaken their base of power—the beast was a rather heavy hitter, you know, in the violence department. We've claimed innocence, of course, but they don't seem to believe us. The fragile peace between our factions is now threatened."

I smiled. "You mean I triggered a monster gang war? Wow. That couldn't have worked out better if I'd planned it."

"Only if you're a fan of chaos."

"I'm not, particularly, but maybe some of my *allies* are."

He leaned forward, and the spongy texture of his flesh was even more apparent at closer range. I caught a whiff of something nasty, old sewage and fresh latrines. "My people are going to be blamed for your behavior, no matter what. As we've already covered, rather thoroughly, I don't know your motives—"

"Simple. I kill monsters, because monsters need to be killed."

"That *is* simple, or at least, simple-minded. But, fine—if that's what you want to do, we can help you. We can point you toward certain monsters, tell you their weaknesses, help you with weapons, whatever you need."

"Uh huh. And why would you do that? Bring *me* into your alliance, when I've caused you trouble?"

He shrugged. "If a war is starting anyway, it's in our best interests if you thin out the enemy. Best case, you make our struggle easier. Worst case, you die, which doesn't bother us much. You're pulling us into a war, so the least you can do is help us win it, and advance your own asinine agenda in the process."

"And if I decline your offer?"

"We can't have wild cards and loose cannons and other clichés meddling in our business. I have been authorized to take preventative steps if you aren't willing to be reasonable."

"You have a boss? A general? Someone you answer to?"

"We are more a loose alliance of like-minded individuals who work together to achieve consensus."

"Huh." I ate a beer-battered mushroom. "That structure never worked for me. I always liked a strong central authority, or at least a first-among-equals kinda deal." Though now that I thought of it, I was technically co-equal with Death during my time in the underworld. I wondered if one of us had ultimate authority, or if we had a system of vetoes or bargains or favors owed, or if we just flipped coins or played Rochambeau to break deadlocks. Probably we had some kind of god-level flow-chart or decision tree my puny human brain couldn't comprehend.

"Yes, you mentioned your time as a one-woman judicial system before. That's the sort of approach beloved by dictators and tyrants."

"Despots get a bad rap. These enemies you mentioned—is one of them called the Eater, by chance? I'm guessing he'd be more equal than the others.'"

The man-thing didn't flinch or twitch or anything, but his total lack of reaction was, in itself, something of a reaction. "The Eater?"

"Just a name I heard. From the thing I killed. Offered up in the form of a threat."

"The Eater is… not one of our allies, not directly. But we have no quarrels with it, either. That's all I'm comfortable saying on the subject at this time." And he actually looked around, as if afraid the Eater might be sitting in a booth, watching him. Which, for all I knew, he or she or it *was*. "I'd rather talk about *you*, and what we're going to do about you—"

"What *you're* going to do about *me*? You don't know who I am, do you?" I was mostly used to fighting people who realized what they were getting into when they fucked with me. What? So I've got a little bit of ego. Then again, I'd once been chief sorcerer of a city, fighting monsters in an official capacity. As a freelancer far from my traditional stomping grounds, my anonymity was a new experience. I couldn't decide if it was liberating or annoying. Probably both. Everything's complicated.

"I don't even know your name, no. We haven't had time to do much research—we just picked up your trail and I came to chat."

"Huh. I'm Marla. What's your name?"

"I don't have a *name* as you understand the concept—"

"I'm curious, how did that thing have allies anyway?" I interrupted. "You know, Mr. tentacles-and-tooth-whorl, the victim, maybe he doesn't have a proper name either. I thought he was some kind of prehistoric dimension-hopper that was imprisoned for millennia, or at least centuries—I half thought 'the Eater' was just the name of his extra-dimensional monster god, some kind of alien divinity. But apparently it's an actual guy, or thing, or whatever. So you're telling me the beast of Sunlight Shores, what, escaped a cavern, hooked into the local power structure, made friends and influenced people, and *then* started eating squatters?"

"Some of our alliances are *very* old, as are some of the creatures who made them. The beast found a familiar face or two when he woke up, as I understand it. Well, not that they literally have faces. But we're always open to promising newcomers, too, Marla. We seldom involve humans in our business, but you're not a typical human, so—"

I held up a hand. "I'm considering your offer, SpongeBob. Let me ask you something. Do you and your allies prey on humans? Drink their blood, or eat their brains, or sap their life essence, or steal their creativity, or suck out their capacity for love, or devour their innocence, or bathe in their sexual energy, or feast on their entrails?"

The monster shrugged. "Everyone preys on something. We act only according to our natures."

"So do liver flukes. And those little fish in the Amazon that swim up a dude's pee-hole and then fill up the urethra with spikes. Not to mention that parasitic fish that eats another fish's tongue and takes its place, then snaps up all the food the big fish tries to eat, until it starves. Every one of them, just doing what comes naturally. Doesn't mean I have to like them."

I took my silver hatchet out of my coat and rested it on the table between us, two fingers touching the handle. "So I pissed off the other crew by killing one of theirs. How about I even things up by killing one of *yours*? I'm not picky about which one, but I mean… you're convenient."

"Did you think I would come here without *protections*?" he said. "I have allies outside, and—"

While he was staring at the axe I whipped my dagger out and jammed it deep into his eye socket. The knife tore through his face like I'd plunged it into moldy bread—part of the hilt got embedded, too, and his whole ocular orbit and cheekbone collapsed inward. I tore the knife out, and watched him wobble a little, then clutch one hand over the injury. "You can't *stab* me," he said.

"Obviously I can, but it didn't appear to do much good. Boots it is." I stood up in the booth, stepped up on top of the table, and kicked his head like I was playing kickball in elementary school. I'd worked some nice inertial magics into my cowboy boots during my enchanting spree the night before, and his head flew free. Nasty sprays of black stuff floated up from inside his neck, some kind of horrible pathogenic spores probably, but I didn't worry about it. Being death-proof had its advantages.

After I got his head off I kicked his body out of the booth to the floor and methodically stomped him to mush. I had no idea if I'd really killed him or not—maybe his actual physical form was those floating black seedpods or spores that came drifting up, or maybe he was a remote-controlled filth golem. I didn't much care. I'd made my point: I wasn't for hire, and I wasn't on anybody's side but my own.

Once he was done, I finished my beer, put on my coat, stowed my weapons, and picked up Nicolette—still sleeping, as far as I could tell.

I didn't go for the front door, but went around the bar, weaving among the statue-like people, and into the tiny kitchen (glad I hadn't seen it *before* I ate—I've been in cleaner crackhouses). The cook, poised over the fry pit, began to move, pivoting in slow-motion, but it was an encouraging sign—the normal flow of time was returning for these people. I found the back door and eased my way out.

I didn't see or sense any sign of life back there, just empty desert night, so I crept around the side of the building, toward the front, and saw a couple of hulking figures watching the door, talking in low grunting voices. I put Nicolette's cage down, then crept up until I was standing just behind and between them.

"Hey." As they turned, I slipped a couple of my mundane knives into their guts, where the kidneys would be. They fell, scrabbling for the hilts, and I got a look at their faces, which were human except for piglike tusks and flat noses and eyes that were all sclera. "So, I stomped the ambassador or lawyer or whatever in there to death. I mean, I think—none of his bits are moving anymore, anyway. You can take that news back to the rest of your mob. And in case they're shaky on the interpretation, the meaning of my radical act of violence is: I don't work for you, or anyone else. Oh, and anyone who fucks with me? I take them apart. Of course, there's a good chance I'll take them apart even if they *don't* fuck with me, but why increase the odds?"

One of them tried to reach into his jacket so I stomped down on his arm until things cracked, then kept on until they stopped cracking and started grinding. "Sorry. Too much? I tend to overreact to negative stimuli. It's a coping mechanism."

"Kill... you..." the one I hadn't stomped said. "I'll..."

"You will? Do you plan on doing it soon, or is this one of those long-term things? Do I have time to set my affairs in order? I have to admit, the suspense is totally killing me." I booted him in the side until he rolled over, then retrieved my knife. His wound was already healing up. Monster-types often heal fast. I retrieved my other blade—better not to give them any possession they could use to magically track me—and spat on the ground beside them, because I always like to get in the last word.

The music came back on inside the honky tonk. I wondered what the clientele would make of the heap of gray mush and flannel beside my booth, and my sudden disappearance. Or the pig-men in the—

But no. They'd crawled off into the dark somewhere. Back to report to their masters, because they were lackeys if I ever saw any. I didn't figure their bosses would be scared away, but that was fine. I was here to make enemies, and if the monsters came to me, that just saved me the trouble of looking for them.

I got Nicolette settled and cranked up my bike, then headed back to the road, toward the highway. The noise of the engine must have woken her up, because she yawned and said, "I smell violence. What'd I miss?"

"I got dinner," I said. "Had a beer. Chatted with a bartender. Some young biker tried to pick me up."

"Oh, gross. You're making me sick to the stomach I don't have. Is that all?"

"Mostly. I also found out I triggered a monster gang war by killing that thing at Sunlight Shores. His allies want me dead—and so do his enemies, since I kicked their messenger to mush."

"Huh," she said. "So was the biker boy cute?"

Then I got a motel room and wrote all this, and tomorrow I'm going to see if I can find the front lines in this war I started.

Or, better yet, bring the front lines to wherever I am. Much more relaxing.

Nojimbo

"GHOST TOWNS ARE BORING," Nicolette said. "They're the *opposite* of chaos, unless you count gentle entropic decay."

"Welcome to Tolerance," I said. "Jewel of the West."

(This was a few days after I stomped the monster lawyer to death, or anyway to pieces. I'd had to do some research first, make some preparations, and sorry, Future Me, but it's too boring to write all that stuff down. I want to get to the part with the traps and tricks and battles. I'll fill you in on any backstory you might need along the way.)

I surveyed the dusty streets and the few sand-eaten structures still left standing. The place looked almost picturesque in the gray morning light. "This is a ghost town, and I mean *ghost*. It's not on the maps or in the guidebooks. Pelly told me about it. It was a thriving little town until the copper mines or whatever played out, and after it was abandoned by humans, other things moved in. Then some kind of major supernatural battle went down here in the late 1800s, and it became doubly-abandoned."

"It stinks of residual magic, all right," Nicolette said. "Why do we care, exactly?"

I carried her cage into one of the nearly-intact buildings. Maybe it used to be a saloon, but it was just a mouse toilet now, full of rotting timbers and broken glass. The walls left standing were riddled with bullet holes, so that was cool. I righted a table that still had all its legs and put her cage down. "All the magic here will muddle things up. They'll have trouble tracking me precisely, and they won't be sure how much power I have, and how much is purely atmospheric. This place is a magical megaphone, too—any workings I do will be made stronger just by the boost of background magic."

"It'll make their magic stronger too," Nicolette pointed out.

I shrugged. "I'm not too worried about that." I leaned against the bar, which creaked but didn't fall over.

"You don't have that white cloak anymore, so I don't know why you're so confident," she complained. "If you get killed, I can't exactly sneak away and hitch a ride back to civilization."

Once upon a time I'd had a magical cloak that healed all wounds I sustained—in fact, Nicolette herself had once set me on fire while I wore the cloak, and I'd ended up with little more than singed hair. The cloak had even let me recover from a bullet to the head, once, though it had taken a few hours. But the garment was cursed, basically, so I was better off without it.

Besides, these days I pretty much wore an invisible cloak of healing, and that was even better, because no one expected it.

"I thought you wanted me to die? I figured you'd be thrilled with me taking on a battle against unlikely odds."

"I don't want you to die while we're in the middle of nowhere, or surrounded by people who think I'm your ally, who'll probably play kickball with me out of spite. I need you to die someplace with a handy innocent bystander or two, someone I can convince or compel to carry me off with them into the sunset. Show some consideration, Marla."

I shrugged. "Don't fret about me. One woman against two rival gangs, in an isolated town—how can I possibly lose? You've never seen *A Fistful of Dollars*?"

"I prefer *Yojimbo*. You know, the classic Kurosawa movie they totally ripped off when they made *Fistful of Dollars*?"

"Thpt," I said, or some similar sound. "Kurosawa? Black and white. Subtitles. What am I, an art house theater? Spare me. Anyway, if you're going to make a Western, let it be a *Western*."

"You're an idiot," Nicolette said. "Eastwood's got a face like a block of wood. He can't emote his way out of a paper bag. Mifune's so subtle, he can convey so much with the tiniest change of expression, one twitch of an eyebrow—"

"Different approaches to the character, that's all. Apples and oranges."

"Apples and vastly inferior apples, more like it," she said. "I bet you prefer *The Magnificent Seven* to *The Seven Samurai*, too."

"Well, duh. Steve McQueen was the first man I ever loved, though I loved him from afar."

"This isn't *Yojimbo* anyway," Nicolette said. "Mifune played both gangs against each other, pretending to switch his loyalties back and forth, and got them to mostly destroy each other. You're not going to double-cross anybody. Both gangs of monsters are just going to kill *you*."

"Don't be silly. It's unlikely *both* gangs will kill me. One of them will manage it first, and the other will be left disappointed."

"They might shed a little extracurricular blood as they fight to see who gets to rip your spleen out personally, but otherwise, I don't see how you're going to hurt them all. And! In *Yojimbo*, he was fighting to save the townspeople from the gamblers and gangsters who'd taken over. There aren't any townspeople here. You're just fighting for… what? Your own self-aggrandizement? General bloodlust? I still don't know what the hell this little road trip is for. Not that I require meaning or purpose—I used to do things all the time just because it seemed like a good, or at least interestingly bad, idea at the time—but I expected more sense and sensibility out of you."

"I'm fighting for hypothetical townspeople," I said. "People somewhere in *some* town who won't get eaten or brain-drained or seduced or ripped off by these things after I kill them. My motives are pure." I strolled toward the front door, such as it was. "How long do you think before they get here?"

"It's hard to tell anything for sure in this place, because of old magic kicking so much noise up in my signal, but… I'd say you have a while. There are forces gathering, but they're a ways off. I don't think anyone will try to murder you until late this afternoon, anyway."

"Good enough. That gives me time to play the good hostess and get some party favors ready."

Let me tell you a little bit about these assholes, these "gangs." You'd think, two big groups of supernatural bad guys, there'd be some kind of fundamental split. Like the classic vampires versus werewolves. (The first don't exist, at least not the classic blood-drinkers with the garlic allergies, not as far as I know, and as for the second, sure, there are people who turn into wolves, just like there are people who turn into jaguars and bears and vampire squid, using all kinds of magical methods, so I don't know why the wolfie ones always get top billing.) Or Seelie versus Unseelie courts. (There are certainly things from a place painfully adjacent to this universe who *present* themselves as fairies or elves, but I wouldn't trust them to accurately identify themselves, or to tell the truth about anything really, or to know what the truth even means.) Or Godzillas versus Kongs, or angels versus demons, or ifrits versus water sprites, or ghost pirates versus giant squids, or *something*.

But these gangs weren't like that. They didn't have some ideological or inherent conflict that could only be played out in the form of a secret war. They were just concatenations of supernatural assholes who arbitrarily aligned themselves into factions for mutual support, until their groups came into inevitable conflict, and then they started a low-level ongoing war. There wasn't a "good" gang or a "bad" gang—they were equally awful. Let me give you an idea what I was going up against.

(Some of this I found out from research I had Pelly do—the man is a whiz with the internet, knows how to access every darknet and private forum for monsters there is, and he's not afraid to make phone calls and do a little social engineering to worm information out of people, either—and some from shady sources Rondeau knows from the casino scene and all the other unsavory things he does.)

On the one side, we had team monster-lawyer—you know, the guy I stomped to bits at Danooli's. His bunch was led by a witch named Orias, who specialized in the satiation of unnatural appetites. Her preferred rackets were prostitution, of the decidedly non-standard kind. You went to her brothels if you wanted to fuck a girl who had a barbed tail she could shove up your ass during the act of love, or to make out with a guy with needle fangs full of hallucinogenic venom, or to get blowjobs from a blob with a thousand mouths and two thousand tongues. Some of the 'escorts' were monsters she hired, some were artificial life forms constructed in her underground flesh lab, and some she acquired through more mysterious means.

Orias supplied ordinary everyday humans to monsters who liked to play with those, too, and she didn't much care if the humans were willing or not. She had fingers in most of the sin industries—exotic drugs (blood, sweat, milk, jizz, and other substances from her employees, mainly), gambling (where the stakes were a little more interesting than cash or cars or houses), and so on. I've got nothing against people having a good time, as long as everything's consensual and nobody gets dragged in against their will, or exploited because they're too young and/or dumb to know better, but Orias had no such qualms. She was teamed up with various thugs and bone breakers and mind eaters who enforced her policies and kept the below-the-line workers focused and on task.

The other gang, the one the beast of Sunlight Shores had been aligned with, was run by a self-styled *loup garou* called Sarlat—name taken from some famous man-eating wolf that only attacked grown men, standing on its hind legs and clawing out their throats. Sarlat was into heavier shit than Orias, mostly. Where Orias served the twisted needs and desires of the people in the Southwestern states, Sarlat believed more in *making* opportunities, and then exploiting the fuck out of them. Extortion, murder for hire, protection, all the standard rackets, backed up with supernatural powers. He was also… let's say a procurer. He was the guy you went to if you were a cultist and your god needed fifteen virgins sacrificed at the next new moon, or if you were a monster who needed to eat the livers of unbaptized babies to sustain your next century of life. For the right price, he'd make sure you got what you needed, and word was he'd wield the ceremonial knife himself for no extra charge.

As a rule, his gang was nastier than the crew Orias ran, but they were also less well organized, more a loose affiliation of independent contractors who bonded together for mutual protection and backup as necessary.

As for why the two gangs hated each other… all the usual reasons. Clashes over turf. Sarlat robbing Orias's people, Orias's people poisoning Sarlat's people in retaliation. There was also some more personal enmity between the two leaders, though Pelly and Rondeau hadn't been able to track down any details, at least not in the few days I'd given them to scrounge up intel. There were rumors that Orias and Sarlat used to sleep together, which was all the explanation I needed, really. There's no hatred like love gone rancid.

Both gangs were using all the psychics and divination specialists at their respective disposals to track me down, and make sure I paid for my crimes. Or, more honestly, to make sure I didn't commit any more. They don't give a shit about justice, but when it comes to self-preservation, Sarlat and Orias are both motivated self-starters.

(You're thinking: what about the Eater, right? I was promised an Eater. But Pelly couldn't find anything about a guy called that, and Rondeau couldn't, either. I could have pestered Rondeau into summoning up an oracle and asking the question, but if he did that sort of thing too often he got migraines, and started barfing, and I was trying to go easy on him. I didn't think it mattered—I figured maybe 'the Eater' was a nickname for Sarlat. I was so wrong.)

The bad guys rolled in around sundown, a line of pickup trucks and SUVs, and creatures moving rapidly on foot (or paw or claw or slime-cushion) in the shadows. I watched and listened from my undisclosed location, through the eyes of various Polaroid photographs of myself I'd secreted all over the ghost town. (Imbuing representations of self with sensory capabilities is pretty basic sympathetic magic. The downside is if someone sticks a knife in one of the photos, it hurts, so I'd hidden them pretty well.)

The monster gangs set up a couple of camps, each at one end of the long main street. Both gangs posted guards, who made occasional forays down the main street toward one another, jeering and shouting threats, each side claiming they would be the one to take my head—I assumed they meant decapitating me, as opposed to taking Nicolette, more's the pity—and so on. Just posturing. It was good to see they hadn't coordinated their plans, teaming up to take me out more efficiently. Given the deep enmity between them, that wasn't surprising, but I'd worried they'd see me as a big enough threat to join forces against the common enemy. I'd have an easier time (and, being honest, a lot more fun) if they were still out to kill each other, too.

Sarlat took up residence in the remains of the sheriff's office, which was pretty much just a tumble of timbers, except for the rusting iron bulk of the cells, the bars still holding firm in stone walls. He set up a chair and table in a cell, which surprised me—animals aren't big fans of being in cages, as a rule—but then, that was the only bit of office that had a solid roof overhead, so it made sense. He barked orders at his lieutenants, telling them to scour the nearby buildings and the surrounding area for any trace of me. There was so much residual magic in Tolerance they couldn't focus on me with the usual pinpoint divination techniques—the best they could tell was that I was somewhere inside a fuzzy circle a mile or so in diameter, centered on the town itself.

Once Sarlat was alone in the cell, jabbing angrily at the screen of his smartphone, I made my presence known.

When I materialized in the office and sauntered to the door of the cell, he tried to kill me straight away—leapt up, threw his phone aside, and just *flew* straight for me, hands extended and already twisting into claws. He passed right through me and rolled in a somersault on the dirty ground before springing to his feet. "Illusion," he spat.

I shrugged in my undisclosed location, and my image standing before him did the same. "Projection, anyway." One of my photos was in a corner of the room, covered with a layer of dirt, allowing me to spy and to project a remote presence into the room. My illusory body only had a range of ten yards or so, but that was more than sufficient for my purposes. "I like how you came straight at me, no posturing, no chit-chat—I'd heard you were a pro. Not like that poser Orias."

Sarlat's hands were just hands again, and he brushed dirt off his body. He looked like a weird cross between a dom and a hipster—motorcycle boots, leather pants, leather vest over a white shirt, and thick leather bracelets on each wrist, but he had absurd facial hair that included a mustache with waxed ends, and his glasses were old-school with big chunky frames. Sarlat might have been handsome, but it was hard to tell under all the clichés he was wearing. "You killed someone I was sworn to protect, bitch."

"Bitch? I'm not one of your litter-mates, wolfman. All human here." (That was true, for the moment. I had three weeks before I'd be a goddess again.) "Which reminds me—what kind of werewolf are you, Sarlat? Are you more like a Basque, or more like a leper, or more like a Tasmanian devil?"

Sarlat circled around my illusion, clenching and unclenching his hands. "What the fuck are you talking about?"

"I mean, are you a human who just happens to turn into a wolf, with your own werewolf cultural traditions and shit—werewolf as ethnicity? Or are you a human who got bitten by a filthy animal and caught a nasty disease that makes you sprout hair in even more places than usual—werewolf as disease, like a leper? Or are you a totally different species, and you just happen to *look* human sometimes, even though you're really no more human than a Tasmanian devil?"

He drew himself up to his full height, which was probably only about five-foot-eight absent the motorcycle boots. "I am *le loup-garou*. My sins were so extravagant that I became heir to an ancient evil, which allows me to transform—and not just into a wolf. I can be an owl, stalking the skies, or a cat, slinking through the shadows—"

"Huh, right," I said. "And a cow, too, right? Sometimes a pig?"

He bared his teeth, which were noticeably yellow, especially the oversized canines. "A bull, and a *boar*."

"Sure, sure. My French-Canadian folklore is a little rusty, but I thought that the curse of the loup-garou thing only lasted for one hundred days or something, and the transformation was involuntary? Why do I get the sense you're just a dude with some shapeshifting magic who decided to come up with a soaked-in-evil backstory to impress the chumps?"

"I will sniff you out," he said. "I will open your belly, feast on your organs, and shit in your empty body cavities."

"Straight-ahead attacking, and weirdly specific scatological threats! I gotta admit, Sarlat, you keep impressing me. I mean that sincerely. How about you and me work something out? Killing your tentacled friend at Sunlight Shores, that was strictly self-defense on my part. I respect the right of a monster to do his monster shit, but I draw the line at letting myself get eaten. You have to cut me a *little* slack there."

"Absolutely," Sarlat said. "All is forgiven. Come over in person and we'll have a drink to celebrate our new friendship."

"Now, now, no need for sarcasm. My point is, I didn't go picking a fight with your people, I just did what was necessary to keep myself alive. I *did* kill Orias's advisor with malice aforethought, though—when he came to congratulate me on killing the beast and to ask if I'd help wipe out your whole gang, since I'd made such a good start."

Now I had his attention. He walked through me like I wasn't even there—which, okay, technically I wasn't—and sat back down on his chair in the cell. "I assumed Orias hired you… until I heard you killed the spore-lord. He's not dead, by the way. His body was a temporary thing made of shit and fungus, mashed up into a man-shape. He's just motes of thinking dust, really."

"Drat. Next time I'll bring a tank of herbicide and put him down for good. Listen—how much do you know about me?"

His shrug was elegant. "Enough. You used to be chief sorcerer of some rust-belt city out East. You fucked up somehow—details are sketchy—and the other sorcerers ran you out of town on a rail. You lived in Hawaii for a while, until some trouble there sent you packing again. You popped up in Vegas a couple of days ago and then proceeded to start fucking with my people for no reason."

"Any such fucking was inadvertent, I assure you. Did you hear *why* I left Hawaii?"

He frowned. "What I *heard* was that you killed Elsie Jarrow."

"You heard right." Technically I hadn't killed her—I wasn't sure someone as powerful as Jarrow *could* be killed—but I'd sure as shit neutralized her. "You sure you still want to fuck with me, knowing that?"

"You killed *the* Elsie Jarrow. Most powerful chaos witch in history. I didn't believe it, but then I heard it from three different sources, two of which I even trust. You really did her in?"

"With these little hands. If I could do that, don't you think I could take out Orias?"

"You've got my attention. What exactly are you saying?"

"I've got some business to do in the Southwest, and I'd rather not have your bruisers bothering me. I can handle them, of course, but I don't want to spend all my time scraping your thugs off the bottom of my boots. I killed one of yours—I'll acknowledge that. Party foul. You've got a need for blood vengeance and all, you can't let anybody fuck with your cohort, I get that. But how about I pay restitution for my crime instead? I'll take out Orias, and you and your gang call it even and leave me be."

He stroked his chin, thinking about it. A normal crook would have just agreed, waited to see if I managed to kill Orias, and then murdered me anyway. You can promise anything when you're a lying piece of shit. But such casual double-crosses are a lot harder in the world of sorcerers—there are ways to make agreements that *stick* in my world, to make deals you can't break any more easily than you could eat your own brain—so if he said yes, he had to *mean* yes, assuming I'd insist on supernatural compulsion to make the terms firm. "So that's it, you kill Orias, and we'd be square?"

"Well, I wouldn't mind having access to some materiel and personnel while I'm in your neighborhood. Give me a few favors to call in, and sure, I'll kill Orias for you, and I'll even help you mop up the remnants of her forces and make sure to take out any of her lieutenants you're especially worried about."

He spat. "None of them *worry* me, they're just annoyances… but life would be more pleasant with a few of them dead, I'll give you that. Okay, Mason. You've got a deal."

"You'll forgive me if I don't just take your word on that?"

He snorted. "Of course not. Give me an hour to set up a circle of compulsion and we'll finalize things formally."

"I'll send my astral proxy then," I said. "You won't blame me if I choose not to come in person."

"I like doing business with cautious people," Sarlat said, which was funny, coming from a wolfman who clearly enjoyed solving problems by tearing out their throats.

I let my illusion wink out of sight, though I still had eyes on him, of course, as he called for his contract sorcerers to set up a circle of binding.

An hour. That was probably enough time.

Orias wasn't alone. She was with her spore-lord, who'd made a new body, just as ugly as the last one. They were using a patch of ground beside a dry well for their base of operations, and she'd had her underlings set up a big tent of dark silk, full of pillows and antique-looking furniture. There was even a full liquor cabinet. Ghost town decadence.

I caused an image of myself to appear. "Boo," I said.

Orias didn't leap up and attack me, though the spore-lord snarled. She arched one drawn-on eyebrow and said, "An illusory body, I see. Afraid to come calling in person?"

She was more perceptive and less prone to leaping without thinking than Sarlat. Good to know. "Oh, I'll be along," I said. "You know, you're not what I expected. I figured, madam of a supernatural brothel, you'd go for the slutty-enchantress look, black lace and red accents, push-up bra and spiked heels." She was dressed more like a weekend warrior on a paintball course, all desert camouflage and black boots, but exceedingly well-tailored.

"There's a time and a place for such sartorial choices. Since I came here to kill you, not seduce you, I dressed appropriately. Your own fashion sense, though… Is that coat made of buffalo leather? Planning to take part in a Wild West show? I can't think of any of my customers who have a dead cowgirl fetish, or I'd offer you a position in one of my houses after I'm done killing you."

"Tempting, but I've got a full-time job and lots of hobbies. Just out of curiosity, how did you know I was an illusion? I thought I faked this up pretty well."

Orias shrugged and tapped the side of her nose. "No smell."

Interesting. You'd think Sarlat, having the nose of a dog, would have noticed my lack of smell before trying to kill me, but I guess he's a "murder now, sniff crotches later" sort of animal. "You're missing out. I smell wonderful."

"Did you want to say anything of substance before my people slaughter you in your hidey-hole?" Orias said.

"Oh, I just wanted to give you a chance to make a counteroffer."

"Triangulating," the spore-lord said, walking around my illusory body in a small circle, motes of black nastiness drifting up from his spongy body. "I'll have her location shortly."

I snorted. "Right. Good luck with that. And 'triangulating' means pinning down a location by finding the position where three lines intersect. Whatever you're doing, you're not doing *that*. Now shut up, Mr. Thrush, the grown-ups are talking—"

"Mr. Thrush?" Orias said, amused.

"Because he's a fungal infection," I said. "I came to talk to the gardener, not the plant life. Here's the thing, Orias: Sarlat has offered me three wishes, pretty much, if I'll bring him your head."

"Ha. I thought you were formidable, but clearly you're an idiot. You'd trust a deal he offered? Sarlat is a cur."

I shrugged. "He's setting up a circle of binding now, so we can make our obligations and responsibilities clear. But I'm not bound *yet*, so you can step in and save yourself. I don't much like Sarlat, to be honest. I went to him first because he seemed to have the stronger crew, and I like to bet on winners, but I think I see a way you can wipe him out instead of going down in a blaze of blood and suffering yourself."

"I am not here to wipe him out," Orias said. "I am here to wipe *you* out."

I shook my head, impatient. "You're living in the past, lady. Circumstances change. The current situation is, I behead you, then I lead Sarlat's forces in an all-out offensive against the remnants of your forces here. Now, most of them are hired mercenaries who'll flee in the face of Sarlat's more passionate and personally-invested murderers, and your lieutenants will be utterly overwhelmed. That's the reality you need to be grappling with, not some imaginary scenario where you kill *me*."

"This is absurd. You can't possibly threaten me, I have a hundred—"

Boring. Deep in my undisclosed location, I snapped a twig in half.

The polaroids weren't the only things I'd scattered around the town. I habitually traveled with satchels full of nastiness, and I'd made sure to sprinkle some of my best liberally across Tolerance. There was a sound like a tree growing at ten-thousand-times normal speed—not a sound most people find familiar, but unmistakable once you've heard it once—and the spore-lord was lifted (or more like *flung*) upward by fifteen or twenty gnarled, thorny spikes that shot forth from the ground all around my illusory form. Seven of the spikes penetrated his body, impaling him through his neck, thigh, and chest, leaving him hanging a good eight feet in the air, up close to the pavilion's ceiling.

My illusory body stepped through the spike garden and strolled toward Orias, who was standing—not cowering, more's the pity—near the far wall of the pavilion. "That could've been you," I said. "You idiots came to ground *I'd prepared*. You let me choose the site of our confrontation, thinking mere numbers would make that advantage moot. Bad plan. I had the best part of a day to get ready here before any of you arrived. Maybe you're used to dealing with idiots, but you're in a whole different kind of fight here."

"Ow," the spore-lord said, dangling on the thorn tree. "This is very tedious."

"You're Marla Mason." Orias hmmmed. "They say you killed Elsie Jarrow."

"That's what they say, and they would know. If you knew about that, you should have known better than to come after me."

"Yes, Marla, I knew you were formidable—that's why I brought a *hundred fucking people* to kill you. Or should I have ignored a deliberate provocation, like stomping my advisor to bits? Would you have just let that pass?"

"Nah. But I'd plan my reaction a little better. Really, the whole big-crowd-of-mercenaries brute force angle? I expect that kind of thinking from Sarlat, but you're better than that."

"Some say you bested a death-god in single combat, and banished another god somewhere in California, before it could fully rise."

"They're easier to kill when they're babies," I said.

"I didn't really believe it," Orias said. "I'm cautious, so I came prepared for a real fight, but in truth, I thought you were some drifter, using a moderately famous name to try and frighten people away."

"And now you know better. Do you want to be on my side, or under my boot?"

"Hmm. I could send for reinforcements. I have favors I can call in, from people who might even make you tremble."

"By all means! Call for help, or hell, just run away. But you should know, I prepared the border, too—or *a* border, anyway, or call it a perimeter. Anyone who tries to enter or leave Tolerance before I turn off the wards won't leave behind enough mortal remains to fill a bucket." That was pure bluff, unfortunately. A working like that wasn't within my powers, not given my current resources and time constraints. Sealing off an area gets exponentially more difficult the bigger the area is. Could I ring a room, or a small cottage, with death? Totally. But a whole town? Not without help. Serious perimeter control was never one of my strengths. I'm better in one-on-one fights. But if Orias believed it…

"*Why*?" Orias said. "Why bait us into this confrontation at all? Why kill the beast of Sunlight Shores, and why on *Earth* did you stomp my spore-lord to pieces, deliberately insulting me? None of us had even heard of you before this, some of us would have respected you, even worked with you, given the chance—"

"My new hobby is killing monsters," I said. "You're lucky, because your bunch isn't quite as monstrous as Sarlat's, so I'd rather kill his gang than yours." Not true, really. Sarlat's guys were more violent, but I found Orias and her affection for human (and inhuman) trafficking more offensive than Sarlat's honest thuggery. "Look, I came here to give you a way out, but if you don't want it, I'll just crank up the murder-engines—"

"What do you propose?" Orias said.

"I promised Sarlat I'd bring him your head. I propose to do just that. Or, at least, to bring him a head that *looks* like yours."

"You'd need an actual head, to make a convincing illusion," she said thoughtfully.

I grinned. "I've got the head covered."

"Even so, he's likely to see through a glamour, or smell through it—"

"I'll need a strand of your hair and a drop of your blood to make a really convincing illusion."

She shuddered. "To give you those things… they'd allow you to enact terrible sympathetic magics…"

I was tempted to tell her to suck it up, take the deal or leave it, but I had a whole elegant thing planned out, so I decided to give a little. "Fair enough. Luckily you've got an attorney present. Have the fungal infection up there lay down a circle of binding and we'll make an agreement right now that I'll only use your precious DNA to concoct an illusion, and not for any more nefarious purposes."

"Very well," she said. She glanced at the creature on the tree. "Are you functional?"

"Of course," he answered querulously. "Nothing essential was harmed." He writhed on the thorns a bit, and a fine snow of black flecks drifted down, like we were underneath the world's largest pepper grinder. The flecks fell in a neat circle about twelve feet around, surrounding both Orias and my illusory body—which was good enough, since I was animating and controlling it directly. For ritual purposes, my illusion was me.

"I heard a name from the thing I killed at Sunlight Shores," I said as we waited for the circle to form. "The Eater. Is that what they call Sarlat?"

Orias shook her head. "No. The Eater… I heard Sarlat mention someone by that name, back when we were friendly. The Eater is a business associate, perhaps, or a kind of mentor? Sarlat can be paranoid, and he never told me much about anything, if he could avoid it." She frowned. "He did say the Eater advised him, though, and I must admit—*someone* is giving Sarlat good advice. I am vastly more intelligent than he is—this I know from intimate experience—but he somehow always seems a step ahead of me, a step ahead of *everyone*, as if there's nothing he doesn't see coming, no eventuality he can't plan for in advance."

I grunted. "Doesn't look like he saw me coming."

"There is that. It's given me hope, actually."

"Any idea how Sarlat might be paying the Eater for all this good advice?"

Orias shrugged. "He never mentioned the details of their arrangement. But Sarlat excels at smuggling, human and otherwise. Perhaps he's helping the Eater transport something? Or perhaps the Eater's name is literal—maybe Sarlat supplied him with whatever, or whomever, it is he likes to eat."

"Anthropophagous take-out? That's a lovely thought." I'd hoped for more useful intel, but that was okay. If things worked out the way I planned, Sarlat would be eager to answer any questions I asked him, pretty soon.

When the circle was done, and the room thrummed with the dark power of compulsion, I said—truthfully—that I would use the blood and hair of Orias only to create an illusion, not to harm her, on pain of painful death.

With that pledge made, the magic fled, and I was free to lie my ass off again. "After I give Sarlat your head—or the head he thinks is yours—I'm going to lead his people against your camp. If you'll allow me to make a few suggestions about the most effective way to set up an ambush, you should be able to kill his goon squad with grace and efficiency..."

Getting Ahead

So after I killed them all, I got on my motorcycle and roared toward Texas singing "Another Traveling Song" by Bright Eyes, just loud enough to annoy Nicolette—

All right, I won't do that to you. For one thing, I know you like the bloody stuff. For another, it's not accurate to say I killed them *all*. Besides, the way I worked it out was pretty sweet, and I want you to admire me, Future Me.

My undisclosed location was several hundred yards down a sharply-sloped shaft in some old copper mine not far from what remained of Tolerance. (I don't actually know if it was a copper mine, but it was some kind of mine, and copper sounds plausible, right?) Somehow I'm more and more comfortable in caverns and dark places lately—imagine that. I was down there in the deep black, so dark even my night-eyes weren't any help, because that's a spell that sucks up every stray photon of light and puts it to use, only there *was* no light in the mine in the dark. I conjured a little red flower of light and stuck it on top of Nicolette's birdcage so I wouldn't go totally crazy and lose track of where I ended and the darkness began. Mostly I was in a trance, looking through the photographs I'd scattered around town, seeing a couple dozen viewpoints at once, so when I pulled all the way back into my own head, the darkness was kind of a shock all over again.

Nicolette was sticking out her tongue at me and generally making hideous faces, but I just smiled at her. "You're going to *hate* this next part," I said.

I could've used a minion just then—it made me wish I'd had Pelly send a couple of death cultists out to meet me. Not that putting their lives in danger in the course of running my errands was really fair, but wouldn't dying in the service of their goddess give them a thrill?

I am so not cut out for the responsibilities of divinity.

With a bit more time, I could have banged together a remote-controlled rock golem or maybe even summoned up a temporary tulpa, but this plan required some pretty close timing, so I took up arms myself and told Nicolette, "I'm going out for a few minutes. I'll be back, and then, guess what? You're getting a makeover! It'll be just like a slumber party." I walked out of the shaft, axe in one hand and dagger in the other, so I didn't quite hear Nicolette's no-doubt-witty rejoinder, apart from something about killing me in my sleep.

I crept out into the darkness, shrouded in spells of bent light and misdirected vision, pausing occasionally to look through the eyes of my scattered photographs for signs of ambush. In twenty minutes I traveled a slow half-mile until I reached a heap of rocks overlooking the drop site.

Orias didn't come to me herself, of course. She sent one of her minions, a petite woman with a squirming fringe of jellyfish tentacles where her mouth should have been. She set down a metal thermos on top of the broken horse trough I'd designated as the drop. She paused, so I shouted, "Get lost!" and she scurried away into the night. After waiting a suitable interval, I slid down the slope, snatched up the canister, and headed back to my undisclosed location, using a roundabout route to make sure I wasn't being followed. I didn't think Orias would double-cross me, since there was no upside in it for her at this point—if I succeeded in killing Sarlat for her, she might turn on me, of course, but she wouldn't try to kill me when there was a chance I might get rid of her worst enemy.

Once I was back inside the mine shaft, I opened the canister and examined the contents. A few strands of hair, complete with skin tags torn from her scalp, and even a drop of blood wetting a tissue. Good enough.

"What are you doing?" Nicolette demanded as I set up a mortar and pestle on a flat rock and started grinding together a few ingredients—butterfly wings, snake scales, the limbs of stick insects, all pretty standard components in illusory spells, part of my basic enchanting kit—along with the bits of Orias's body I'd acquired.

I lifted the cage off Nicolette's head and held the mortar up to her mouth. "Here, spit in this."

Nicolette tried to spit on my hand instead, but I was ready for *that*, so I got a little of her saliva in the mixture, as needed. A little water from my canteen sufficed to make the mess into a mushy paste, and I said the right words (which, really, could have been any words, as long as they acted to focus my will), then dabbed the mixture onto Nicolette's forehead, cheeks, chin, and the tip of her nose.

"I hope whoever you're trying to make me look like doesn't have a *body*, or this isn't going to be too convincing."

"It's okay. All you have to do is play dead. I promised Sarlat I'd bring him the head of his enemy. That's going to be you."

"Play dead?" Nicolette crossed her eyes and stuck out her tongue.

"Maybe a little more subtle than that. Not that I'm entirely counting on your acting skills." I watched as the illusion shimmered into place—at first it was like looking at Nicolette through a sheen of greasy water, but after a few moments the structure of her face changed, and the severed head of Orias was looking at me—high cheekbones, pouty lips, dark eyes rendered glazed and staring, hair a little less stylish than before.

I nodded. "Looks good. You can blink if you want, and even lick your lips or wiggle your nose or waggle your eyebrows—the illusion is tailored to look all dead and staring-eyed and slack-jawed, but he'll hear you if you talk, so keep your swear-hole shut, all right?"

The face was blank and expressionless, of course, but there was plenty of scorn in her voice. "You bitch. I can't believe you're delivering me into the hands of the enemy. Bad enough I have to be your bloodhound—now I have to be some asshole's trophy?"

"Please. I'll be risking my life, committing mayhem and treachery, and all you have to do is sit on a shelf and listen to Sarlat rant about how he's vanquished you at last. Worst case, he'll use you to reenact that scene with the skull from *Hamlet*. Keep your ears open, though, especially if he says anything about someone or something called the Eater. I think there might be a bigger monster for us to hunt once this is all done."

"I am your obedient servant," Nicolette said.

"Good. Hold tight for a minute." I went back to the comfiest spot in the mine to sit down—hardly any rocks digging into my ass at all—and dropped into a trance of telepresence. I shimmered into Sarlat's jail cell office.

"You ready yet?" I looked around at the candles and chalked lines and the circle of salt. This set-up was a bit more involved than the binding circle I'd used with Orias, because that had been a simple "I promise" situation. This was a complex bargain with conditions that needed to be binding on both sides, so the magic was more complex.

"Just step into the circle there." Sarlat flapped a hand toward the east end of the cell without looking up from the rune he was drawing on the wall. I was a bit surprised to see him doing his own paperwork, as it were, but his work looked deft and accurate enough. I didn't see any traps or tricks in the set-up, not that he could do much to me through my illusory body anyway. He could theoretically try and trace the illusion back to my actual location, but the general magical haze over Tolerance and the dozens of charmed photographs I'd scattered through town would make it practically impossible.

This binding circle was actually shaped more like an infinity symbol, two ovals that joined in the twisted middle. I stepped into my circle and felt/heard the hum of binding start up, but at a low idle. "You've got pretty good penmanship for a ravenous beast," I said.

"I am a monster of many talents." He dropped the chalk and stepped into his oval, and the compulsion took hold more firmly. "Now we make promises to one another."

"Okay. I swear to do everything in my power to kill Orias." Lying wasn't allowed in that circle, but that was okay: I wasn't lying. There was the *click* of something locking into place, so loud it almost made me flinch, though the sound was only in my head.

Sarlat nodded. "After you kill Orias, I swear I will not harm you, or cause you to be harmed. I will, further, offer you three favors, if I can fulfill them without harm to myself."

"So our bargain is made," I said, "on pain of painful death."

He repeated the words, and then scuffed out the circle of salt, and the low buzz of binding magic vanished.

I got the murder-itch immediately. There are a couple of different kinds of binding circles: restrictive ones, and prescriptive ones. With Orias, we'd used a restrictive circle, which meant there would be consequences only if I performed a certain act—namely, if I tried to use the witch's blood and hair for anything but the promised illusion, I would be subjected to untold torments. That was a magic that limited my behavior.

The deal I'd just made with Sarlat was *prescriptive*, though: it was a promise to perform a certain act, namely, doing my best to murder Orias. Until I did that, I would feel goaded—there would be a pressure in my head, a tingle in my bones, a need somewhere between a starving man's hunger and a junkie's urge to fix: the murder-itch. Prescriptive bindings are nasty. The pressure builds and builds the longer you go without fulfilling the requirements, and if you don't do what you're supposed to do in relatively short order, madness is inevitable. (Well, in most cases. I'd once wriggled out of a prescriptive binding, namely a promise to bloodily avenge the death of an old friend, but getting out of it had required the intervention of godlike entities to cancel the compulsion, which had mostly taken the form of my dead friend's voice screaming at me in my mind.) I'd left myself a little wriggle room by promising only to do my *best* to kill Orias, allowing for honorable failure—but the binding was rooted partly in my perceptions, so I couldn't fool the magic. If *I* didn't think I was doing my best to kill her, the binding would know I was cheating, and I'd suffer.

Which meant it was time to get the whole bloody climax thing started. "I'll be back with Orias's head shortly. I'll try to be subtle so I don't stir up her camp or put her people on guard, but no promises. Either way, once she's dead, you should be able to launch a full assault against her. You're willing to give me a strike force to take out her more dangerous lieutenants, the spore-lord and so on?"

"Some of my best and darkest will be at your disposal. Assuming you make it back with her head in your hands." He shook his head. "Orias isn't as tough as I am, but I'm not convinced you're as tough as *her*."

"I did kill Elsie Jarrow."

He sat on a stool and took a long sip of water, then shrugged. "Maybe you did. I didn't have time to confirm that story. But Jarrow was *crazy*, by all accounts, and not too concerned about self-preservation. Orias only cares about Orias." There was a doleful tone to that last line that hinted at a deep history between them, and I was briefly interested, but I had things to do, so I just winked out of sight.

I strolled in from the outskirts of town, and Sarlat's baddies murmured as they looked at the dusty old sack swinging in my hand. "Move aside," I said, and the hairy, scaled, chitinous, over-muscled men and beasts and man-beasts shuffled out of the way, making a path to the collapsing remnants of the jail. I had dagger and axe both in my coat, and I was ready to drop the sack and fight if it seemed prudent, but Sarlat's boys—they were nearly all boys—stayed in line.

This was a delicate point. I had to make it look like I'd fulfilled our agreement, but it was tricky, because Sarlat hadn't *actually* been bound against harming me yet, since Orias was actually still alive. His binding was purely restrictive—after I killed Orias, he couldn't harm me, or deny me three reasonable favors, without suffering a painful death—so there would be no buzz of compulsion to tell him whether or not I'd held up my end of the bargain—only consequences if he tried to break the deal. In theory, Sarlat could test whether or not the head really belonged to Orias just by just trying to kill me: if the binding let him murder me, that meant the head was a fake. I didn't *expect* him to do something that clever, but it was a worry.

I shouldn't have worried. Sarlat was obviously used to getting his way, and to people doing his bidding. Shit like that can make you complacent. (Believe me, I know.) I stepped into the remains of the jail, and Sarlat rose from his stool with a grunt. "You're dustier in person." He nodded toward the sack. "Is that for me?"

I tossed the bag toward him, and he caught it deftly. He peered inside, chuckled, and lifted out Nicolette's head—which looked like the freshly-severed head of Orias, complete with dripping blood. Blood that would match Orias if he did a DNA test or magical divination. That was the advantage of getting her genetic material for the spell; a *really* convincing illusion.

Sarlat held the head before him, palms pressed against her cheeks, gazing into the apparently lifeless eyes. The illusory blood dripped from the stump and spattered on the floor and his boots. "Oh, you beautiful bitch," he said. "I put you on a pedestal, you said? Now I'll put you on my mantelpiece."

Mr. Loup-garou didn't do any kind of magic to test the head's identity, as far as I could tell. Oh well. I was still glad I'd taken the necessary steps to create a nearly impenetrable illusion. Just because your adversary is an idiot is no reason to be sloppy.

"So we're good?" I said. "Ready to move against Orias's camp?"

"They don't suspect anything?" Sarlat said. "You got in and out undetected?"

"I'm basically a ghost, Sarlat. If ghosts had big knives. No one noticed me, but they'll notice their boss's headless corpse stuffed in a hole in the ground sooner or later, so we should move now, before they go on alert."

He made a "shoo-shoo-go-away" motion. "Fine. Your squad is waiting for you outside. Tell them you're ready, and the general assault will launch. Go, kill her whole camp, I don't care. I've got the only one that really matters here." Sarlat never once stopped staring into the head's eyes. I wondered what kind of faces Nicolette was secretly making at him.

"Off to war, then," I said, and it was true, though the only side I was fighting for was my own.

Knowing Squat

I LOOKED FOR THE BIGGEST swaggering asshole in the general area and walked up to him. He stood about eight feet tall and had a sixteen-point antlered helmet and a necklace of animal fangs and baby teeth. "Hey," I said. "I'm supposed to lead a team in this attack."

"Then you should be talking to me," said a voice at my elbow. "I'm Squat."

I looked down into the froglike face of a non-human—I'd never seen anything like him before, but the world is full of mysteries. "You certainly are," I said. Squat had skin the color of rotten crabapples and the bumpy texture of a diseased tongue, and his overall shape was that of a brachydactylic thumb standing four feet high, the whole wrapped in white bandages seeping with fluids in surprising and unexpected colors. "You're the big bad killing machine I'm leading into battle?"

"More of a small bad killing machine," Squat said, and gave me what I assumed was a smile, though the mouth was on sideways and instead of teeth there were rows of tiny wriggling pseudopods in there, tipped by oozing bulbs. He had arms like a stevedore, or more like if there was a superhero called Captain Stevedore, with biceps on his biceps. He saw me noticing and flexed. "I can lift a Humvee over my head, and every morning my shit is full of the bones of my enemies."

"That's the greatest OK Cupid profile I've ever read," I said. "You're hired. Where's the rest of the team?"

I was introduced to antler guy, and some kind of potion-addled man-beast who reeked of earthy musk and had boar tusks, and a roughly humanoid creature made of globular, tar-like shadow, and a demon wearing the body of a mountain lion grotesquely altered into a bipedal form, with spines pushing up through the pelt. "Okay," I said. "You look like a pretty formidable lot. We're going to circle around back and penetrate the enemy's defenses, the same way I crept in when I took out Orias. Only this time, we're going to blitz her lieutenants. Got it?"

For a motley bunch of malcontents addicted to alien drugs, they were fairly well-organized when it came to mayhem, and they fell in behind me as I slipped off into the desert brush. Squat walked alongside me, his short, bandy legs keeping pace remarkably well.

"I don't know what the fuck most of those guys are," I whispered to him, "but I *especially* don't know what the fuck you are."

"You mean my species?"

"If that's not too personal a question, yeah."

"Cursed human," Squat said. "I wasn't always this ugly. I used to be just *ordinary* ugly. But I got cursed to become repulsive to anyone who cared about me. At first it was just my skin color changing, and the bumps, which was enough to pretty much knock me out of willing human company. But I fell in with a different crowd, one with greater... tolerances... for physical variation, so the curse made me even *uglier*, to repulse the new friends and lovers I made. Sometimes it's pretty specific—my last girlfriend was a sort of swamp-monster, and this fucked-up sideways mouth and the venomous cilia are physical attributes shared by some ancestral prehistoric cryptozoological predator of her people. She could put up with a lot, but not with fucking someone who looked like the thing that ate her brother-father. And the effects of the curse are cumulative, so the ugly just piles up." He sighed.

"Dude. That is fucked up." I felt pretty bad about planning to smack Squat in the head with a magical hatchet. Then again, he probably did something *really terrible* to get hit with such a nasty curse.

"Eh. It is what it is. All these assholes in Sarlat's crew hate me. Some of them I literally make vomit—apparently I emit super offensive pheromones only certain supernatural creatures can sense? But I've got good qualities. I'm as strong as two Kodiak bears having a hate-fuck, and since nobody likes me anyway, I don't ever bother holding back my nasty impulses, you know? Sarlat gives me dirty work, even though he says I look a lot like the thing his father turned into after he drank a tainted love potion."

"There's something to be said for doing work you enjoy and doing it well," I said, pretty tactfully, aware of the words tattooed on the inside of my wrist. I might have to kill Squat soon, but I could be polite in the meantime. The guy was miserable enough. Piling more misery on wasn't necessary.

"Of course, Sarlat always tries to send me into certain death." Squat's tone was more philosophical than doleful. "That's just life when you're cursed, though."

I signaled to the other nasties as we approached the rear of Orias's camp, and we slowed down and stretched out in a loose line, staying close to the ground, watching for sentries.

There was a lot of screaming in the distance—Sarlat's full-frontal assault had launched, and his goons were presumably walking right into the kill zones and ambush sites and overlapping fields of fire I'd recommended to Orias. Most of Sarlat's gang would get chewed up, though I'd left a few gaps in my suggestions, places where some of Sarlat's guys could get a few licks in. I didn't want this massacre to be entirely one-sided. Most of Orias's mercenary guards had broken at the sounds of violence, but there were a couple still pacing the perimeter: a guy dressed like a casino pit boss, tuxedo and all, with curling ram's horns on his head, and a bleached-blonde, ghost-pale woman in a thin tank-top scratching her bare arms so hard she bled. Her wounds smoked like her blood was made of acid, which it probably was.

"Okay. Bambi and The Shadow, you take those guys out," I whispered. "Mr. Whiskers and Babe Pig in the City, you creep up to the tents and do recon, see if there are any big bad guys lurking around. Kill anybody you see along the way—we're aiming for the central pavilion, where the remnants of Orias's leadership are probably managing the battle." The baddies flowed away across the desert, fanning out to go about their appointed tasks. I love monsters who do what you say.

Squat snickered. "Cute pet names, there. I'd hate to think what you'd call me."

"'Squat' pretty much covers it," I said.

We watched as The Shadow flowed up the acid-blooded woman and smothered her with his malleable form, and Bambi actually no-shit *impaled* the ram's-headed guy with his antlers, right through the chest, in a shocking piece of horn-on-horn violence. Then they joined the others, peering in-between the closely-packed tents of Orias's camp.

"So what are you, anyway?" Squat said. "Baseline human? Doing shit you learned, not shit that got inflicted on you?"

I glanced at him sidelong, because he wasn't the kind of guy you wanted to look at straight on. "Sarlat didn't tell you about me?"

"Sarlat's not big on interoffice communication," Squat said. "He's more of an order-giver. Like, he says, 'Shit,' and we say, 'On whom?'"

"Good use of grammar," I said. "Yeah, I'm just your average ordinary witchy woman. I couldn't work a curse like the one that got laid on you, though. Who did it—and why? Or is that impolite, like asking somebody in prison what they're in for?"

I was hoping he'd murdered a bunch of children or something. I had my hand on the handle of my hatchet, and I figured I could bury it in his head pretty quickly, here and now. He was probably the most dangerous of the bunch, so it made sense to take him out first.

"Is that impolite?" he said. "I've never been to jail. The curse, well, it was a long time ago, like forty years. I was on the East Coast, in law school, bright future ahead of me. I was driving along, and there was this crazy woman in a convertible, driving like a nutcase on the expressway. She'd slowed down to something like fifteen miles an hour in the passing lane, so I started to go around her, passing on the right." He sighed. "She turned her head and stared at me and said, 'That's *rude*. I hate rudeness. And so everyone will always hate you.' I could hear her voice like she was whispering in my ear, even though I passed her in a second, and my windows were rolled up, and then she *spat* at me, and despite the distance and wind and windows, the spit hit me on the cheek, a big nasty wet glob."

I closed my eyes. "This woman. Did she have red hair?"

"You've heard of her, huh? Once I started running in sorcerous circles, I found out I'd been cursed by a *famous* crazy witch. Elsie Jarrow. I heard she was locked up in a loony bin, but then I also heard somebody killed her, not long ago."

"I heard that, too." I gritted my teeth, but loosened my grip on my hatchet. Okay. So what if Squat and I had a tormentor in common? He was still a killer and a thug, right? But then, what the hell was *I*? In theory, I was trying to kill in order to save innocent lives, but Squat was living the only life he could. Elsie's curse hadn't left him with a lot of options. "Too bad her dying didn't break the curse."

"Those chaos witches build spells to last, except when they don't," he said. The other baddies gestured to us that they were planning to advance, and then they faded into the tents. "Shall we?" he said. "Otherwise they won't leave anyone for us to kill."

"Sure." I could always cut Squat down later. Might as well let him do some work for me first.

When we got into camp proper, I was glad I'd kept him with me. The ground was littered with the dead, mostly Orias's defenders who'd been taken by surprise from behind—they'd been entirely focused on breaking the front line of Sarlat's attack, which I'd told them to expect. Tents were slumped and tangled, and the whole place stank of blood and fire and monstrous fluids, the grisly scene lit by moonlight and torchlight and the odd bioluminescent corpse. But Sarlat's A-team hadn't fared all that well: Bambi's head was resting on the ground some distance from his body, The Shadow had been reduced to several weakly-pulsing puddles, the cougar was moaning and holding its guts in with a clawed hand and lots of confused mewling, and the boar-faced man had taken a spear through the chest and been transformed back into a pigeon-chested twenty-something wearing a filthy pig-skin cape.

Only a handful of Orias's people were still standing, but they were formidable: a teen in a pleated skirt with a scarred face who I took for a poltergeister, especially when a cloud of broken glass and nails began swirling around her. A purple-skinned woman with three faces and fanged mouths all over her body. Another woman with iridescent wings and arms that ended in preying-mantis claws, like something out of a China Miéville novel. They surrounded Orias's white pavilion like an honor guard.

"Kill 'em all?" Squat said.

"Sure." I activated all my polaroids at once, so that high-resolution copies of myself popped up all through the camp, all drawing a knife with one hand and an axe with the other, all converging on our enemies. Only the original me could actually hurt anybody, but the others added to the general confusion.

We waded in. I got my axe into the mantis-girl, but only sheared off her scythelike-forearm. Then Squat was there, pulling her head off just like I'd tug a ripe lemon off a branch, then tossing it aside. I looked around for another target and saw he'd already killed the other two. In, like, a *second.*

"Squat. You're like a murder virtuoso."

"I'm short," he said. "So I try harder."

Damn it. I was starting to like the repulsive little monster.

The sounds of fighting in the camp had pretty much ceased—the people I could see who were still moving were racing off into the night at great speed. It was a shame I didn't actually have a death-wall erected around Tolerance, or I could have made sure all the pests got exterminated—but most of these were hired goons anyway, who wouldn't cause much trouble without central leadership.

Which meant I just had to finish taking care of the central leadership.

"Let's see if there's anyone left in the big tent," Squat said, and rushed the white pavilion.

I went in after him, and found him gaping at Orias, who was surrounded by a shimmering sphere of light, rainbow-colored like an oil slick, her eyes closed, in some kind of deep magical trance.

"She's *alive.*" Squat looked at me. "They said you brought Sarlat her head…" He grimaced. "So it's a double-cross."

The spore-lord was in one corner, muttering and fuming—really fuming, puffs of black mold rising from his body like smoke. "You!" he shouted. "This ambush was a *disaster*, Sarlat sent some of his people to circle around from behind and take us hard in the rear—"

I really missed Rondeau right then. He would have gotten a kick out of all this talk about people taking it in the rear.

"Not so much a double-cross," I said to Squat. "More of a triple-cross, really."

The spore-lord realized I wasn't actually his ally pretty quickly, and raised his hands to enact some nasty magic. I didn't give him the chance. I knew my blades were useless against his faux-body, and blunt-force-trauma, though satisfying viscerally, was also ineffective against his sort of distributed biology.

But that doesn't mean there's no way to fight things like him. You just kill them with fire. I took an enchanted Zippo from my coat pocket, flipped it open, and blew on the flame.

A cone of fire billowed out and consumed the spore-lord. The fire passed over Orias's shimmering sphere—her Hamster Ball of Invincibility—too, without causing any notable effect, but I hadn't expected it to hurt *her*. The fire was a lot hotter than your average butane flame when it hit the spore-lord, and he collapsed in on himself with a noise like burning styrofoam, a sort of shriveling squeak. His spores tried to escape but flared into orange sparks as the heat ignited them. When the flames subsided, there wasn't much left but ashes and the half-melted buttons from his shirt.

"I know it's a cliché," I said. "But I never did like lawyers."

"I, myself, never even took the bar exam." Squat backed up, putting some space between us, but not running away, which was either threatening or interesting or both.

I drew my dagger—the one my dear husband gave me—and began carving through the shield of magical force surrounding Orias. The compulsive murder-itch got *really* bad now that I was so close to her, and I admit I went into something of a frenzy, slashing at the magical wards as fast as she could erect them. But my dagger was forged in the underworld by the god of death. It can cut through flesh, and bone, and steel, and lies, and light, and ghosts, and magic. (It can cut through nearly anything, except all the bullshit. There's no reliable way to cut through all the bullshit.)

I could tell Orias wanted to talk to me or claw my eyes out or something, so I just gritted my teeth and gave into the geas and let my dagger take her head off, messy and awful as that was. When she gasped her last breath, the murder-itch subsided instantly, and my mind once more felt entirely like my own. (As much as it ever does, especially lately, with big hunks of memory torn out.)

I turned to Squat. I was covered in Orias's blood and assorted muds and dust and other foulness, but I was still nowhere near as ugly as him.

He raised his hands. "Hey. I've got no loyalty to Sarlat, okay? He's just the only one who'll give me work anymore, and a guy like me needs work. I'll keep your secret, I'll say Orias was dead all along—"

"It doesn't matter," I said, and it didn't. Sarlat was bound now that I'd fulfilled our bargain by slaying his enemy. He didn't have to like me, but he couldn't harm me, or cause me to be harmed—he even had to do favors for me. Favor one would be telling me about the Eater, because I am the curious type. "Here's the thing, Squat. It's not your fault, not entirely, but… you're a fucking monster. You've killed innocent people, right? You've done terrible things?"

"True, but—"

But nothing. I brought out my silver axe and buried it in the center of his hideous head, then twisted the blade and wrenched it out. Squat sat down hard on his unsightly ass. I'd left a giant split that ran between his eyes and met up with his sideways mouth. I turned away, feeling vaguely ashamed of myself. He'd been a monster, but maybe not such a bad *guy*—

"That hurt," he said, and I turned, chilled. The wound in his head was sealing as I watched, and I was reminded of the way I'd taken an axe to the head myself not so long ago, and to similarly little effect. "The thing is, I can't *die*. It's part of why I'm valuable to people—or things—like Sarlat. That's part of the curse, too. No one will *ever* like me—and that means I have to be around forever, so I can be forever unloved."

"Shit, Squat," I said. "*I* like you. At least so far. You're gross, but so's almost everything."

"Huh." He rubbed the place on his face where a gaping hole had been. "So, what now?"

"Well, I could put you in a hole and fill the hole with concrete and leave you down there for a million years. But I got into the monster-slaying business, not the prison-industrial-complex business. The problem is, I don't feel good about letting you run around loose doing more murder for whoever—sorry, *whomever*—cuts you a check or gives you a bag of cheeseburgers or whatever it is you take in payment."

"Look, I'm not ideologically committed to working for evil people," Squat said. "They're just usually the ones who have suitable job openings. So, I mean, what I'm saying is..."

I groaned. I wanted to tell him to fuck off before I *really* tested his immortality. I'm pretty good at killing things that are conventionally considered unkillable. But I thought of my tattoo: Do Better. I deserved a chance to redeem myself, right? Would I deny this guy that same chance?

"Fine," I said. "Consider yourself an unpaid intern. Come with me to deal with Sarlat. And don't think about doing any treacherous shit—I know you think you're hard to kill, but you're an amateur next to me." I started to walk out of the tent, then paused. "I am *not* getting a sidecar on my motorcycle for you to ride around in."

"You're the boss," he said. "So... are we going to kill my old boss now?"

"No need for murder in this case," I said. "Sarlat works for me now."

A Plan is a Thing that Fails

THE STREET WAS FILLED WITH THE DEAD, mostly Sarlat's people, cut down by Orias's crew. Nothing was moving, not even scavenger birds, though I imagined the buzzards would be along in time to eat whatever corpses proved edible—many of the dead were so inhuman their flesh probably wouldn't be compatible with a vulture's stomach. We picked our way among the fallen, Squat pausing occasionally to mercifully dispatch the not-quite-dead-yet from both gangs.

Tolerance was a ghost town again, pretty much. I kept expecting Sarlat to emerge from the jail, transforming into a wolf as he came—and I gave it even odds that Squat would turn on me to help his old boss, in that case. He wasn't bound to me, and I didn't have time to put him in a circle just then.

But the loup garou didn't come out, which was odd. He didn't strike me as the lying-in-wait type. More the fools-rush-in type.

"So Sarlat can't kill you?" Squat said, standing beside me just a dozen yards from the yawning-open door of the jail. "Maybe that's why he's holding back, hoping you'll just go away?"

"I've heard crazier ideas." I crept up to the door, trying to think of loopholes in the geas that prevented him from acting against me. Could he set a booby trap? Not if he had any expectation that I'd be the one to trigger it, not without dying himself in agony for breaking the deal. But maybe he'd tried to do it *anyway*, pain of painful death be damned? He seemed too conceited to give up his own life just to kill me, but it wasn't like I knew him all that well.

"Marla," Nicolette shouted. "If that's you, get me the fuck out of here. I didn't think it was possible for me to hate you any more, but I hate you *so fucking much* right now—"

I stepped into the jail. The only light in the room came from a lantern inside the cell, but I could see well enough. Nicolette, still disguised as

Orias, was on the floor, resting on one cheek. Sarlat was also on the floor, in a pool of blood, very much dead.

"Gods *damn* it." I'd had such a clever plan. Trap Sarlat in the geas, force him to tell me about the Eater, and then force him to help me take *out* the Eater, assuming the Eater was someone that needed to be taken out. Gloat a little and rub it in his face that I'd outsmarted him—petty, sure, but I didn't think it was a failure of character to act like a jerk to someone who sold virgins to cults for ritual sacrifice. But Sarlat was dead. So much for being clever. "What happened here, Nicolette? Did one of Orias's people get in and kill him?"

"*I* killed him!" she said—or screamed, and for the first time, I realized she was *really upset*, not just being ill-tempered or pretending outrage to amuse herself. "Do you know what that sick fucker tried to do to me? I don't know who this chick you made me look like was, but her and Sarlat had some kind of messed-up relationship. He kept *talking* to me, telling me I should have loved him the way he needed to be loved, that I brought this on myself. Creepy as fuck, but I went along with things, I played dead, because I'm your goddamn slave oracle bloodhound and that's the task you gave me. But then. Then he *kissed* me, Marla, he thought I was dead, and he still stuck his tongue in so deep I almost gagged on it. I could have stood that, but I could tell he was getting excited, and I was pretty sure he was about to move on from kissing to something a *lot* worse, so…"

I looked at Sarlat again. Most of the blood seemed to emanate from the vicinity of his mouth. "You tore out his tongue?"

"Aren't you fucking perceptive. Get me a drink of water, right now, and *fuck you*."

I just stood there, looking at Sarlat's corpse, but Squat took the initiative and found Sarlat's bag and took out a bottle of water. I shook off the horrified skin-crawlies and set Nicolette's head up on the table. Squat gave her sips of water, which she spat out, twenty or thirty mouthfuls as the water went from bright red to pink to finally clear.

"Hey," Squat said. "I'm Squat."

"Did Marla enslave you, too?" Nicolette said.

"Uh…."

"Squat was cursed by Elsie Jarrow," I said.

Jarrow was the woman who'd beheaded Nicolette, so I was thinking there could be some shared trauma bond thing there. Or that, being a chaos witch herself, Nicolette might find the nature of the curse interesting or instructive. But Nicolette was still a Jarrow fan, the way some twisted assholes revere serial killers, so instead she said, "Holy shit, did you *know* her? Like, were you a friend of hers, did you do her wrong, or..."

I walked outside. All the monsters were dead, except Squat, and killing him might require breaking his curse first, and it seemed like a shitty thing to do, breaking a guy's curse and then murdering him. Like if, in *Beauty and the Beast*, Belle had shoved a knife in the Beast's eyeball as soon as he turned into the handsome prince again. Maybe Squat was in the market for redemption, and we could work something out. I wasn't exactly experienced in the rehabilitative arts, but it's an article of faith for me that I can do anything.

I'd once overhead a guy in a comic shop trying to explain the difference between a superhero and an anti-hero to his young son. He said, "An anti-hero wants the bad guys to be dead. But a superhero wants the bad guys to turn into good guys."

I didn't have much hope of being a superhero, but maybe it was worth a try. Redemption over execution. All part of Doing Better.

Speaking of doing better, I knew I should figure out some way to make things up to Nicolette. She was supposed to just be a head on a mantelpiece, a prop in my plan, but instead she'd gotten monster-tongue in her mouth, and the legitimate fear of getting something worse. What she'd endured had gone way beyond the call of duty. The hard part was figuring out something I could do to make it up to her that wouldn't constitute a crime against humanity.

But first I let Nicolette take it easy while Squat and I disposed of the bodies. There were about a hundred dead—hardly a massive battlefield, but way more than we could easily deal with. A fire would have been visible for miles, so we decided to go the mass-grave route instead. Squat didn't know a damn thing about doing magic—he just *was* magic—so his job was picking up the strays and outliers and piling them up in the middle of the street. Me, I just concentrated on a bit of sympathetic magic. There were plenty of deep holes in the area, because of the old mines; I just needed to convince the dusty main street of Tolerance that *it* was actually a deep hole, too.

After Squat had heaped the bodies into a mass, I let the two thoughts held in opposition in my mind snap together, replacing over *here* with over *there*, and a sinkhole formed, the dead from Orias's and Sarlat's gangs tumbling down like sand disappearing into the lower chamber of an hourglass. Once all the dead were below the level of the ground, I gestured casually and a great wave of earth swept over the hole, burying the bodies and leaving no sign beyond a mass of churned-up dirt with shredded bits of scrub brush poking out haphazardly.

I looked at the covered hole for a moment, satisfied with myself, then I started blinking and twitching and shivering and had to sit down right there in the sand, my head between my knees, sucking in great gasps of breath.

I was freaking out because I *shouldn't have been able to do that*, especially the last part. Covering a huge mass grave with a thought and a gesture was pretty big magic. Such mastery over earth was not one of my skills. I've never specialized as a sorcerer, as necromancers and pyromancers and technomancers and biomancers and so on do, preferring to be a utility player, or a "rag and bone shop sorcerer" as my old mentor called people like me. I was a jill of all trades, master of none; pretty good at a lot of things, not amazing at any of them. Insofar as I had a particular strength it was probably enchanting, because I had the strong will and stubbornness necessary to spend hours imbuing objects with magic to be released in a sudden torrent or flash as needed.

What I *didn't* have was the power to be a human bulldozer. I could maybe fool myself into thinking I'd mastered sympathetic magic enough to make a hole spontaneously appear where there was no hole, but waving my hand and covering over the grave had been pure telekinesis or geomancy or, I don't know, earth-bending.

"Uh, are you okay?" Squat said.

"This is part of my magical process," I mumbled. "Go check on Nicolette, would you?"

Squat shrugged and wandered off. As far as he knew, I could move heaven and earth with a twitch of my fingers, so he wasn't surprised by my grave-digging abilities.

I remembered something I'd read once, about people who suffered brain damage and lost the ability to form new memories. Some researchers had gotten such patients to play that old video game Tetris for hours, spinning colored blocks around on screen and forming them into lines. Every day, the patients were offered the chance to play Tetris again, and even though they didn't remember playing it before, and acted as though they were encountering it for the first time every time, their game play *improved.* Their brains were forming new pathways and connections on levels far below consciousness. Some of the patients even reported dreams of colored shapes falling, just like they did on screen, though they had no idea why.

For a month, I'd been a chthonic goddess, co-regent of a metaphorical underworld, and even though my conscious mind had been stripped of the memories, and I assumed I'd lost all those goddess powers… maybe something was lurking underneath the thinking part of my brain. Not power I could access intentionally, but only in a casual, thoughtless act, with a distracted mind and a wave of my hand. World-class outfielders don't *think* about catching pop fly balls—they don't work out the angle of descent and lift their glove accordingly. They just *do* it, the same way I'd just unthinkingly moved a ton of dirt, by will alone.

Of course I wasted about ten minutes trying to make the earth move again, but thinking about it made it impossible. Like the old joke about a grasshopper asking a centipede how it managed to walk with all those legs, making the centipede so aware of its milling limbs that it promptly got tangled up in its own locomotion and fell over.

I stood up, glared at the hole, and wondered whether I should call Death, to demand an explanation. I felt like yelling at him, though there was no reason to, really. My response to being annoyed and confused is often to spread that annoyance and confusion around, which was probably one of those things I need to Do Better about. So instead of pitching a fit, I took a deep breath and decided to get on with my life on Earth.

I retrieved my bike and all my stuff from the undisclosed location, and got Nicolette settled in her cage on the rear seat again. Her illusion was fading, Orias's face sloughing away like mascara running in the rain. She'd gone all quiet, which worried me. A constantly bitching Nicolette was something I knew how to cope with, but a silent and unsleeping Nicolette was weird and creepy.

"I don't think there's room on this bike for you to ride bitch, Squat," I said. "You're going to have to make your own way home."

He snorted. "I'll take one of the twenty trucks left parked outside of town."

I swore. "Damn it. I buried the bodies but left the vehicles. I didn't even think about that."

"Eh, most of the cars were stolen anyway," Squat said. "I wouldn't worry too much."

"Where are you headed after this?" I asked.

Squat shook his head. "Fuck if I know. Sarlat's operation is all but wiped out, and the few guys left aren't too fond of me. When they hear I'm the only survivor, that's not going to make them like me any better. I seem to be unemployed and basically fucked." He looked at me expectantly.

"What do you want me to do about it? I spared your life. That's a pretty good favor you owe me already."

"You couldn't kill me anyway." He sighed. "Look, do you need some muscle? I know you managed to wipe out about a hundred people pretty much solo, but I work cheap, and when I don't have work to do, I tend to get myself in trouble."

"Hmm. I don't much need a thug. I'm pretty good at thuggery myself. But maybe… What do you know about the Eater?"

He blinked his eyes, which were the most human part of him, and actually kind of pretty in isolation, a sort of greenish-blue—

As I looked at him, his eyes changed, pupils elongating into goat-like slits, irises clouding and becoming a sort of bruise-purple color I found especially repellent. I flinched away from him, entirely involuntarily.

He grunted. "You had to like my eyes, didn't you? One part of me that hadn't changed much since I was human. Fucking curse." He sighed. "The Eater? I've heard the name, sure. Sarlat had dealings with him, though I never met him. If it is a him. Could be a her, or an it, or something else."

"Any idea what *kind* of dealings Sarlat had with him-her-it?"

"I want to say… human trafficking," Squat said. "I saw a couple of trucks loaded up with drugged people, mostly runaways and stuff, and I heard the Eater's name mentioned."

"Cannibal?" I said.

"I'm talking, like, a dozen to twenty people, on three or four occasions, within a few months. If the Eater is literally eating people, dude has an *appetite*."

"He could be eating their life-essence or something. You have any idea how Sarlat contacted him?"

Squat spread his hands. "Sorry. I was just a leg-breaker, with a sideline in other limbs. I could take you to his office and we could snoop around, check out his computer or whatever. Maybe we'll find something. You planning to go after the Eater?"

"It's a way to pass the time," I said. "Beats wandering around looking for monsters to slay at random. Sure, let's ransack Sarlat's shit, see what we can find." I glanced at Nicolette, who was still silent, and then covered her cage with the drop cloth. "But I need to get some sleep while there's a little night left, and I need to take care of some other business tomorrow… Give me the address and we'll meet there, not tomorrow morning, but the next day."

"You're the boss," he said.

"Don't get ahead of yourself. We'll call this a probationary period."

Crushes

Somewhere in there I found a motel room and slept. The next morning my smartphone obligingly showed me the location of both a local truck-rental place and a nearby scrapyard. I'd always been resistant to technology, but I had to admit, having the world (or a digital analogue thereof) at my fingertips was more convenient than calling up Pelham and demanding he research everything for me.

I tried to talk to Nicolette as I motored toward the rental place, but she wasn't talking back. Either she was sulking, or she was genuinely disturbed by what had happened with Sarlat. Having somebody shove their tongue into your disembodied head had to bring home a sense of powerlessness, and Nicolette didn't like having no power. Sure, she'd killed the guy, but in a pretty ugly and brutal and personal way. It had to be rough on her. Moreover, she'd only been in a position to be assaulted that way because I'd *put* her there. She had to be filled with a powerful cocktail of anger, disgust, revulsion, and the realization of her own helplessness at my hands, all combining to make her the next best thing to catatonic. Or else plotting my downfall.

Nicolette aspired to be chaos embodied like her hero Elsie Jarrow, but she still had a core of reason and rationality, and was driven by her own personal interests. Jarrow might have killed me one moment and crowned me queen of the universe in another and ignored me entirely in another, but Nicolette just wanted me to suffer. She was a fairly powerful witch, probably my equal (goddess stuff notwithstanding), at least when she wasn't reduced to a head in a cage, but she didn't have the deep irrationality necessary to be a master chaos practitioner. She had too many axes to grind, too many grudges and aspirations for personal gain. She'd always had dreams of greatness, but instead of becoming one of the most deadly and powerful forces on the planet, Nicolette had been reduced to my magical bloodhound, radiation detector, and dowsing rod. She was good at fooling herself, spinning a narrative in her own mind, making herself the hero of her own story, sure… but the shit she'd gone through in Tolerance, being reduced to an abused prop in one of my plans, might have shaken her illusions a little.

I couldn't fix Nicolette. I wasn't even sure what "fixing her" would mean—if there was a decent person inside her somewhere, I'd never seen a sign. But maybe I could cheer her up, and give her a jolt of chaotic power, and at least give her back enough of her delusions that she'd continue being useful to me.

I rented a fourteen-foot truck, using one of my fake IDs and another wedge of cash. My pale horse rolled easily up a ramp into the back, leaving lots of room for all the other crap I needed to buy. I put Nicolette on the front seat next to me and said, "Want to go shopping?"

She did not reply, just dully stared at the dashboard, so I slipped the cover back over her cage and went for a drive. I was afraid I'd have to go all the way to Tucson to get what I needed, but there are plenty of antique shops and people selling stuff on Craigslist even in the small towns on the outskirts. I kept hoping Nicolette would take an interest, wonder where we were going, why I kept stopping, what I was loading into the back of the truck (often with attendant cursing and swearing and the assistance of shop employees or people happy I'd helped transform their family heirlooms into cash). She didn't pay any attention at all.

It was creepy. She was also useless to me if she wouldn't *talk* to me, but that wasn't the only reason I wanted to snap her out of this. I really was trying to do what my stupid tattoo said.

It took half my remaining cash and damn near the whole day, but I was finally satisfied with my haul. When the last item was securely locked up in the truck, I got back in the cab. "Off to the main event," I said, more chirpily than I've said anything ever, and Nicolette didn't so much as grunt.

I followed my phone's glowing dot and robotic verbal directions to a scrapyard south of Tucson, the most isolated one I'd been able to locate. I felt a twinge as I approached the place, which, like so many junkyards, resembled the citadel of a postapocalyptic road warrior: high fences made of scrap board and corrugated steel topped with barbed wire, huge metal buildings, and rows upon rows of junked cars. My old friend Ernesto had owned a junkyard, a literally magical place full of folded space and strange magics. He'd died because of something I did. One of the many fuck-ups I needed to atone for.

I drove my truck right through the open gate, parked near the office—an airstream trailer streaked with bird shit—and then climbed out, holding a plastic soda bottle full of reeking potion. I dribbled the fluid all around the gate, then screwed the lid back on and put the bottle away in the truck. The keep-away potion would give any potential customers who approached a sudden, strong desire to be elsewhere, giving me two or three hours to do my thing.

The manager came banging out of the trailer, shading his eyes from the late afternoon sun with one hand. "Help you?" he called. My friend Ernesto had usually worn a black tuxedo (the lapels stained with axle grease, for ritual purposes), but this guy was dressed in a practical gray jumpsuit, hair sticking up like the bits of hay that didn't get mown down in a field.

"Yeah, I need the run of the place for a couple of hours."

He cocked his head. "You want what?"

"I need to use the crusher. Don't worry, I know how. Will five hundred bucks do?" That was all I had left. I should've looted the bodies in Tolerance for spare cash.

"Lady, are you *crazy*? I can't let you run the crusher."

I grunted. "Don't worry, I'm not trying to dispose of a body or anything, I just need to turn some shit into splinters, you know?"

"No. I do not know." He pointed to the gate. "You need to leave."

"Okay then." I started to turn away, then turned back, tossing something at him underhand.

I expected him to try and catch it—people tend to do that, instinctively—but he just stood there as the cloth-wrapped sachet smacked him in the chest, sending out a little puff of aromatic dust. It worked anyway, though: he smelled it, and his eyes closed, and he started to sway. I stepped in and caught him before he fell, then dragged him up the short steps into the trailer and dumped him on a couch that smelled like eight or ten cats had copulated, urinated, and died on it, possibly simultaneously. He'd be unconscious for the rest of the afternoon. Sleep charms are kind of annoying to make—it helps to be exhausted when you enchant them, but when you're tired you tend to make sloppy mistakes, and I'd created a lot of cloth packets of lavender and other ingredients that didn't do a damn thing except smell like the bedrooms of old grandmas. But such charms were handy, and a vital part of any solo running witch's toolkit. They don't have the nasty long-term effects that some other charms useful against ordinaries do—charms of compulsion and forgetting, especially—though I had some of those in my bag, too. Sometimes you have to balance the need for success against the chance of giving some innocent bystander brain damage.

I drove up and down the lanes to make sure there were no other customers lurking, but I was lucky, so I found the car crusher and parked near it.

Ernesto had taught me how to use the big junkyard machines, and even though this one wasn't identical to the one I'd learned on, the general idea was the same. This was a hydraulic vertical press—a "pancake" crusher—basically a big-ass metal box the size of a garage, with a heavy plate that would descend and crush anything you put inside. The press was striped in yellow and black danger lines, and there was a shimmery scatter of shattered safety glass all around it, but no car inside at the moment. This kind of press was designed to flatten junked cars so they could be stacked more easily on trucks and hauled off for disposal. I was glad it was a pancaker. A baling press—the kind that first squashes a car flat, then squashes in from the sides, and reduces a car to an astonishingly compact cube—would have been too fucking scary for what I had in mind.

I moved stuff out of the van and got everything set up. Some of it was hard to move solo, but I've always been pretty good at inertial magics, so I managed to manhandle everything into place, though it turned me into a sweaty, sore-muscled wreck in the process.

Once I was satisfied with the set-up, I removed Nicolette from the cab of the truck, set her cage on the hood with a good view of the crusher, and removed her drop cloth. "Ta da!" I said.

I stood beside her and took in the scene. The car crusher looked like a diorama of a pleasant living room. An antique Persian rug covered most of the crusher's floor, and there was a leather armchair, a beautiful carved-wood end table holding a Tiffany lamp, a dark mahogany sideboard bearing several old and lovely vases and an old-school phonograph, complete with the big horn. A curio cabinet stuffed with awful porcelain figurines, and a pie safe with a mismatched bunch of wedding china, depression glass, and Fiesta plates and bowls. The piece de resistance was an upright player piano, maybe a little too honky-tonk for the vibe as a whole, but in amazingly good shape for its age.

Nicolette made a little noise, almost just an exhale, but it was something.

"Pretty nice, huh?" I said. "I know you always got a kick out of destroying beautiful things. I feel bad your enjoyment of the giant massacre in Tolerance was spoiled. I realize you couldn't really savor the chaos in the street because of, ah, all the… stuff… going on with Sarlat. So I thought—"

"Smashing up some antiques isn't going to make me feel better, Marla," she said, voice dull and monotone. "Not noticeably."

"Ah, but the antiques, they're really just the garnish," I said. "You just watch and see."

The controls were an issue I'd puzzled over a bit. It would have been useful to have an accomplice, again—it made me wish I had Rondeau with me, but I didn't, for two good reasons: he wouldn't want to do all this shit, and having him with me would make all this too much like *fun*, and I wasn't convinced I was supposed to be having much fun. Maybe I should have brought an annoying-as-shit death cultist to act as general dogsbody. Or told Squat to come along on this errand. That was a pretty good solution, actually. His presence was *guaranteed* to be kind of unpleasant—the curse required it—so he'd contribute to my general misery. (Maybe it's stupid to punish myself this way. But the thing is—I'm a part-time goddess. I'm unkillable. I deserve to be punished, to suffer a little for the suffering I've caused, but there's no one else qualified to punish me—or capable of making it stick. Like always, if I want something done, I have to do it myself. I've never been good at forgiveness. Apparently not even when it comes to myself.)

Shit, introspective digression there, those are getting more frequent. Anyway, the controls: the crusher was run via levers and buttons on a panel at one end of the machine, and I didn't have anyone to operate it. I realized I should have used a pebble of compulsion on the shop owner after all—then he could have pulled the levers and pushed the buttons, transformed from autonomous being with his own hopes and dreams into my own little remote control. Instead I had to do something far creepier.

I still had one of the polaroids from Tolerance, so I scrawled a rune across my own face, using blood from my index finger—a bit of my flesh to lend the simulacrum solidity—and then lit the photo on fire. (The telepresence illusions were re-usable, minimal magic, just bent light to create an image and displaced air waves for sound, but for something more substantial I had to let the components be consumed.)

After I tossed the burning image to the ground, smoke rose up, thick tendrils of gray, far more than a burning bit of plastic could have supplied through ordinary combustion. The smoke seemed to fill an invisible mold, forming a life-sized but not even remotely human-looking copy of me, wearing the leather coat and boots I'd left in the truck, all rendered in shades of dark gray. The edges of the figure swirled and eddied, but there was enough solidity at the core to run some heavy machinery—

And to run its mouth, apparently. "Are you sure you want to do this?" my smoke-golem said.

I frowned. "What the fuck? Since when do things like you talk?"

"You invested me with a piece of yourself," it said, smoke flowing out and up as its mouth opened and closed.

"I've done this sort of thing before, and I never got any chatter in the old days."

"You're more full of life than you used to be. Your blood is more potent."

Was this more goddess shit? Or a bizarre consequence of being unkillable? It made me wonder if *all* my blood-based magics would be more powerful now. "You're just temporary though, right?"

"How should I know? You created me."

I glanced at Nicolette, hoping the sight of two Marlas would sufficiently enrage her to prompt a comment, but she barely seemed to notice. "Huh. This is a little bit new to me, too. So are you, like, an independent entity, or a reflection of me, or..."

The smoke-creature looked amused, I thought, but it was hard to tell with its shifting face. "Whatever I am, I'll run the controls, if you're sure you want to go through with this."

"Why not?" I said. "It's worth a try."

I climbed up into the car crusher, the part of my brain that had not yet internalized the fact of my immortality screaming at me that this was a *bad bad bad* idea, a transgression against good sense and self interest. But I fought those feelings down, walked across the rug, and sat down in the armchair. I glanced up at the immense, rust-pocked metal plate above my head. "Here goes," I said. "You might want to watch this, Nicolette."

"Wait, what?" Nicolette's flickered from me to the plate above my head, her face alive with interest and confusion at last.

Then the squealing roar of the hydraulics started up.

Look, I got crushed. I don't know how much detail I really want to go into here. I was terrified, deep in my backbrain, despite my intellectual knowledge that I'd be fine. I was terrified in my forebrain, too, when I thought about the pain, because I knew being crushed was going to hurt, a sort of hurt almost no one has ever experienced and lived through.

I thought of stories I'd heard of thieves and mobsters hiding out in the trunks of cars, waiting for the heat to die down, only for the cars to be crushed with them inside. At least those poor bastards hadn't seen it coming. I had to deal with the *suspense.* I hunched down as the plate descended, tried to pull in my neck like a turtle, a totally involuntary action, but it happened, inevitably, the rusty plate touching the top of my head, the pressure, the slowly mounting *pressure*—

I heard the jangling sound of the piano being crushed, its strings snapping and setting off a last discordant symphony, the kind of chaotic, irreproducible music that Nicolette most enjoyed. I heard the vases shatter and pop and the curio cabinet crunch. The chair I was sitting in broke and squeezed to splinters and fragments around me, adding stabbing and scratching to the crushing.

The last thing I heard before I lost consciousness was Nicolette's howling laughter.

I opened my eyes and then wiped the blood out of them. The enormity of the pain—I mean the classic sense of "enormity" here, of something bad on a vast scale—was already fading from my mind. I stood up, looking around at the pulped and smashed remains of the antiques, and at all my blood—drying puddles of apparently very magically potent blood. My clothes were torn to pieces, ground and scraped into shreds by the armchair I'd been sitting in, but basically I felt fine. I stepped out, wobbly, and nodded to my smoke ghost twin standing by the controls.

"How in the *fuck*," Nicolette said. "You could do this trick on stage in Vegas. You were sitting there, I *know* it was you, I can sense your reality, throbbing like a rotten tooth in my jaw. I saw you get squashed, I thought you'd lost your mind and decided to end it all in the crazy painfulest way ever, I was so *happy*—and now here you are, looking like you really *did* get crushed, clothes ripped to shit, but not a mark on your body. *How*?"

I coughed, shrugged, cracked my neck. "A magician never reveals her secrets. You know I'm good with illusions."

"And that chatty smoke golem over there, how'd you manage—Wait, that's it, isn't it? You disguised yourself as the golem and switched places, so it was the golem who got squished and you who ran the controls, then you swapped back. That has to be it. All smoke and mirrors."

"Exactly," I said. "I figured seeing me in agony might perk you up, so I wanted to make it convincing."

"The screams were very authentic," Nicolette said. "And knowing it was all bullshit, that you didn't get crushed at all, sort of spoils the thrill, retroactively—but I admit, in the moment, seeing you get pulped, gods, yeah, that made me happy. And all those nice antiques getting smashed, too, like the olive in a martini or a cherry on a sundae, not necessary really, but a nice addition. Good trick. Feel free to stage shows like that for me nightly."

Nicolette would never know how I *had* suffered in my attempt to do penance. It crossed my mind that this atonement stuff was arguably a little crazy—I was basically a monk whipping himself to ribbons with a thorny branch and then putting on the old hairshirt for good measure—but I felt a little better, too. I'd fucked up by handing Nicolette over to Sarlat, and I'd paid a price for that mistake. The only books being balanced were the ones in my head, but it still mattered.

The crusher kind of put things in perspective, too. I wasn't likely to moan over a stubbed toe any time soon, not after experiencing that kind of pain.

My smoke ghost started to walk toward me. "Marla," it said, producing ribbons of gas like a fog machine at a metal show. "Your heart's in the right place, but it's not a competition, this whole self-improvement thing. Don't get obsessive or become an overachiever, you know how we can be—"

Then a gust of wind blew through, spinning my ghost into shreds of nothingness, leaving behind a smell of burned chemicals and blood.

I looked at the car crusher. Shit, yeah, blood. The manager of the yard would wake up soon, and he'd find a crusher full of weird stuff and lots of blood, and there would be panic and cops and even though it was unlikely any of it would trace back to me, it'd be better if this place looked like less of a crime scene.

Without thinking about it, I gestured, and flames appeared in the crusher, casting an invisible shadow of heat so powerful I stumbled back a few steps. The flames burned blue and white, seeming brighter for a moment than the sun, and when they abruptly winked out of existence there was nothing in the crusher at all but ash. Even the bits of metal were gone, flashed to toxic steam.

"Since when did you become a master pyromancer?" Nicolette demanded.

"I've been taking night classes at the community college." I kept my voice light. I'm capable of making big fires, but I do it in the usual ways: pull heat from the atmosphere, or strike a match and use amplification and sympathetic magic, or splash some gasoline around and flip open a Zippo. I don't just wave my hand and summon… hellfire.

Covering up mass graves and calling up flames that burned with the contained heat of stars. Okay. It seemed I'd learned a few tricks during my month in the underworld. A shame I couldn't make this stuff happen at will. The battle in Tolerance would have been over a lot faster if I'd been able to intentionally summon a fire so intense it turned metal into gas. Then again, I was known to lose my temper and do destructive things without sufficient forethought, and the idea of having that kind of power at my command was a little worrisome even for *me*—

Suddenly it seemed a lot more plausible that my goddess-self would decide to limit access to my memories, if they included the knowledge of how to wield power like that. I could recognize my own thought processes at work: never trust anybody else to do anything right. Even when that "anybody else" encompasses another, arguably lesser, version of yourself.

"I guess you're stuffed with chaos, but I could use something to eat, and some sleep," I said. "I'm going to change clothes, then let's ditch the truck and find a place to hole up for the night."

"And tomorrow we go looking for this Eater thing?" Nicolette said.

"That's the idea."

"Good. Maybe he can kill you for real."

"Hope springs eternal, with feathers on," I said.

Getting Clean

We were in yet another crappy motel—there were no shortage of those in the Southwest—but the water pressure was good and hot and I spent a long time filling the bathroom with steam while Nicolette watched TV in the other room.

I'd killed a bunch of monsters, and caused a bunch of other monsters to be killed. Filthy work—literally, not figuratively—and getting squished in a hydraulic press hadn't helped my cleanliness. Hence the endless hot scouring torrents of water. The curtain was a flimsy thing, and I knew someone else was in the bathroom with me the moment he appeared. I knew who, too.

"Peeping Tom," I said.

"I look upon mortal bodies with disinterest," Death replied, sitting down on the closed toilet next to the shower. "All flesh is grass. Though admittedly yours is very tender and delectable grass."

"Are you planning to check up on me every week?"

"Just on days you cheat death," he said mildly. I peeked around the edge of the shower, though I could barely see him in the swirling steam. "I assumed some enemy of yours loaded you into a car crusher, but, no, it was self-inflicted. May I ask why?"

"I screwed up, and something unpleasant happened to Nicolette—something I didn't *mean* to happen. She was pretty upset about it, and I felt bad, so I figured I'd make her feel better. There's nothing she likes more than the idea of me dying horribly, so."

Death clucked his tongue. "You couldn't have taken her out for an ice cream cone or something less violent instead?"

"She says eating real food isn't satisfying anymore, since it just falls out of her neck-hole. Don't worry. I'm fine. Unless, what, do I only have nine lives or something?"

"No, death is withdrawn from you during the time you dwell on the Earth, until you've achieved a reasonable human old age, or until you decide you don't want to bother with being alive anymore. You could drown yourself for breakfast every morning and you'd be spitting up water and breathing fine mere moments later. Granted, if you were incinerated utterly by the blast of a hydrogen bomb, putting you back together again would prove difficult and time-consuming, so try to use *some* discretion in your choice of deaths, all right?"

"So you're saying, don't piss off anybody with access to nukes. That's pretty good advice in general."

"If you'd let me, I could take away the pain when you—"

"Life is pain," I said. Then winced. "Sorry. That came out way too emo. But pain is an important part of life, and I want to *be* alive, really alive, during the six months of the year I'm here on Earth."

"Dying is *also* an important part of life," he said, his tone only a little bit insufferable. "Or at least, awareness of the possibility of death. You don't seem too bothered about giving that part up."

"I make exceptions when it comes to survival. I'm pragmatic that way."

"I just worry that you're hurting yourself because you think you deserve to be hurt."

"Maybe I do. More than most people do, anyway. Sure, there could be a streak of mortification-of-the-flesh going on here. I won't deny it. But crushing myself… that sucked. I think I'm going to get out of the physically masochistic self-punishment business."

"And the psychological punishment? Like traveling with that horrible head-in-a-cage woman?"

I adjusted the water temperature a little, inching it a bit closer to boiling. "Part of that's self-punishment, sure. But part of it's also, like, a *test*. I want to be a better person than I used to be—more thoughtful, more compassionate, less selfish. Except, it's easy to be a good person when your life doesn't have any obstacles or complications. So I stack the deck against myself a little—travel with a companion who hates me, instead of Rondeau, who loves me, or Pelham, who almost worships me. Go to territory I don't know and pick fights with nasty bastards who are bigger than me. Eat shitty food, and sleep rough. Save people who'll never know I saved them, who'll never be grateful or owe me a favor. If I can be a better person under *those* circumstances, then, damn—that means something. Maybe I really can change."

"You do like to make things more difficult for yourself than they need to be," Death said.

"What's life without a challenge? Hard mode or go home, motherfucker."

"I suppose this enforced misery means you would refuse the comfort of your husband's touch."

"In theory. But maybe, for today, I've suffered enough. This time I'll make exceptions for survival *and* sex. Come on in. The water's fine.

"And you're even better."

"Damn right," I said.

That cheered me up a little.

Now that Nicolette was no longer half catatonic, she became irritatingly chatty again. After my long and quite refreshing shower, I was sitting in the armchair of the motel room, reading more about Zen and motorcycle maintenance, when she said, "Are we really going to team up with this Squat guy?"

I closed the book and squinted at her, where she sat on the table in her cage. "I don't know. Maybe? I feel like I killed a bunch of gangsters and then an ugly puppy came wobbling out of the bullet-ridden house, looking around all confused, wondering what those loud noises were and where his master went. Like I have some obligation toward him now, maybe. The poor bastard's cursed."

"Speaking as an undying head stuck in a bird cage and forced to serve the will of a woman I repeatedly tried to kill, let me tell you about all the vast bucketloads of sympathy I have for him."

I thought about that. Making Nicolette be my bloodhound and oracle had seemed to serve two purposes: punishing her for her numerous crimes, and punishing *me* for mine. But now I began to wonder: was it also another kind of test, from my more enlightened goddess-self? Maybe I was supposed to learn something about forgiveness or the folly of revenge for revenge's sake or simply about using people like they were tools and nothing more. Was I supposed to *stop* hating Nicolette?

"I think of you hating me the way I think of the sun rising in the east," I said slowly. "It's just... part of the natural order. But, you know, it's been so long, I can't even remember why you *started* hating me—"

"It hasn't been that long," she interrupted. "I always thought you were awful, snobby, arrogant, and way too full of yourself, but I don't think I graduated to full *hate* until you had my mentor killed. I was supposed to succeed him as one of the leading sorcerers of the city, and instead—"

I frowned. "Nicolette. Your mentor was plotting to murder me. Assassinate me, depose me, stage a coup, take over as chief sorcerer. And he collaborated with truly monstrous forces to try and get his way. Damn right he was executed for his treachery—he put the whole city, *my* city, in danger. And anyway, you *got* your seat on the council after he died, you fooled me into thinking you could be trusted—"

She rolled her eyes. "Oh *goodie*. I had the chance to serve under the bitch who killed my friend. The *incompetent* bitch. My boss thought you were a terrible chief sorcerer, and you know what? Less than a year after you murdered him, you got your ass deposed and exiled for your *own* crimes against the city, abuse of power, whatever. Proving he was right about you all along. But before you pissed off to the islands, you got me locked up in an insane asylum—"

"You were a danger to yourself and others, Nicolette. You were irrational, you couldn't even be trusted to act in your own self-interest—"

"Oh, puh-*leeze*. You just described every chaos witch ever. If I behave too predictably, I lose my mojo. Besides, you weren't locking me up for therapeutic purposes. You used the Blackwing Institute as a place to put your political prisoners. Don't deny it."

I squirmed a little. There was a tiny bit of truth to that. But it's not like Blackwing was a gulag, some nightmare horror-movie asylum. If you had to be locked up somewhere, it was even sort of a nice place, maybe... I thought of further arguments. Like the fact that Nicolette still worshipped Elsie Jarrow, even though Jarrow had literally cut off her head, on the sort of whim beloved of chaos practitioners. But you couldn't *argue* someone into not hating your guts.

I sighed. "Okay. You've got legitimate grievances." Along with the illegitimate ones. "I did some bad stuff. I know that. I'm trying to... never mind. Look. Do you want me to let you go?"

"What?" Never had a single syllable been so filled with suspicion.

I ran a hand through my damp hair and grimaced. "Death was withdrawn from you. I can probably arrange to... withdraw the withdrawal. Let you die in peace."

She belched. "Fuck you, Marla. I was just starting to feel a little bit *good*. I will always choose life over death, even this kind of half-life. What I *want* is to get my body back, or if that body's not available, some *other* body will do. I'd take yours, for instance, if only because of the opportunities for self-mutilation."

I shook my head. "Nicolette, even if I could get you a new body, you'd just try to kill me again, right?"

"Most likely. You haven't given me a lot of reasons to be nicer to you, that little snack this afternoon notwithstanding. Don't get me wrong, I appreciate the gesture, and I'm sure I'll have some erotic dreams about you in the car crusher next time I fall asleep, but that whole act of contrition just brought me back from depression and restored our old status quo—I hate you, and you get hated by me."

"How about if we made a truce? I get you a body, you go on your way, and you leave me alone?"

"Sure," she said. "I double-dog swear."

"Would you swear that in a circle of binding?"

"Fuck, no," she said. "I don't like being subject to a geas. Besides, have you ever been in a circle of binding? The whole point is you *can't* tell a bald-faced lie in one of those, so there's no way I could promise not to kill you."

I couldn't say her reaction entirely surprised me. She hated being with me, sure, but that hate was counterbalanced by another force. Nicolette has always wanted desperately to be my nemesis, but she's seldom risen above the level of an annoyance. Oh, she'd allied herself with people who *could* reasonably qualify as nemeses—Jarrow, my dark doppelganger The Mason, maybe even her dead mentor Gregor—but she'd never been more than the sidekick or lieutenant or chief thug of the various big bads I'd faced. My refusal to dedicate myself to destroying her as I had some of those other figures had wounded her in her most sensitive spot, a part of her that remained intact even after her body was lost: her pride.

I *almost* told her I felt sorry for her, but that would have only made things between us worse.

Instead I spread my hands. "So what can I do? You don't want to die. I can't risk letting you have bodily autonomy." Not that she could *succeed* in killing me, but she sure could make my life unpleasant. "You don't want to travel with me—"

"I never said *that*." She smiled slyly, a familiar expression, like a clever child thinking she was smarter than all the adults around her, not recognizing the limits of her own cleverness. "This is pretty great in some ways. I mean, I hate your *company*, but you drag chaos and horror around with you wherever you go, and since I can't have orgasms or eat lobster or punch people anymore, feeding on chaos is one of the only two pleasures I've got left."

"What's the other pleasure?"

"Complaining incessantly and annoying the shit out of you, and always devoting at least part of my attention to how I might engineer your eventual ultimate downfall."

Ah. She got joy out of depriving me of joy. I could see that. "Okay. It's a deal."

"What are you talking about? What's a deal?"

"Nothing," I said. And from Nicolette's point of view, nothing would change. She'd bitch at me, and I'd bitch back—we'd snap and snipe at each other. But I'd be doing it because I knew the viciousness made her a little bit happier. It was bad enough to make Nicolette serve me in her undeath; making her suffer more by trying to treat her with sympathy and kindness was just cruel. I'd give her more fuel for the hate that sustained her.

I embarked on my new policy immediately: "Why don't you shut up? I'm starting to think I should have reanimated your body as an oracle and left your head in that fish pond. I could've stuck a motorcycle helmet on your neck-stump and let your body communicate with me by sign language."

"I'm going to sing you a song I made up about how much I hate your guts," Nicolette said, and proceeded to do just that, caterwauling and wildly out of tune.

I put in my earplugs and went to sleep feeling like I'd done some good.

Cold Trail

"**THAT HOLE FULL OF ASHES AND RUBBLE** used to be Sarlat's office." Squat was dressed like it was the depths of winter instead of Southwest summer, bundled in hat, scarf, ugly brown parka, gloves, shapeless pants, big boots, and additional layers of clothing, like he'd put on his whole closet at once on a dare. He looked like an ambulatory pile of dirty laundry, which was better than looking like an ambulatory demon thumb wrapped in pus-covered bandages, which was the look he'd been sporting last time I saw him.

I kicked a blackened fragment of the devastated building in the general direction of the rubble. The structures on either side were intact and unharmed by fire, which suggested either the actions of an incredibly talented arsonist or the use of magic. "Was anyone hurt?"

"Nah, the place was empty. Used to be a little import/export office, small warehouse on site, loading dock in the back. Nobody there last night when it got torched. All the computers and papers and stuff are totally gone, though."

"You think it's the Eater trying to cover his tracks?" I said. "Knowing someone might come looking and find a clue about his identity or whereabouts?"

Squat stuck a finger in his ear—at least I think it was a finger, and it was probably an ear—wiggled it for a moment meditatively, and then shrugged. "You're asking the wrong guy. I just beat people up for a living. I don't, like, *deduce*."

I'd never been good at deduction, either. I'd tried to be an occult detective, for a while, but I'd sucked at the detecting parts. "So what do I do now? Place some ads online? 'Dear Eater, I'd like to discuss your future prospects?' I don't even know what kind of bad guy this is—the revenge-taking sort, or the going-to-ground type?" I sighed. "Crap. I need an oracle."

"What, I'm not good enough for you?" Nicolette said.

"Just because you're a severed head doesn't make you Mimir," I said.

"Who the fuck is Mimir?" Squat said.

"Sorry," I said. "Sorcerers tend to be mythology nerds. Mimir is from Norse mythology, a legendary wise man who got his head chopped off. After that Odin, the father of the gods, carried Mimir's head around, and it whispered secrets to him. Whereas Nicolette mostly shouts obscenities."

"Living severed heads are full of wisdom," Nicolette said. "There's the Brazen Head, the Baphomet head, the singing head of Orpheus, Bran the Blessed—read a book, uggo. We're chock full of wisdom, I think because when you're missing your stomach and sexual organs and all that you don't have so many distractions, so it frees up the brain for thinking."

"Nicolette's good for leading me into generalized trouble," I said. "She can smell chaos, especially the bad unnatural kind that we might as well call evil. But for tracking down one particular monster, if that's what the Eater is..." I shrugged. "Time to call in the big guns."

"That rat fuck Rondeau?" Nicolette said. "He's even uglier than you, Squat."

"I'd like to see that," Squat said. "It might help my self-esteem."

"Too bad," I said. "I'm not dragging him out here. He can find an oracle for me just fine in Vegas." I pulled out my phone and rang him up.

When he answered, his voice was blurry with sleep or possibly booze. "Wha?"

"Good morning, sunshine," I said.

He groaned. "Marla. It's... not even noon yet. I am not awake before noon. And I had all kinds of fucked-up dreams."

I perked up at that. "Did you have... one of *those* dreams?" Rondeau was a powerful psychic, known to have occasional prophetic dreams about potential futures. They tended to be of the annoyingly cryptic variety—surreal images that only made sense as prophecy in retrospect—but sometimes they contained useful clues.

"Nah. I just hit an all-night buffet right before bed. Eating so much before I go to sleep always gives me vivid dreams. You know I usually only have *those* dreams about stuff that impacts me directly, so your decision to leave me here instead of dragging me around the desert—thanks again for that, by the way—means I'm not expecting any useful visions."

"Too bad," I said. "I need you to summon an oracle and find something out for me."

"Gahhhh," Rondeau said, or syllables to that effect. "You know doing that stuff wrecks me, I get the shakes for days. You sure this isn't something you could just look up on the google?"

"We tried that already. I hit a dead end trying to track down this guy or thing or whatever, the Eater. It's trying to hide from me, I think. Or else I'm just no good at knowing where to look for it. Go summon up something horrible and ask it to tell me the Eater's whereabouts, all right? And I'm sorry in advance for your headaches."

"If you really need it, I guess I'll do it."

Having gotten what I wanted, I remembered to try and be pleasant. "How are things there?"

"They were pretty good, until I got this phone call. Just gambling and sleeping and keeping myself entertained, pretty much pure perfection. Pelly's doing all right, I guess—he's back in Vegas now, though he wants to go back to Death Valley to check on the cultists this weekend. Apparently none of them have died on their spelunking expeditions yet."

"I really need to figure out what to do with those lunatics," I said.

"Taking all their money and having sex with the attractive ones is pretty traditional," Rondeau said. "But whatever makes you happy. When do you need this oracle summoned?"

"I don't have any other plans, and my time is limited." Both Squat and Nicolette looked way too interested when I said that—neither one of them knew I was going to turn back into a pumpkin at midnight, so to speak, when my month on Earth ran out. "So, you know. Make it a priority."

"Yes'm," he said. "I'll be in touch."

I switched off the phone. "My associates are going to chase down a lead," I said. "Buy you lunch, Squat?"

"I usually just crouch in an alley and eat rats and garbage."

"I was thinking cheeseburgers."

"Sometimes when I go into places where there are lots of people the curse gets extra-active, and there are, uh… unpleasant consequences."

"Drive-through it is, then."

I expected Rondeau to call me up and tell me what the oracle said, but instead Pelham sent an e-mail. It's weird to get an e-mail composed of complete sentences, but that's Pelly for you. I'll just stick his message in here so you can read it if you want, Future Me, instead of trying to paraphrase. I've been writing in this diary a long-ass time, and I'm going to see if I can find the House of the Eater soon, so I want to kind of wrap this up.

Being an Account of Certain Oracular Visitations

Dear Mrs. Mason,

As you have repeatedly chastised me for my alleged tendency to "bury the lede" or "beat around the bush," and in keeping with your frequent suggestion that I "get to the [expletive] point already," I will begin with the details I believe will interest you most: you should go to West Texas to continue your search for the Eater. Alas, the Eater is not necessarily *in* that location, but we are informed (reliably informed, Rondeau assures me) that you should be able to pick up his trail there.

You will, of course, be disappointed that we were unable to obtain more precise information regarding the Eater's location, or, indeed, his nature, abilities, and "threat level," as the saying goes. In order to explain this failure to acquire more useful intelligence, I beg your indulgence: allow me to describe the events of this morning in some detail.

Rondeau knocked on the door to my bedroom shortly before noon, and I was immediately alarmed, for he seldom rises before "the sun is over the yardarm," as he says—a vague term, and a peculiar semantic choice given that Rondeau is not and never has been a sailor—but one which seems to corresponded in Rondeau's mind, at least, to approximately midday. I inquired as to whether anything was wrong, and he said, "No, everything's fine, but Marla needs me to summon up an oracle and I want you to come along in case I pass out or start choking on my tongue or something."

Though I found that explanation not at all reassuring, I dressed and accompanied Rondeau downstairs to the garage. He suggested that I drive, so that he might "concentrate on catching the right vibe," and so I selected my preferred conveyance—a Bentley, not unlike the one you once used as chief sorcerer of Felport, though Rondeau insisted on putting "spinning rims" on it, for reasons which escape my understanding—and followed his directions.

Soon we turned away from the unspeakably gawdy area near the so-called "Strip"—truly, living in this crass place is an affront to my sensibilities; I think I genuinely prefer being in Death Valley with the cultists—and wound our way through residential areas until finally moving south into the desert. I never fail to be astonished at how swiftly the glittering eyesore of an oasis that is Las Vegas gives way to genuine wilderness.

Rondeau complained bitterly about the journey, however. "Why couldn't I just go summon up the spirit of Lady Luck in a slot machine or something? You're telling me in all of Vegas there's not a single useful oracle?"

"I'm afraid I don't know," I replied. You will recall, Mrs. Mason, that though I am familiar with Rondeau's ability to "call spirits from the vasty deep," as the bard so memorably put it, I have rarely had occasion to witness such summonings, and as such felt both curiosity and a certain amount of apprehension at the prospect. "Did you feel no, ah, 'vibes,' in the city itself?"

"Not a twinge, not a tickle," Rondeau answered. "But there's a definite sort of tugging sensation from the desert in the south, and maybe, I want to say, *underground*, too. Hell. I hope there's a shovel in the trunk."

I did not answer that, though I was a trifle offended. Of course there was a shovel in the trunk. I would no more set out on such a journey without a shovel than I would without a tire iron and jack, jumper cables, toolbox, rope, pickaxe, burlap sacking, sewing kit, or any other item that a reasonable person might expect to be of use. Working with sorcerers has taught me the value of being prepared, and all of our cars are amply provisioned. (I was very saddened by the limited storage space available on your motorcycle, Mrs. Mason, but even then I found space in your "saddlebags" for a collapsible portable shovel and other essentials.)

After several miles of sitting slumped and staring out the window, Rondeau finally lifted his head and said, "There, take that road."

The "road" in question was clearly suited more to rugged off-road vehicles than to a luxury vehicle like the Bentley, but the tires and suspension had been suitably enchanted to make travel over such a rutted and potholed ruin of a track relatively easy, so I complied without complaint. (I confess I winced a bit, if only inwardly, at the thought of how dusty and filthy the Bentley would become. I know our business can be a dirty one, but must the dirt so often be *literal*?) Rondeau did not look well—his skin was pale, droplets of sweat forming on his forehead and running down his cheeks, and he developed a twitch in the muscle of his cheek. "Holy fuck, this is a big one," he said.

"What do you mean?" I asked.

He shook his head. "Sometimes you can conjure up a little oracle, something small, and it doesn't take too much of a toll. But if the revelation you're after is a particularly momentous one, it takes a... larger summoning. Usually a steeper price, too."

"I'm afraid I don't entirely understand the nature of your power," I told him, as we slid smoothly across the battered ground, deeper into the desert. "When you summon these creatures, are you *genuinely* locating supernatural creatures and pulling them into our mundane physical reality, as in the old tales of sorcerers summoning demons to do their bidding? Or are the things you summon more like... hand-puppets, merely a way for you to directly interrogate and interact with your *own* psychic powers, which are actually responsible for uncovering the information you receive from the oracles?"

"Better minds than mine have debated that question, Pelly," he replied. "Whichever it is, I get a bastard of a headache most times, and sometimes nose bleeds, and often bad dreams. Marla thinks it's just my brain, plucking the information out of the cosmos or whatever, and that when I summon an oracle I'm pretty much talking to myself. But there's this *transactional* element, you know? The oracle always demands a price, and you have to pay it, and if you don't, there are consequences—strictly psychic ones, your mind starts to crumble and fold in on itself, but still. The fact that there's a bargain struck, a price paid, a deal made—that makes me think the creatures I encounter are real, even if they maybe *weren't* real in the moments before I called them up. If *that* makes any sense—you know I'm not a major philosophical thinker. Marla herself has summoned minor oracles, is the thing. It's not as easy for her as it is for me, she doesn't have the natural knack, but there are rituals you can do, and she's done them. Marla's about as psychic as a block of wood—there are times I think she doesn't even have a good understanding of what's going on deep down in her *own* mind, let alone anybody else's—so I find it hard to believe that she was just focusing her own energy and unlocking her own psychic perceptions when she, like, called the demon Murmurus into existence in an alleyway to ask it for directions." He paused. "The world is a lot scarier to contemplate if you believe the things I'm calling up have real, independent existences, isn't it?"

"I suppose so," I said, considering his words, which cast a shadow of apprehension across my mind.

"And there's some monstrous big desert spirit here for me to call up," Rondeau said. "Pull over here. About that shovel—"

"I have one."

"How about a pickaxe?" he said, and I nodded.

We spent the next half an hour or so toiling, some hundred yards from the place where we'd parked the Bentley. The desert has a certain beauty, I will admit, but there are times when it seems quite alien to me, and as I looked around the bleak and, to all appearances, lifeless expanse around us, I felt as if we had been transported to some distant planet, one inimical not just to human life but to any sort of life at all. I used the pick to break up the stony Earth, and Rondeau the shovel to remove the stones, and in this way we dug a hole some three feet deep. ("It's about a half a grave down," Rondeau told me.)

Eventually the shovel revealed something quite different from the beige and gray sand and rocks: something black and reflective as volcanic rock, probably spherical (it was actually an ellipsoid, as we found when we dug it up entirely later), the size of a soccer ball, its revealed hemisphere cratered and pitted but nevertheless lustrous. We stood at the bottom of the hole, barely large enough for the two of us together, and looked at the incongruous rock. Even I could sense within it some power—perhaps even malevolence, or worse, a cold curiosity.

Rondeau knelt down, grunting, expression that of a man trying to bear up under considerable pain. "This thing, Pelly… it came from beyond the back of the stars."

It could have been a meteorite—and I believe, based on what happened next, that it was, at least of a sort—but I found the phrase "beyond the back of the stars" to be a strangely chilling one.

"You be ready to ask the question, Pelly. Sometimes it takes all my attention just to keep a hold on whatever I've called up, and this might be one of those times." I nodded my assent, and he reached out with both hands and clasped the sides of the stone, like a faith healer grasping the head of a worshiper.

He screamed, then, or *keened*, a sound uncannily like the howling of a boiling teapot, but his face remained bizarrely expressionless.

After that, Mrs. Mason… this may be hard to credit. I am painfully aware that I can convey to you only what my senses conveyed to my *mind*, and we both know that senses can be fooled, both by illusions created by others and by our own human tendency to seek patterns and order and reasonable forms of cause-and-effect. But I will report what I remember seeing, acknowledging that memory, by its very nature, is hardly reliable.

The sky turned black. Above us, stars burned, but they were not cool distant pinpoints of whiteness, as they are in our Earthly sky. They were red, and sometimes green, and I call them stars only because it seems that's what they *must* have been. In truth they looked like nothing so much as welts, wounds, festering sores on the utterly black skin of the sky. They were so numerous that, despite the fact that they glowed only faintly, I could see my surroundings easily.

We remained in our respective positions—Rondeau kneeling, hands on the stone, and I standing beside him—but everything around us was changed. We were no longer in a hole, but standing on a plain, the surface identical to the lustrous black stone we'd unearthed. The place should have been cold, but it was actually warm, and moist, like being in the jungle again. The plain stretched in all directions as far as I could see, but the *horizon*... the horizon was wrong. Have you stood on the beach, Mrs. Mason, and looked out over the water, and perceived the roundness of the earth, a subtle curve on the horizon? I could perceive the curvature of *this* world, too, but the horizon curved *up* at the ends, you see, turning up at the edges like a faint smile, and as I scanned the distance in all directions I perceived that same distortion everywhere I looked.

It makes no sense, of course. Unless we were on the *inside* of a sphere. Unless the sky above was just more interior surface. But if that's true, *what* were we inside?

It is more likely that my eyes were deceived, or that the place had no literal existence at all.

Before I could worry overmuch about our altered surroundings, Rondeau threw his head back, and his mouth began to work in a terrible fashion. His jaw fell open, mouth distending so widely I was afraid the bones in his face would crack, or the muscles tear, and his tongue writhed in his mouth like a thrashing serpent.

Nevertheless, a *voice* emerged, a voice both booming and viscous, the voice of the god of an ocean of blood:"Little things," it said. "Why have you called to me?"

Normally, I know, the oracles our friend summons manifest externally—they appear as ghosts, or gods, or monsters. But this one seemed to be using Rondeau as a medium instead, a conduit for its words. Or perhaps the thing he'd summoned was all around us—perhaps we were in its belly, or some other cavity—and we could only hear its voice if it spoke through Rondeau.

I was sorely afraid, but I kept my wits about me as best I could. "We have a question," I said. "We are trying to find someone—ah, someone on Earth—called the Eater."

A vast rumbling came from all directions, for just a moment, then ceased. "A piece of me is lodged on that distant lump," the thing said from Rondeau's mouth. "A splinter of me, spun away and fallen through a tear in reality, traveling through eons and vastnesses, to land on an unremarkable ball of mud and teeming life... And you touched that part of me. I see, I see. You wish me to turn my gaze upon this ball of mud and rot and find the one you seek?"

"Ah. Yes. If it's not too much trouble."

"Mmm. But there must be a price, yes? Will you pay the price?"

"We will," I said, having been briefed on the importance of transactions when dealing with oracles.

"The Eater... ha. Yes, you had to find me, to come all this way, because no Earthly being could help you to find him at all. He can *hide* from them, you see—hide in among all the possibilities, picking and choosing and twitching unwelcome futures aside. But I stand above and outside and away, so I can see the whole... but even so, I cannot tell you precisely *where* he is, or *when* he will be there, because it shifts. I can give you a thread, though, a reliable thread you can find and seize and follow inward, to the center. Will that do? That will have to do."

"It... will be acceptable," I said, unsure what else I *could* say.

"Go to... West Texas. Tomorrow. Interstate 27, about halfway between Lubbock and Plainview—do these words mean anything to you? I am... translating, you might say... across several levels of comprehensibility."

"Ah, yes," I said. "It makes perfect sense."

"Good. Go there. Search for a thread of chaos, and follow that thread where it leads."

"I understand," I said.

"Good. Now, the price. The piece of me that is lodged in your world: break it up, smash it to sand, and send some of that sand to distant places: sift some into the seas, drop some at the poles, some in the mountains, some in the caves. Do you understand?"

"I do, but why—"

"My reasons are not for you to know," it roared, and Rondeau's jaw *did* stretch too far, then, the skin on both sides of his mouth tearing and beginning to bleed, and I flinched back. "Obey!"

"Of course, we will obey!" I shouted, and with that, we were back in the desert again. Rondeau fell backward, unconscious, and in kneeling to attend to him I happened to glance at the stone. . .

For just a moment, Mrs. Mason, it seemed to be a monstrous human *eye*, the size of my own head, the white of the eye crawling with veins that were actually living worms, the iris a deep and mottled purple, the pupil a blackness pinpointed by red and green stars… but then the eye closed, the lid just lustrous stone again.

Perhaps I have gone on too long. Rondeau was fine, after a few moments, waking up with no memory of the experience at all, though he did not doubt my interpretation of events. He did experience a profound compulsion to dig up and smash the stone, and so we fetched a tarp from the Bentley, set the stone upon it, and set to breaking it with pick and sledgehammer. I was terrified that we would crack the outer layer and discover an eye inside, soft and full of fluid and pulsing and warm and alive, but it was mere stone all the way through, and surprisingly brittle and easy to break up. Seeing the eye may have been a trick of my senses after all. I hope so.

When we were done we had a few pounds of black sand, which we carefully tied up in the tarp. Rondeau says he will begin mailing packages of sand to people he knows throughout the world tomorrow, to fulfill the bargain. He does not seem eager to speculate about the nature of the oracle we consulted, or its motives in making the demands it did; I feel no particular eagerness to do so myself.

You have said, Mrs. Mason, that there is nothing humankind was not *meant* to know, because that implies there is some reliable higher power doing the *meaning*, and you do not believe in such things, as you know from experience that even gods are limited creatures. But I think there are things humanity would find it unhealthy, or at least deeply unsettling, to know, and the true nature of the oracle we summoned strikes me as one of them.

I hope the information we provided proves to be valuable, and worth the price; whatever that price truly turns out to be.

I remain your humble and obedient servant,

Pelham

East of Nowhere

That Pelly. He writes like he's a time traveler from the Victorian era, though he was born and raised in Felport. (Admittedly, he was raised in captivity and trained to be an ideal omni-competent servant for a family of snotty nobles with supernatural lineage, but still.) That story was pretty fucked-up, and I might not have asked Rondeau for the oracle intel if I'd realized it was going to be such a traumatic experience.

It did make me think the Eater was bigger prey than I'd realized, if we'd needed to summon an oracle with *that* kind of mojo just to get a *clue* about how to find it. I'd been assuming he was some kind of anthropophagous magical crime boss… but maybe I was dealing with something more dangerous here.

If so, good. Killing magical thugs is a public service, but it's not a particularly interesting challenge.

After I read the message from Pelly on my smartphone, I looked up to find Squat staring at me expectantly. We'd eaten our nasty fast food at the picnic table beside a rest stop that otherwise consisted of two bathrooms and a knocked-over garbage can. Squat had a motorcycle of his own, a beat-up old Harley, parked beside mine. We were well on our way to being a biker gang. (Maybe "The Brides of Death." I could picture the logo on the back of a leather jacket already. Though I wasn't sure Squat would go for that.)

"Ever been to West Texas?" I asked.

Squat shrugged. "Sure. Looks a lot like East New Mexico."

I poked at my phone some more. "Hmm. If I really pushed it, I could get there in ten hours or so."

Squat whistled. "Ah. Okay. Will you be coming back, or…"

"Not necessarily. It's not like this is my home base—that's Vegas, if it's anywhere. I might just keep rolling on the roads."

"Huh. I have a place here, some stuff, some affairs to set in order, but... would you mind if I caught up with you?"

"You've gotten a taste for the monster-killing life, huh?"

"Let's say I'm hearing the song of the open road. And you've gotten me kind of curious about this Eater guy. He burns down Sarlat's place to cover his tracks? Must have something interesting to hide. Plus I have a lot of rage, on account of being cursed, and following you seems like a great way to find people I can beat up."

"Never people, Squat, just monsters. Unless they're monstrous people. The lines get a little blurry sometimes, but I'll be your guide. As for being my tagalong..." Like I mentioned before, having Squat around sort of appealed to me. A sidekick with opposable thumbs had obvious advantages. "I guess having a tough unkillable cursed guy could be a tactical advantage. Sure. Sort out your shit and then give me a call. But I have to get on the road—this lead I've got on the Eater has a time limit attached."

He saluted with his gnarled fingers. "I'll be in touch." He leaned over and spoke to the covered cage resting on the table between us. "See you, Nicolette."

She mumbled something not very nice, and Squat shrugged and went on his way.

I went to throw my burger wrapper on the ground, in the existing pile of garbage from the spilled can, then sighed, righted the container, scooped up most of the garbage (using a bit of newspaper as a makeshift glove/dustpan), and only then threw my own trash away, in its proper place. "Doing Better," I muttered. "Dirty business."

I stood in the broken remnants of a town somewhere in West Texas at twilight, motorcycle saddlebags slung over my shoulder and a birdcage in my hand. The cage rocked and swayed in my grip. She'd gotten restless on the long drive—not just the ten hours racing from Arizona to Texas, but the subsequent going up-and-down the freeway all night and through the next day, sniffing for chaos. "Be still in there," I said, bumping the birdcage with my hip. A muffled snarl emerged from under the heavy cloth, but I ignored it.

My motorcycle was parked some distance away, locked down with magic to keep it safe and make it less likely to be noticed. I didn't want to ride it right up into town, because the bike stank of magics, and I didn't want to tip off my prey. Bad enough I had a bag full of enchantments, and a living head in a cage, but both bag and cage were charmed to muffle the emanations, so maybe they'd go unnoticed.

The town wasn't much to look at, and if it had a name I never noticed. There was a stoplight, but it didn't look like it got much use, even though we were just off the highway. The few shops, huddled together as if for warmth, looked ignored if not abandoned. A gas station with ancient red-faded-to-pink pumps that had never even heard of credit cards. Everything on this side of the highway looked desiccated, like flies after days in a web.

The gleaming oasis of a modern truck stop shone a little ways off on the other side of the highway, and I figured it had sucked most of the life out of this place like a well-lit, colorfully-packaged vampire. There was a motel over here, though, with a couple of big rigs in the parking lot, for drivers who wanted more than a shower at the truck stop and a nap in their own cab.

And somewhere, in or under or above or running through this town, there was something that might as well be called evil. My thread, I hoped—the one that would lead me to the Eater. We'd driven all the damn day, Nicolette sniffing for chaos, and finding nothing noticeable, and I'd almost started to despair. The oracle had said my lead on the Eater would be located somewhere in the fifty miles between Plainview and Lubbock "tomorrow," but "tomorrow" was a long ass day, in practice, and fifty miles of highway was a lot of territory to check over and over again. Nicolette and I had both gotten pissy and impatient and I was starting to think I'd missed the lead entirely, or that the oracle was full of shit, when she said, "Wait, there, something, it's *moving*, no, wait, it's slowing down, it stopped, there! *Here*!"

So here we were. Nicolette said the evil was in this vicinity, but couldn't (or wouldn't) narrow it down except to say it was somewhere near the truck stop, motel, or wasteland environs. Alas, there were no sixty-foot-high goat-headed demons or enormous carnivorous blobs with visibly entropic auras in the area, so we'd have to wander around and play hot-and-cold until Nicolette's chaos-sense could get a better fix on whatever we were looking for.

I checked into the motel, paying with some cash Pelly had messengered to me. My room was surprisingly clean, though old and worn. At least, I thought so until I saw a roach scurry from beneath the bed and into the bathroom. Yuck. If a place had roaches, it didn't seem beyond the realm of possibility that it would have bedbugs, too. I set the birdcage on the table, then opened my bag and fished out a napkin wrapped around a chicken bone I'd saved from a hasty roadside lunch. I muttered an incantation, snapped the bone in half, and send a low-level pulse of death through the room, enough to kill any six-legged vampire bedbugs, shit-footed roaches, or other vermin.

The birdcage rocked on the table, and I sighed and pulled off the dirty brown cover. "So," I said. "You got a better fix on our mystery monster yet? North, south, east, west? Up, down?"

Nicolette bared her teeth at me. "Hungry."

I sat down in the chair and glared right back at her. "There'll be plenty of time to eat *after* I deal with—"

"Not if you get killed. And I'm hungry *now*."

"You don't get to make ultimatums, Nicolette. You're a head in a cage. You don't even have the classical dignity of being a head in a *jar*. Do your job, and speak."

"Oh, I'll speak, but you won't like what I have to say, unless you've got a fetish for humiliating insults. You rode up and down a highway with me for ten fucking hours today, a linear path cut through the desert, so orderly it made my follicles ache. I need chaos if you want me to do any fine work, pinpointing locations—so *feed me*."

"Seriously?"

"*Hungry*!" Nicolette shouted.

Shit. I hated being in thrall to her moods, but this lead on the Eater was obviously mobile somehow, so I couldn't waste time arguing—it might move on, and I wasn't about to ask Rondeau to summon up an oracle that big again. I went to my bags and pulled out a messily taped-up, bubble-wrapped package. Unwrapping the plastic, I removed several antique blue glass bottles, ranging in size from beer bottle to test tube, and then dug out a small ball-peen hammer. I'd purchased the glassware for the crusher trick, and decided to hold them back in case Nicolette got peckish later.

I lined up the bottles in front of Nicolette's cage and smashed them, one by one, with the hammer. Nicolette's eyes rolled back in her head, and she gasped and shuddered, less like someone eating a meal and more like someone having an orgasm. I really hoped she was exaggerating her response just to make me uncomfortable. Otherwise I hated to think of the ecstasy she'd experienced watching me get crushed to death.

"Mmm, delicious entropy," she said, once I'd swept all the broken fragments into a trash can. "Nothing tastes as good as destroying something beautiful."

"Chocolate's not bad either, sicko," I said. "So speak. Where's this evil?"

"Hmm? Oh, that. It's in the room right next door."

I have been criticized for being too direct in my approach to problem solving, but many of the subtle, tricky, deceitful people who made those criticisms are dead, and I'm still alive, so I see no reason to change my ways.

I turned on the TV, both so the noise would make the room seem occupied and to keep Nicolette more-or-less entertained. She was a lot less dangerous than she used to be, but she was still capable of making trouble, and I wouldn't put it past her to try and fuck me up at any given moment.

I opened my bathroom window and climbed out, dropping down to the weedy ground in back of the motel. Then I crept over to the next room, listening at the bathroom window—frosted glass, so I couldn't spy more directly. I couldn't hear anything, except the low murmur of the TV, so I tested the window. Locked.

I took a tarnished old key out of my pocket and gently drew the outline of a rune on the window. The key dissolved into powder in my hand—four hours spent enchanting it, and only seconds to use up the magic. Isn't that always the way? This time when I pressed my palms against the window and pushed upward, it moved.

I stared through the open window at the astonished face of a man sitting on the toilet, pants around his ankles. He had thinning wisps of brown hair, big brown eyes, and a generally fishlike aspect. "Wha—" he began.

I reached into my coat and drew my most mundane weapon—just a little .22 target pistol, but a gun is a gun—and aimed it through the window. "Don't speak, and don't move." I preferred to use my knife or axe, of course, but they weren't much of a threat when I was standing *outside* the room. I never used to carry firearms at all, since blades were fine for close work and magic seemed sufficient for all other purposes, but I'd had a run-in with an anti-mancer capable of nullifying magic not long ago, and Pelly had convinced me to carry something with a little more range and intimidation factor for certain eventualities.

Have you ever tried to climb through a chest-high window without taking your eyes *or* your gun off a prisoner? It's not easy, but I managed—it helped that he had his pants around his ankles and his hands in the air. Once I was upright in the bathroom I slid the window shut behind me with one hand. I was no more than three feet away from the man on the toilet, my gun pointed straight at the center of his chest.

"Hi," I said. "My name's Marla Mason. I hear you're a bad person. Tell me about the Eater." I looked him over carefully, but there wasn't much to see—he looked like a middle-aged guy who'd spent a long time on the road and was now experiencing a totally reasonable moment of terror in the face of a stranger with a gun interrupting his bowel movement.

His face was slick with sweat, his adam's apple bobbing, his eyes fixed and wide. "Listen," he said, "I don't have much, but you're welcome to it, my wallet's in the other room, just—"

"Let's not do this. It's so tedious, the part where you pretend you don't know why I'm here. You're a monster. I'm a monster-hunter. Today, you're lucky, because I don't so much want *you* as the guy you can *lead* me to—the Eater. Cooperate, and I might let you scuttle off into the night alive."

"Lady, I swear, I don't know what you're talking about—"

"The fuck you don't." But I didn't shoot, or kick, or draw my blade to make him a little more talkative... because this just looked like a *guy*. Sure, lots of monsters were indistinguishable from humans—lots of monsters *were* humans, though I was focusing on the inhuman sort these days—but confirmation was nice. He could be a mind-controlled slave, or even just a dupe unwittingly in the Eater's employ—the oracle had promised me a *thread*, something I could follow to the Eater, but it didn't necessarily mean that thread was going to be another bad guy. If I'd found him eating a baby or wearing a hat made of human eyeballs, I would have been more comfortable bringing some enhanced interrogation techniques—fuck it, I mean torture—to bear, but he just looked like an idiot taking a crap. It was always possible Nicolette had misread the cues, too, or—

"Shit," the man said. "Did you say Marla *Mason*? Did Nicolette send you?"

I didn't quite lower my gun, but I confess my hand wavered. "What do you know about Nicolette?"

He ran a hand through what was left of his hair. "Ah, hell, we used to date in high school, before she got into all that witchy shit. Things between us never worked out, in fact we had a nasty breakup, but a few years back I was passing through Felport and she somehow knew—magic, I guess—and she invited me out for dinner. I thought, you know, she wanted to rekindle an old flame, but it was all a trick. She poisoned my food—just a little, enough to make me puke and shit myself all night long. The whole time I was sick she stayed in my hotel room, laughing at me, and she never stopped *talking*, and mostly she bitched about you, Marla Mason, how much she hated you and wanted to get rid of you. I passed out eventually and woke up in a cornfield wearing nothing but a pair of pink lace panties, and one of my kidneys was missing. *Crap*. And now she's told you some bullshit about how I'm a monster?"

I gritted my teeth. That was all alarmingly plausible. Nicolette was nothing if not whimsically vindictive, and we *had* been ruinously bored tooling up and down the highway. I could easily believe she'd scented an old lover and decided to have some fun at *both* of our expenses. A guy she knew being in the same part of the country where we were was kind of a big coincidence, I'll grant you, but I've noticed that bizarre coincidences seem *way* more likely when you're in the company of a chaos witch.

I lowered the gun, but I didn't put it away, because, well. Like I said. Better safe.

The guy was a little less terrified-looking, now, and he went on with renewed energy. "I don't know what Nicolette told you, Marla, but I'm just a *guy*, I drive a truck for a living, you know? She's just fucking with both of us. I think ever since she got her head cut off she's gone even crazier—"

And the gun went back up. The man—if he was a man—winced. "Damn it," he said. "I shouldn't have known she got her head cut off, huh? Must have happened too recently. But it was such a strong image in your mind… I'm a decent telepath, but I can only skim the surface. Oh, well. I guess we'll do this the other way, then. At least I can read enough of your mind to know you don't have any idea what the fuck you're dealing with here."

He started to stand, and I shot him in the shoulder, just by way of discouraging him. I would have gone for the face, but I wanted answers before I took him apart.

A .22 doesn't make a very big noise, but in the confined space it was loud enough to make my ears ring. It didn't do much *except* make a big noise, though. The bullet passed through his shoulder like a rock dropping into a pond, his flesh rippling for a moment and then smoothing out again. He went "Ouch," but I clearly hadn't hurt him a bit.

I realized he was cloaked in an illusion, just wearing the semblance of humanity. That was confirmed when he finished standing, and I saw his crotch was entirely bare, smooth as a doll's. He hadn't bothered to make the illusion complete. I wondered why he'd been sitting on the toilet at all. Did he even shit? Or maybe he kept his real mouth down there and he'd been drinking the water out of the toilet bowl. Who the fuck knew?

The monster grinned at me, his jaws and lips contorting, at least half a dozen mandibles—they looked like crab legs—unfolding from within his mouth and wriggling at me, dripping what I could only assume were assorted toxins. He reached out with an arm that was rapidly mutating into something multi-clawed and hard-shelled.

I kicked him right between his hairless legs. The inertial charms in my boot gave my kick the impact of a battering ram, and I hit something solid that *crunched* with a sound like a stomped eggshell. His body flew upward hard enough to hit the ceiling, then crashed back down on the toilet. The illusion draping him wavered and vanished, revealing his true form. Man-sized crab-spider-octopus, more or less, with a thin veneer of slime eel. I'd seen worse, though it was certainly nothing you'd want to share a bathroom with.

"Doesn't matter," it slurred, human voice emerging from the grinding nightmare of its mouthparts. "My hive-mates are legion, and they gather at the House of the Eater. The work will go on."

"The work always does," I said. "So about this House of the Eater. Where can I find it?"

The thing chuckled, I think, or maybe it was just choking on fluids, but then it spoke: "You have attacked one of the Eater's tribe. That will not go unpunished. You will see his house soon enough: when you are brought there, laid bare before him, all your possible futures flayed away. "

"Huh. Hurting you will make him track me down, huh? Would killing you accelerate the process? I only ask because I've got an immovable deadline coming up, there's someplace I've got to be next month, so I don't have a lot of time for cat-and-mouse back-and-forth."

"To kill me would earn you nothing but a lifetime of servitude and suffering—"

"Good enough," I said, and stomped down on its head. There was no reason to assume a thing like that kept its brains in its head, so I stomped the rest too, until all the bits stopped wriggling, and they were no longer recognizable as parts of a coherent whole. Dismemberment-by-stomping is pretty tedious work—this guy's carapace was a lot tougher than the spore-lord's spongy form had been—and my legs got tired, but it was easier than ruling an entire city or being an occult detective, at least.

I didn't envy the maid who'd have to clean that bathroom. It didn't look like a murder scene, exactly. More like a dozen people had used the contents of a sushi bar for a mosh pit.

I climbed back out the window and returned to my room, washing off my boots in the sink, making the little embroidered skulls and scythes shine.

"Well?" Nicolette said. "Are they okay?"

I frowned, poking my head out of the bathroom. "Are *who* okay?"

"The monster's captives," she said. "Or didn't I mention there were captives? I'm totally getting a captives vibe."

"You *bitch*," I replied.

I went back to the monster's room, doing my best to jump over the nastiness in the bathroom, and searched his belongings. I found a set of keys and took the risk of slipping out his front door—it was dark, and as far as I could tell we were the only two guests on that side of the motel anyway. I made my way through the parking lot, to the far end where the big rigs were. There were two: one gleaming black with a shiny refrigerated trailer, and one smeared with mud and muck, with a dirty white trailer. I took a wild guess and tried the keys on the dirty truck. The door opened right up.

The trailer in back was locked, of course, but flipping through the keys I soon found the right one to open it. I tugged the trailer door up and open, and found.... Nothing. Empty trailer, just a big dark echoing space.

Remembering the illusion the monster had cloaked itself in, I grimaced. I'm capable of seeing through illusions, but it gives me a nasty headache if I overdo it. Oh well. Some things can't be avoided. I closed my eyes for a moment, and when I opened them, the truth inside the trailer was revealed.

It looked like a child's bedroom. Giant fluffy stuffed animals, mostly bears of various kinds; a child-sized pretend kitchen, complete with stove and oven and sink and cabinets and little dishes and fake food; a miniature table and chairs, with a plastic tea set; three sets of bunk beds with brightly-colored sheets all done up in superheroes and princesses; and the whole scene lit by whimsical lights in the shape of ladybugs and smiling suns and flowers stuck on the walls and the ceiling.

Half a dozen children sat in a circle on the colorful rug, eating candy bars, faces smeared with chocolate, a litter of discarded juice boxes all around them. I'm no good when it comes to guessing ages—kids all look like lumps of uncooked dough to me—but the oldest couldn't have been more than six or eight. They had dirty hair and wrinkled clothes, ranging from footie pajamas to Sunday dresses. One little girl stood up and waved at me, tentatively. "Is this the farm?"

"Farm?" I said, wondering if I sounded as stupid and stunned as I felt.

"The farm where mommy and daddy are waiting for me," a little boy said. "The man said it was a surprise."

"We will ride ponies," the girl said solemnly.

One of the younger kids wailed. "No farm! Want mama!"

I swallowed. Some things you couldn't fix with guns or knives or magic boots. "This man—did he hurt you?"

The oldest boy and girl shook their heads; the others were too young or distracted to notice my question, but I took their two responses as a good sign.

"Did this man… take you?" I asked.

"He said it was okay to come with him," the boy said.

"He's my mommy's friend," the girl added. "He knew the secret code, so it was okay to go with him."

I closed my eyes, this time because it hurt to look at them. Secret code. Right. I'd heard about that sort of thing—you teach your children a secret family pass phrase, and they know they shouldn't go with anyone who doesn't know the magic words. As far as security precautions went, it had a few flaws, especially when you were dealing with a telepathic monster who could pluck the words right out of your head. He'd probably skimmed *all* their minds and come up with whatever info he needed to lure them in. But why take all these children?

Then again, who cared why. There weren't a ton of *non*-horrifying reasons to steal children, especially when the kidnapper was a monster in the employ of something called the Eater. "Come on, kids," I said. "You'll see your parents soon."

Getting them across the parking lot was a little like herding a bunch of lizards on meth, but I got the kids settled into my room—after nipping in real quick first to cover up Nicolette, because the little ones didn't need *more* trauma. Once they were happily ensconced in front of the TV (little kids maybe shouldn't watch Godzilla movies, but it was the best I could do), I said, "Be right back." I left, and took my saddlebags and the birdcage with me.

I unhooked the trailer from the truck, then climbed into the cab. I put Nicolette down on the passenger seat, and after I took her cover off she looked around and whistled. "Do you know how to drive this thing?"

"I know how to do everything worth doing," I said.

She snorted. "Sure you do. What are you going to do about the kids?"

I took out the pad of stationery I'd liberated from the motel room, then turned on my cell and dialed the number on the letterhead. When the bored-sounding clerk answered, I said, "Hey, this is the lady in room 6. I came back from dinner and found six little kids in my room. What the hell?"

The clerk squawked in disbelief and surprise and annoyance but I cut him off. "Look, I don't *care*, that shit was too weird. Consider this me checking out." I hung up, and just to be safe, I dialed 911—confident my cell couldn't be tracked or called back, since it was magicked up one side and down the other—and told them I'd seen a guy in a mini-van dump a bunch of little kids in the motel parking lot and then drive away. I disconnected before the follow-up questions got too personal. Between the two calls I was confident *somebody* would look into things and get the kids back to their parents.

"You're not going to deliver them personally?" Nicolette said as I started up the truck and eased out of the lot, trying to get a feel for the sticky clutch and loose gearshift. "You'd be a terrible mother."

"No argument there."

"So where are we going now?" Nicolette said.

"To park this truck someplace where it won't be noticed for a little while. I can do some divination magic, figure out where it's been, maybe track the Eater that way—"

"Or you could come screaming into the present century," Nicolette said, "and just check the fucking GPS."

I noticed the LCD screen on the dash. "Oh. So I could just look at his travel history and see where he's been, and maybe where he's going, if it's a place he's been before. This 'farm,' the kids mentioned, or the House of the Eater." I shook my head. "Kids. He was stealing kids. Shit."

"The great savior on a children's crusade," Nicolette said. "Let's say you save, oh, twenty kids. Make it thirty. Will that make you feel better? Wash away some of the guilt for all the people you've killed and screwed over?"

"What are you talking about?"

"You think I'm stupid, don't you? I know you're on some kind of quest for redemption, or atonement, or whatever."

"Like I've got anything to feel sorry for. I enjoy beating things up, that's all, and if I beat up monsters, I make the world a better place in the process, so why not?"

"Now who's spouting bullshit?" Nicolette chuckled nastily. "There are two dozen ways you could track down monsters to kill, Marla. You're not the most talented sorcerer in the world, but even you can do the kind of divinations that would lead you to disturbances in the Force or what-the-fuck-ever. You've got rich and powerful contacts, gifted sorcerers who could line up worthy victims to keep you busy for decades. Instead, you wander around like a vagrant, with the head of your worst enemy in a cage, choosing to travel with somebody who hates your guts. And you want me to believe you *aren't* punishing yourself? Of course you are. Don't get me wrong—I'm *glad*. You deserve to be punished. I'm no angel, but you've fucked things up for people on a scale I could never match. But don't pretend I'm the only one in a cage here. You're bad, at least as bad as I ever was, but you don't have the guts to live with yourself, to *embrace* it, so you do all this bullcrap to convinced yourself you're *good*—"

I braked as hard as I dared—with no trailer hitched up, there was no risk of jackknifing, and the street was pretty empty here. The truck lurched, jerking me forward hard, banging my chest painfully against the oversized steering wheel. Nicolette's cage flew forward, hit the dash hard enough to dent the bars, and then fell into the footwell on the passenger side, bouncing her head around a lot in the process—painfully, I hoped.

Nicolette started cursing like she does, and I turned up the radio loud enough to drown her out, and felt a lot better. For a little while.

A mile later I took the GPS unit off the dash—it was one of those portable ones, not built-in, so I didn't have to break anything—and left the truck parked not far from where I'd stashed my motorcycle.

I couldn't do anything about the Eater right then, though. I needed sleep—I'd spent the past day driving, which was exhausting enough, and my recent exertions hadn't exactly re-energized me. I needed sleep, but the motel I'd paid for was obviously no good anymore. I wasn't too far from Lubbock, so I got Nicolette strapped in, dragged myself onto the bike, and set off along the hated freeway, rumbling along in the full dark.

I prefer to stay in that vanishing breed, grungy little roadside non-chain motels—the clerks tend to value your privacy there—but I was sufficiently tired that I pulled into the first gleaming chain motel I reached on the outskirts of Lubbock. The clerk really wanted a credit card, but I bullied him into accepting a cash deposit with a sob story about how I'd had all my cards stolen. I snuck Nicolette into the room—no pets allowed, natch—and stuck her in a closet, then collapsed on the bed, staring at the ceiling.

I couldn't sleep, tired as I was. I was on the *hunt*, now, I had the scent, so I picked up the GPS and tried to make sense of its history, which went back months. A lot of destinations had been punched in, but one got returned to several times, a tiny town in New Mexico called Moros. (Not to be confused with El Moro or Mora County, both also located in New

Mexico—a stunning lack of originality on the part of place-namers there.) Moros was practically next door—I'd damn near driven past it on my way to Texas in the first place. I could check it out the next day, and see if there was anything worth murdering there.

I still couldn't sleep. Too keyed-up. So I started writing again instead, filling more pages in the notebook that Pelham was kind enough to leave for me.

And, uh, here we are. This is getting crazy long. Luckily, I'm done—that brings us up to date, dear me. I'll write more after I'm done wiping the Eater, whoever he is, off my boots.

Deader than Ever

Reader, he killed me.

I took the fight to the Eater, but I did not know what the fuck I was getting into. Fortunately, he didn't know how to deal with *me* properly, either, or I'd be down at the bottom of a well in captivity instead of writing this from the comfort of Pelham's RV.

So let me back up and tell you how I got into this situation:

I got a call from Squat shortly after I finished the last chunk of this real-time memoir. He'd settled whatever he had to settle—somehow I doubt he had to sublet an apartment or cancel a newspaper subscription, but we've all got our shit to deal with—and was ready to come roaring across the state to see me. I told him to meet me outside Moros instead, and we'd formulate a plan of attack.

That was a lie, pretty much. My plans can usually be summed up in a single word: attack. I'm good at improvising, and plans always fall apart *anyway*—witness the debacle in Tolerance—so why waste a lot of time formulating an approach that's going to be rendered irrelevant by circumstances anyway? Sure, rampaging into a town and trying to find a hornet's nest to knock down was arguably foolhardy… but I was *immortal*, and so apparently was my new assistant Squat. I could make the earth move and call up hellfire with a wave of my hand (as long as I didn't think about it too hard). I was armed with a dagger that could cut through ghosts and an axe made of a shard of moonlight (probably). I had a bag full of nasty enchantments I hadn't yet had the opportunity to employ. How could I lose? I was the Terminator. I was Freddie Krueger from *Nightmare on Elm Street*.

I was an idiot.

Moros, New Mexico was a little piece of nowhere, and it was surprisingly hard to find. In the course of my frustrating travel across the state I saw signs for places with names like Angel Fire and Elephant Butte and Bottomless Lakes and Wink and Texico, but no Moros. Eventually I got closer to my destination, in a part of the state that was more woods and mountains than rocks and sand, but despite trying to follow the directions on the GPS, I kept getting turned around. Roads would curve in great slow loops, sending me back where I started, the dot on the map on my phone drifting around aimlessly instead of moving consistently toward my destination. "Shit, Nicolette," I said. "There's some kind of topological crumpling going on here, or a spatial distortion field. But it can't be absolute, obviously the truck driver was meant to make his way through with his cargo—maybe there's a magical beacon on the truck, some fetish-bag stuck under the hood that lets it penetrate the border. Think you can see your way through to the center?" I was stuck in a repeating pattern of asphalt and curves, and chaos witches have a knack for tearing patterns apart.

"Oh, fine. Let your conscience be your guide," Nicolette said. "In this scenario I'm your conscience. And, by the way, speaking as your conscience, I'd just like to say, you're a terrible person."

"If you guide me off a cliff or into a tree and send me to my doom, you'll be stuck in a cage in the middle of nowhere," I said.

"And yet, it's still so tempting. Okay, turn left up here, in about a hundred yards."

"Turn left onto *what*?" The road was a straight shot, lined by pines, with a soft shoulder on either side.

"I'm stuck under a drop cloth back here, so I'm not distracted by what you see with your lying eyes," she said. "I see what's *really* here, and there's a path through the trees."

I slowed the bike to a crawl, then a stop, parking it on the shoulder near this supposed left turn. I walked into the trees, frowning—and then I was through the illusion, standing on a well-maintained blacktop road that branched off the path I'd been following around and around. I walked back out again, and the illusion didn't recur—once I'd gotten past it once, I was immune, apparently. I gave Nicolette a grudging "Good job," then called up Squat.

He answered after a few rings, the sound of his idling engine almost drowning out his words. "Where are you?" I said.

"Driving in fucking circles!" he said. "I'm parked on the shoulder now, and I swear I've been past this same spot four or five times already. I recognize this beer bottle in the ditch."

"It's good to have old friends," I said. "Keep riding, you're sure to run into me eventually. I think I've been circling the same loop, but I found a way in."

"Will do." He hung up, and I busied myself checking my supplies, casting occasional glances down the newly-revealed blacktop track—it ran straight as a rich man's teeth for a quarter mile or so and then dipped over the horizon and dissolved into the blur of distant trees. After ten minutes I heard the big aggressive growl of Squat's engine. His bike had been nice once, but it hadn't been well maintained, and when I'd asked him about it, he'd shrugged and said he won it off a guy in an arm-wrestling contest and didn't know shit about motorcycles, really. I had the distinct impression that if it ever stopped running he'd leave it where it fell and acquire other wheels by a similar method. I wondered if the guy he'd arm wrestled still had his arm attached.

Squat saw me and pulled over, and I walked him through the illusion, too, holding his hand, even though touching him was repulsive in some deep way I couldn't articulate. He grunted when he saw the road. "One way in, and hard to find. Even so, if I was a hypothetical bad guy, and this was my home base, I'd have somebody watching this road, just in case."

"Good thing we're indestructible," I said.

"You know how some tombstones say 'Too beautiful to live?' Mine would say 'Too ugly to die.' Except I guess I'll never get one, on account of not dying."

"You could write it on a welcome mat or something. Maybe one of those samplers people sew and hang on the wall."

"I am full of inspirational teachings. So what's the plan?"

"Drive into town," I said. "Look around. See if Nicolette's chaos-sense can lead us to the guy we're looking for. I doubt we'll find a sign that says 'Here Lies the Eater,' but you never know."

"What are you planning to do when you find him? Or it?"

I shrugged. "The guy stole a bunch of kids, and from what you've told me about Sarlat's dealings with the Eater, he's stolen other people, too. I doubt he's rounding them up for an ice cream social. 'Evil' is a slippery word. People have called me that, for some pretty defensible reasons. But for me, the definition of evil is simple: it's treating people like objects, and working against life. I've got every reason to believe the Eater's doing that. I could try to threaten, or bargain, or whatever, but… probably I'll just kill him."

"Simple and direct, I like it," Squat said. "Mount up?"

"Mount up."

So then we rode into utopia.

Moros was nestled in a valley surrounded by hills and trees. It was a picture-postcard kind of small town, the kind that doesn't exist anymore, and maybe never did, outside of the movies. I'm talking picket fences, lush green lawns—yeah, in New Mexico—perfectly maintained streets, every building freshly painted and pristine. The weather was gorgeous, and people were out enjoying it, riding bicycles, trimming hedges, mowing the grass. The place was so familiar-looking, from a thousand TV shows and paintings, that your eyes kind of slid across it without friction, but there were a couple of jarring notes. We passed a church, but it didn't have a cross on the steeple, and instead it bore a strange sigil—a single vertical line that split into a Y-branch at the top, and then each branch split again, and each of those branches split yet again, so it looked like a child's drawing of a tree or a diagram of a neuron.

There was also the way everyone *looked* at us, from every front porch and sidewalk, through the windows of the diner and the hardware store—children, adults, old people, teenagers, they all turned their heads in unison to silently follow our progress.

"Nicolette," I said, as we rode slowly through the streets, obeying the posted twenty-five-mile-per-hour speed limit. "What're you getting?"

"You're heading in the right direction," she said. "There's something up ahead, like a tumor growing on reality."

"You're not getting… I don't know, a weird vibe about the whole town?"

"I don't get even a whiff of chaos here," she said. "In fact, it's weird how *little* disorder I'm sensing. It's almost like nobody lives here at all. It might as well be a town in a model train set."

I paused at a stoplight—the only one we'd seen so far, at a four-corner intersection with a gas station, a grocery store, a gym, and a bank, though the latter was closed, the windows boarded up. I noticed there were no prices on the sign at the gas station, either. Definitely weird. People came out of the gym and store and garage, sauntering with no great haste in our general direction.

"This is some Stepford wives shit," Squat said, drawing up beside me. "Also Stepford husbands, sons, daughters, neighbors, mailmen—"

"No mailmen," I said. "Or so I assume. Because there are no mailboxes. Didn't you notice? Not in front of a single house, and this is the kind of town that should have lots of mailboxes, novelty ones shaped like covered bridges and St. Bernards and shit. No mailboxes, the bank is closed, no prices on the gas station sign, a weird church…"

"I am missing a lot being under this stupid cloth," Nicolette said.

"That stop light isn't changing," Squat said. "It's just sitting there, red."

"I noticed that, too," I said. "Let's be scofflaws before the welcoming committee reaches us."

We drove off—it's not like there was any other traffic, though there were plenty of gorgeously gleaming cars in the driveways—and the crowd converging on us all seemed to lose interest and wandered back toward the buildings they'd emerged from.

Okay. What the fuck? This was more like a model of a town than a real town, like Nicolette said—not a place where real people, with their families and dreams and jobs and adulteries and stupid hobbies, would live, but a place that would pass for a town at first glance, but not much beyond that. A dollhouse sort of place. So were the citizens of Moros the dolls? If so, what was the nature of their particular damage? Hive mind? Kidnapped slaves under mind control? Androids? Just cultists worshipping the Eater the way my own handmaidens (and, I guess, footmen?) of Death tried to worship me? There were various explanations, all terrible. If these *were* real people in some kind of thrall, then maybe killing the Eater would free them. It was a theory worth testing, anyway.

"Up ahead," Nicolette said. "There's something like… a spiderweb made of tumors, it feels like, but there's this M.C. Escher vibe, impossible shapes, angles that don't make sense, strands that appear from nowhere and go nowhere…"

We were approaching a beautifully landscaped central park with a bandstand, surrounded by civic buildings. The city hall was done in neo-Classical style, columns and marble, and it was *way* too big for a town this size. I had a suspicion that was our ultimate destination. Maybe the Eater was mayor of this place, or god king, or whatever. Beyond the city hall there was a hospital, much more modest in size, and seemingly appropriate for a community of a couple thousand, tops. The hospital didn't interest me much, then. It would later.

But in order to reach the city hall, we had to ride past an elementary school. I assume it was an elementary school, anyway, because of all the children. There were at least a hundred of them, ranging in age from five to ten years old (as I mentioned, I'm crap at judging stuff like that), standing in front of the school in neat ranks, seemingly ordered by size. They were all dressed in the same school uniform, white shirt and blue pants or skirt, and they were holding... well, all sorts of things. Yardsticks. Hockey sticks. Flutes. Wooden spoons. Brooms. Rakes. Hammers. Clarinets. Some of them had rope, and some had what looked like fishing nets, and one kid, who seemed big for his age and uncomfortable in his body and uniform both, was just holding a large damn jagged rock.

I stopped the motorcycle, and Squat paused beside me.

"Uh, Marla?" he said. "I'm getting a Lord of the Flies feeling here. Or maybe Children of the Corn, minus the corn."

"Nicolette." I reached back and tugged her drop cloth off. She didn't need to be able to see in order to sense things, but I figured she deserved to get a look at what we were facing. "Can you tell if they're really kids? They're not, I don't know—demons, or whatever, in kid form?"

"I don't consider children human," she said. "Not technically. But... I'm not sensing anything out of the ordinary, except for a big central focus of power in city hall. The kids are just kids. Except they look like they're preparing to re-enact some kind of violent peasant uprising."

"Shit. Squat, don't hurt them. Let's just ditch the bikes and run through the park and try to get into city hall. Deal?"

"Deal," he said.

I reached back and unhooked Nicolette's cage. I *really* wanted my saddlebags—they were full of goodies—but I could get by with the dagger and hatchet and a few treats I'd squirreled away in my pockets. We put our kickstands down and climbed off the bikes—and the kids seemed to take that as their signal to launch. No one gave them an order. There were no lurking adults, no gym teachers blowing whistles, no guidance at all—they just *surged*, a wave of humanity that topped out at about four feet high, barreling off the school lawn and down the road toward us.

Squat and I made a run for it. I'm in pretty good shape, and Squat was no slouch, either. But kids... those little bastards are *fast*, and they hunted us like a wolf pack, splitting up to flank and encircle us. We made it about halfway across the park before they reached us. At first it was just little fingers plucking at my pant legs, or ineffectually hitting me in the shins with rulers, but there was a definite cumulative effect. And since I wasn't willing to straight up murder a bunch of children—I was pretty sure that was contraindicated by my attempts to be a better person—there wasn't much I could do besides shove them away. I saw Squat disappear under a wave of children. They were literally *climbing* him, the ones with ropes and nets trying to bind him, and I was afraid he'd freak out and snap and start tearing their arms off, but he didn't. Maybe he wasn't a total monster after all.

I rolled and dodged and shook and dove, trying to hold on to Nicolette and get away, but eventually one of the kids tripped me up, forcing me to take a knee, and then they were just *on* me, a wave of them hitting me in the back and driving me down.

Then the big kid with a rock saw his chance, and hit me on the head, and I was done.

But not dead yet. That came later. After I met the Eater.

I woke up in chains, which is never fun unless you've negotiated it with your lover first, and even then I usually prefer to be the one holding the keys instead. My shoulders were screaming from holding up my weight, and when I tried to put my feet down, I could only touch the floor with the toes of my bare feet—enough to take some of the pressure off my arms and keep me from dislocating my shoulders, but only barely. I lifted my head—which hurt like I'd just been hit with a rock, aptly enough—and took in my surroundings.

They were not very comforting.

I was strung up in a spiderweb of chains, bound at ankles and wrists, arms and legs at full extension, with a few chains looped around my waist and in an X across my chest for good measure. At least I wasn't naked or dressed in a slave Leia outfit. I seemed to be in some sort of ballroom (or throne room), presumably in city hall—my chains were attached to stone columns, the floor was buffed marble, and the ceilings were high and vaulted. There was nothing in front of me except an empty chair, but it was quite a chairchair: clearly handmade, of polished dark wood, and the back was made in the shape of that Y-branching symbol I'd seen on the sort-of-church roof.

People were standing around *just* on the edge of my peripheral vision, where I couldn't quite see them clearly no matter how much I turned my bashed-up head. The place was silent except for the whisper of cloth as the barely-glimpsed people moved.

"Nice town you've got here," I said, going for a tone of cocky confidence, and was thus disappointed when my voice emerged as a broken croak. I soldiered on, though. "Not too welcoming to outsiders, obviously, but clean streets and neat lawns count for plenty."

Squat walked out of my peripheral vision, holding Nicolette's cage in his hand, but her head wasn't in it. "Marla, this place is amazing." He spread his arms wide and spun around like a little kid twirling in a field. "My whole life I've been so confused, especially since the curse and everything, but even before that, really. But now, here, in the kingdom of the Eater, it's all so *clear*, there's one true path laid out before me—"

I didn't bother arguing with him. When a friend has been mind-controlled there's not usually a lot of point in saying, "You've been mind-controlled! Look deep inside yourself and see the truth!" Exceptionally strong-willed people can resist such compulsions, sometimes—but the Eater was apparently powerful enough to take over a whole town full of people, so I would imagine he could tear through most wills like tissue paper. Which made me wonder why *I* hadn't been turned into a mind-slave. Probably more wonderful side effects of goddesshood. Not that having a free mind was a lot of good when my body was bound this way.

"There's a saying," I said, talking over Squat's joyful babblings. "Something like: I want to talk to the organ grinder, not to the monkey. No offense, Squat. But where's the guy holding your leash?"

"You bewilder me, Marla Mason." An immensely tall and broad figure wearing a brown robe with a hood glided into my field of vision. Squat shut up and walked away, leaving me alone with the new guy. He looked like he should be singing the bass part in a Gregorian chants choir.

"You're the Eater? What's with the Friar Tuck get-up? I was expecting, I don't know, a stained apron and a barbecue fork."

"Some call me the Eater. I encourage that nomenclature among those who help keep me… supplied… because it makes for an intimidating persona, and inspires obedience even in those I do not take into my service. Most of my procurers think me a cannibal, but they misunderstand my nature." He stood before me, hands tucked away in his sleeves, face in shadow. The voice sounded human, but he could have been anything under those robes—snake monster, three were-rats standing on each other's shoulders, sentient cancer, whatever.

"Oh yeah? You're not a cannibal because you're not a human, is that it?"

He ignored me. "You disrupted those supply chains, you know. Killing Sarlat was rude of you. He was a very reliable business associate, despite his dramatic trappings. I would take vengeance for that alone, purely as a practical consideration—no one can slay my allies with impunity. But I have more personal reasons to want you punished. The so-called beast of Sunlight Shores was an old friend—we came to this continent together. He was foolish in those days, too hungry to exercise caution, and as a result he was imprisoned for centuries. I'd hoped it would be a learning experience for him."

"You knew he was imprisoned in a hole and you just left him there? Wow, you're the best friend ever."

Still nothing. I wasn't getting a rise out of him. But it was early yet. "You killed the beast. That is impressive, in a way. But I am not so easily slain. My protections are vast. Understand, though, that I don't actually *want* to kill you. I would rather have you serve me. And yet… you are strangely intransigent. My devotees call me the Guide, or the Way, or the Path, or the Opener. But you… you seem resistant to my guidance."

"I've never been good at group activities," I said. "I sucked at intramural soccer, too. I see you've recruited my buddy Squat to your team. That's too bad. But what about Nicolette?"

"That severed head you traveled with? I have put it aside to study more closely. I have never seen death defied in precisely that way before. It's very curious."

"I hope you have more fun with her than I usually do. So what's the deal here? Psychic domination? Brain parasites? How do you do it?"

"You persist in misunderstanding my nature. I do not control these people. I simply show them their ideal path, and they choose, willingly, to follow it—having been shown truth and perfection, they can do nothing else, for perfection contains its own compulsion." He turned and gestured toward the throne. I saw his hand for a moment, and it looked human, though the skin was unhealthy-looking, the color of dirty dishwater. "Do you see my sigil? At the top, there are many paths, all divergent, and they gradually come together, as tributaries flow to a single river, and in time they become the *true* path: my path. I am gifted at looking into the future, you see, Marla Mason, into seeing what *might* happen… but you confound me. I begin to peer into your probabilities, and at first all is blurs and shadows, as if *anything* could happen, which is patently nonsense—and after a few weeks, I see nothing at all, as if you've vanished. I have seen this before, of course: that is the future of one who is almost certainly going to die. And yet this darkness is absolute, as if you *must* die, as if there are no other possibilities open to you, no matter what—I have seldom encountered such a thing in someone who is not obviously terminally ill. But that is not the strangest thing. The strangest thing is, that if I peer a *bit* farther—you appear again, still shrouded, but present. And then you vanish again. And appear again. I confess, I have never anything like it."

"What the fuck do you *eat*?" I said, but I was half thinking out loud, because I already had a decent idea. Any decent sorcerer could see the future—hell, I could look through my wedding ring and do that. Mostly 'the future' just looks like a kaleidoscope in a blender, though, because the future isn't *fixed*—all you can ever see are possibilities, and it takes a lot of practice or natural skill to discern the likely futures from the whole whirling mass of possibilities. Every life is full of a finite-but-vast number of possible choices, which can lead to wildly divergent worlds. This guy, apparently, could look ahead more clearly than most, and see futures out to an almost unfathomable distance… but his power didn't work on me, because I would vanish from Earth every month and go to the underworld and cease to be human for a while, only to return later. My future was full of possibilities, too, of course, but it was rare in that it was also full of some rock-hard *certainties*.

"What I eat is none of your concern—"

"You eat their futures, don't you?" I said, gazing into the darkness in his hood. I saw him flinch, slightly, but definitely. "Or, I guess, just *most* of their futures. You eat all their choices, subtracting all the decisions they might make, narrowing their possibilities to a single line and forcing them onto one path: where they're devoted to you, cultists and willing slaves. You feed on all that potential energy. But there must be some victims who won't serve you in any possible future—what do you do with those?"

"You… I am impressed."

"I'm good at intuitive leaps," I said, but in truth, I wasn't sure *how* I'd locked onto the idea so quickly, and with such certainty. There were all sorts of things happening deep in my mind, way below the level of consciousness, and this revelation felt like a bubble rising up from those goddess-haunted depths. "Answer me. What do you do with the ones who won't be your slaves?"

"They are not slaves, they are *happy*—but I may as well answer you. What harm can it do? Those who would never become my devotees, in any possible universe, I simply send back out into the world, to live the one possible life left to them in peace. I always choose to leave them a pleasant life, one without undue stress—"

"Except they aren't really people anymore," I said. "They're totally deterministic automatons. They're philosophical zombies—they *look* human, they *act* human, but there's nothing inside them. They don't have any *choices* left, they can only do… whatever it is you decided they could do."

"They believe themselves to be perfectly real," the Eater said. "They still *think* they make choices. If they don't mind, why should you?"

"Them not minding when you steal their possibilities? That's even more fucked up. What do you do with the energy you get? Consuming those possible futures… you're getting into some multiverse-level shit, there, shutting down branching timelines before they're born, harvesting all that potential energy—what do you *do* with it all?"

"I made this town. This society. I keep it perfectly maintained. The weather is ideal, the people are ideal, *everything* is ideal—it is the one perfect place in the world."

"You're a selfless cult leader-slash-dictator, that's for sure. But come on. All that power? What else is it for?"

He pushed his hood back. His head looked like a rotting melon, almost entirely bald, apart from stray tufts of gray hair poking up here and there. His ears were gone entirely, his nose was like a squashed zucchini, his eyes two rat turds stuck in a wad of dough. But as I watched, he raised his hands, and his face gradually transformed. It was a bit like watching a skyscraper demolition in reverse. His skin tightened up, his eyes widened, his ears grew back, and his hair came in, thick and lustrous. Within moments, he had the sort of unremarkable face you'd never glance at twice. "I am four thousand years old," he said. "Don't I look good for my age?"

"I've seen prettier things stuck on the heel of my boot," I said. "You have to do that level of plastic surgery every day? Every five minutes? I know it gets harder and harder to maintain your looks as you get older." He didn't respond. "So, you steal futures in exchange for crass immortality, great. I've got nothing against assholes living forever, but when you start to mess with *people*, that's when I get—"

"Your friend, Squat," the Eater said. "I took away his futures, all but one: one in which he serves me, loyally, of course. But also one in which he does something else. It is inevitable. No pleading can change it, no bribery, no sudden violence: I close my eyes, and I *see* the action performed, shining and golden, the one true path. It might as well have happened already."

Hellfire. Earthquake. I tried my best, I really did, but whatever trick of the mind allowed me to bring down unearthly quantities of violence on a whim wasn't working today.

"I look forward to seeing what mysteries lurk inside your brain," he said.

"And I look forward to seeing *your* brain spattered on the—"

That's when Squat ran at me and twisted my head literally all the way around, my neck snapping with a sound like a branch breaking under a weight of ice. Apart from a moment of blurred motion, it was instant darkness. Again.

Slabs

I WOKE UP IN THE MORGUE, presumably at the Moros hospital, on a cold metal autopsy table. I was naked, but covered with a sheet, so that was something. My head was on straight as far as I could tell, and I felt as refreshed as if I'd just had a good night's sleep.

"Good morning, sleepyhead," Death said. "You were very nearly sleepyheadless." He was laying on his side on the table on the other side of the room, propped up on one elbow, dressed in an immaculate suit, with a lazy smile on his face. But I wasn't fooled. I could tell by the tap-tap-tap of his many rings against the metal surface of the table that he was anxious or annoyed about something.

I sat up, letting the sheet fall to my waist, and glanced around the room. I've been in a few morgues in my day, and this was definitely one of them: lots of closed white cabinets, a wall of square doors for body storage, bottles, scales, and assorted scary-looking tools. This room also featured a doctor in a lab coat slumped (but breathing) in the corner. "Why the divine intervention?" I said. My throat wasn't even raw. "Are you going to show up *every* time someone kills me? Don't you to have better things to do?"

"I was perfectly content to let your natural immortality take care of itself, darling, but this person was going to take out your brain, cut it up, and take a close look at the slices." He gestured toward the doctor. "Your body is capable of growing you a new heart and liver and kidneys, all new and even better than your old ones, and I have every reason to believe you'd grow a new brain, too—but I don't think you'd like that. A new brain wouldn't have all the old wrinkles and folds and neural connections, so in a very real sense it wouldn't be *you*, despite being made of your own genetic material. While I could have let your old brain be removed without violating the *letter* of our agreement, I thought allowing your mortal body to be reduced to the intellectual level of a newborn would be a violation of our bargain's spirit. You get to be mortal for half the year, and I'm interpreting 'you' to mean something more than 'someone with Marla Mason's DNA.'"

I whistled. "I hadn't thought about that. I took an axe to the brain, and I was okay afterward, I was still me—but that was the original organ."

"The difference between a repair and a replacement, yes," Death said.

"Still, you didn't have to come yourself. Don't we have underlings to do this sort of thing?"

"I'm plenipotentiary and omnipresent, love. You and I can be our own underlings. This form you see here before you… think of it as a finger poking through a knothole. Just a piece of me, not the thing entire."

I grunted. "Is it the same for me? Is my goddess-self hanging out somewhere, and I'm just, like, a walking, talking fingernail?"

"Not at all. You wanted to be human—it's a bit silly to say you're 'mortal,' really—for half the year, and so you are. The Marla Mason in the room before me, looking so fetching in autopsy-table chic, is all the Marla Mason there is."

"That means all the goddess stuff is *in* me somewhere, then," I said. "Which explains why I keep getting little… glimpses. I have powers I didn't used to, and sometimes I have… call them insights, I guess, intuitions that are more reliable than usual."

"That makes sense. Your memories and self-knowledge were suppressed, but it's all still inside you. Or folded up in adjacent dimensions. It's complicated."

I mulled that over. It was giving me ideas. "I don't suppose you've seen my clothes?"

"Sliced off you," he said. "In a plastic bag over there, though they won't do you much good in so many pieces. I took the liberty of bringing you some clothing." He pointed to the floor, at a paper bag I hadn't noticed before, possibly because it had just appeared. Who the fuck knows what gods can do?

"It better not be anything slutty," I said. "I know you enjoy roleplaying, pretending to be a human who gets off on human things."

He snorted. "While a black leather corset and stockings are perfectly suitable attire for an avatar of death—at least in some of the comic books I've seen—I went a more practical route. I know better than to offer you any help—"

"This is enough deus ex machina for one day," I interrupted. "What I'm doing is important—but it's just as important that *I'm* the one doing it."

"Of course," he said, entirely too soothingly. "Allow me to give you some information, at least: Your wedding ring, dagger, and axe are with the Eater, I'm afraid—he could sense the magic radiating off the objects. The ring is my gift to you and you alone, and no use to him—though since it only shows possible futures, he hardly needs it."

"Tell me the dagger sliced off his fingers, at least." It had nasty effects on people who picked it up without my permission.

Death shook his head. "Alas, he must have seen that outcome was likely, because he picked the dagger up with tongs and put it inside a metal box. That blade is worthless to him as well, of course. The ring and the dagger are from *our* realm… but the axe is an artifact of some other origin, and he may be able to wield its power."

"Oh, good, because he didn't have *enough* of an advantage."

"You have an advantage, too. The Eater is used to seeing the future with trivial ease, and he *can't see you*, not in any useful way. You defy cause-and-effect. Someone who becomes that accustomed to knowing the future—"

"Is probably shit when it comes to improvising and dealing with surprises."

"Which are two of your strengths," he said. "I fear your cursed friend Squat is lost to you, at least for the moment, but I think Nicolette is giving the Eater trouble—she is resistant to his control, for some of the same reasons you are. He can't cut away and feast on her possible futures, because her future is *spoken* for—we have decreed that she will serve you for as long as you see fit, and since her futures are tangled with yours, he has difficulty penetrating them as well."

"Any idea where she is?"

"In the Eater's office, at the moment," Death said. "In what we might as well call City Hall, though locally I gather it's called the House of the Eater. They use the same name for the church where they worship him."

I grunted. "How'd we miss this guy? Living for four thousand years? Aren't we supposed to pay attention to unnatural lifespans?"

Death chuckled. "He has not lived for four thousand years. He exaggerates for effect. More like a thousand."

"Oh," I said. "Is *that* all."

"Anyway, we don't police immortals," Death said. "For one thing, no one's definitively immortal—time has not ended, after all, and they could still die *sometime*, so that's all right. It's not as if we have a shortage of the dead back home. So what if someone defies death for a while? It would be like worrying about a single salt molecule missing from the whole ocean."

"Fine, but if it's not our department, shouldn't it be *somebody*'s? This guy is stealing possible futures, cutting off whole branching *universes* from being born, right?"

"Indeed. And feasting on the energy from those aborted timelines."

"Well? I've dealt with this multiverse crap before, I've even *been* to worlds where other choices were made and new timelines formed, and I know there are people in charge of that stuff. Except not people—gods. Except not *gods*. Things that are to you and me—well, you, at the moment—as we are to ordinary mortals."

"Meta-gods, you might say, yes. Very scary. Well above my pay grade. Comparatively, we are mere custodians. They are architects."

"So shouldn't the architect in charge of maintaining the integrity of reality and the safety of the multiverse be pissed about the Eater devouring possible timelines? That seems like a pretty major violation to me." I was particularly pissed because I *knew* the guy who watched to make sure the fabric of reality didn't get ripped up; my old apprentice Bradley. "I think it's the drop-in-the-ocean problem again," Death said. "With every moment, with every decision made, new universes are born, trillions per second, no doubt—why would the guardian of the multiverse notice a few hundred universes that never came into being in the first place? Universes that *don't* happen can hardly threaten the integrity of the multiverse. In a field growing full of wheat, the farmer doesn't pay much attention to the seeds that *don't* sprout."

"So I'm the only one who cares about the *people*, then. Great."

He shrugged. "You're human. At least part-time. It's right that you should care about individual humans. And I'm proud to see you meddling. I think it's what you were born to do."

"Come on. To you, I'm panicking about mayflies, right? Why bother going to all this effort to save people, when they'll be dead in the blink of an eye anyway? I bet your clocks measure in centuries instead of seconds."

"It's true I have a different perspective than you do. Though with our month-on, month-off schedule, I spend rather a lot of time engaging with the world on the level of human time. But all that aside—even I find the Eater's actions abhorrent. I don't think death is so bad, really. The underworld is no more terrible than those who die believe it to be. Sometimes it's quite lovely. But these poor people aren't being allowed to die—they are being turned into objects. Machines. Death is my domain, but there is no death without life, and so I believe life is precious. Give them back their lives, Marla. And if that's not possible, keep the Eater from taking anyone else's life."

He slid off the table, stepped lightly toward me, kissed me on the lips, then strolled away, as always, opening a door that didn't exist and stepping through.

This time, though, I caught a glimpse of the place beyond the door. You're probably thinking fire, or dank caverns, or something like that, but no—it was a perfectly ordinary foyer, maybe a little posh, walls paneled in dark wood, with a little table that held a vase full of pale flowers. And above the table there hung a mirror. I saw my reflection in the mirror, or something like my reflection. It was my face, except paler, and the eyes were dark, as if they were all pupil, no iris or whites. My reflection opened her mouth—even though I didn't—and revealed a mouth full of pearl-white canines and a black tongue. She mouthed, "We should talk," just before the door closed (and then ceased to exist).

"Yeah, no shit," I said.

But first I had to escape Eater Memorial Hospital. I hopped off the table and opened up the paper bag Death had brought me. Loose cotton pants, button-down short-sleeved shirt, jogging bra, socks, and hand-made running shoes, all in black, of course. I rolled my eyes at the underwear, which had little black bows at the sides, but at least they covered my whole ass and didn't have any unnecessary lace. Everything fit me like tailor-made, which they probably were, assuming the underworld had tailors.

Once I was dressed, I looked over the tools in the room, considering scalpels and saws, but the problem was, I didn't want to *kill* any of the Eater's thralls—I had enough innocent blood on my conscience for a lifetime. I settled for a steel hammer with a wicked hook at the bottom of the handle, figuring I could drive it into someone's gut or tap someone on the temple without offing them in the process.

Before I slipped out of the room, I had the bright idea of checking the doctor for a phone, and lo, he actually had one. I'd worried the Eater communicated with his disciples telepathically or something—or that their lives were *so* deterministic that they didn't even need to receive orders, just doing whatever the Eater wanted them to automatically. Maybe that was the case usually, but my arrival had disrupted things. The phone was old-fashioned and dumb, only good for making calls, and it didn't get any reception here in the bowels of the building, so I pocketed it and peered into the hallway. A boring white corridor, tiled walls and gleaming floors and fluorescent lights overhead. I walked out like I had every reason to be there, looking for signs marked Exit, but I guess OSHA didn't ever visit Moros, because there was basically no signage at all. Fortunately there were no patients, either, at least not down here, and eventually I found a stairwell, and from there, an exit.

The outside was bright and hot, and I wondered if it was the same day I'd arrived, or the next. Who knew how long it took to recover from having your head twisted nearly right off? I'd emerged on the far side of the hospital, away from City Hall, near an empty parking lot. I kept a lookout for terrifying hordes of children, but so far my revivification and escape had gone unnoticed. I lit out for the steep hillside behind the hospital, scurrying up into the trees and making my way up to the ridge. The sightlines were a bit shit, but I'd probably notice if an army of philosophical zombies came charging up the hill toward me. I found a flattish rock, sat down, and dialed Pelham's number from memory.

It rang and rang, which was weird, because he was usually the type to pick up before the first ring even finished—but then, he usually knew it was me calling, and with this random-ass phone… Finally I heard his voice, sounding harried and impatient: "Yes?"

"Pelly? It's Marla."

His tone changed instantly. "Oh, dear, Mrs. Mason, has something happened to your phone?"

"Oh, yeah. My phone, my weapons, my potions, my charms, my oracle in a birdcage, my stalwart companion, my just about everything. I took the fight to the Eater, and he kicked my ass. I got away, but only just. I'm in the woods near his lair, and since I don't like to say I'm *hiding*, let's just say I'm regrouping."

"Rondeau and I will be there in—"

"No, no, I'd just lose you, too—the Eater has some heavy mind-control mojo, that's how he took over my buddy Squat, and every other person in this little toy town. You'd better stay clear. I've got a plan, sort of, to take down the Eater and maybe even save Nicolette and definitely to get my shit back, but I need a safe place. I can get out of town, but I need a hidey-hole up, someplace I'll be hard to track magically. You did so well finding Tolerance for me…"

"Of course. I will call you back as soon as I can. *Please* be careful."

"I can't imagine why I'd start being careful now. Thanks, Pelham."

I started walking down the other side of the ridge, into the wilderness, wondering how far I'd have to walk before I felt safe, wishing I had my motorcycle. I had no doubt it was still standing in the street where I'd left it—not even the Eater's magics were sufficient to overcome all its protections—but I wasn't about to walk over and get it. I should have enchanted my pale horse to drive itself toward me whenever I whistled. The dagger *did* have that kind of enchantment, and would spring into my hand when called, but the trick only worked at short range, like if it got knocked out of my hand in a fight. I wouldn't dare put a long-range enchantment on a weapon like that—if I whistled for it from a mile away, it would slice through walls, trees, cows, cars, children, lawnmowers, horses, cattle, mailmen, whatever, on the way back to me. A neat trick, but hardly worth the rather awful possible consequences.

No, I was on my own, with just my wits… and whatever secrets were buried deep inside my mind. But I was going to excavate those secrets soon.

Another Great Escape

I HEARD PEOPLE COMING so I climbed up a tree, or rather up a pair of trees standing so close together that their branches overlapped and formed a ladder or a cage. Fortunately the pines were thick with needles so I was able to hide myself pretty well. Unfortunately, the pines were thick with needles, so I couldn't see a thing. I was only a few feet off the ground, and considered going higher, but if the Eater did have hunting parties out for me, I didn't want to give my position away by making the branches shake and sway.

For a while there was silence, and I started to wonder if maybe I'd just heard a deer, or whatever fauna calls woods like these home. I was standing on two branches, and had my hands on two others, and I discovered that pine trees bleed sap, which is pretty gross and sticky. (You know I'm not a country girl.) The approaching footsteps got louder, and I was ninety percent sure they were human, but they weren't *talking*. I realized I hadn't heard any of the Eater's thralls speak, except for Squat, and wondered if that meant Squat still had some unshredded shred of agency, or if the Eater had just wanted him to talk in order to demoralize me. Probably the latter.

The footsteps were just starting to move away when my stolen phone rang, an annoying up-and-down trilling sound. I fumbled for the phone as fast as I could, trying to figure out how to silence it, cursing the unfamiliar controls.

Gunfire boomed. Sounded like a shotgun, and from the explosion of pine needles up and to my left, it had been aimed at the tree. None of the shot hit me, but I didn't want to give the bastards time to reload, so I played dead and just let myself fall out of the tree, tucking in my arms so I wouldn't bang too many branches on the way down. I hit the ground—which was plenty hard, and not cushioned much by a scattering of pine needles—and tried to look mortally wounded while peering through slit eyelids. I was on my side, one arm tucked under me (with a surprise in my hand), the other flung out in an awkward fashion that I hoped would sell the whole "unconscious" thing. The phone had fallen not far away, and it was still ringing.

Two people approached—a man in a flannel jacket and a petite teenage girl in, I swear, a frilly white Easter Sunday sort of dress. The girl was the one with the shotgun. The guy just had a baseball bat.

Clearly they were not trained in the arts of war, because she didn't unload a point-blank shot into my chest or face to make sure I was dead. Instead they just walked up to me, and stood so close I could have reached out and grabbed their ankles.

"I don't see any blood," the man said. He prodded me with the end of his baseball bat, and I didn't react.

"Maybe she healed," the girl said. Totally missing the fact that my clothes were intact, too. At least I wasn't dealing with genius detectives here. "She was definitely dead before, we saw her head get twisted around, and she somehow got up again."

"It's strange the Eater didn't know she would rise from the dead." I wanted to hear a hint of doubt or defiance in his voice, a questioning of his living god, but instead it was a simple observation.

"We need not understand to obey." The girl spoke with the confident devotion of the very young or the thoroughly brainwashed. "Do you have the handcuffs?"

"I do."

If they'd had any sense, she would have covered me with the shotgun while he cuffed me. Instead, she leaned the shotgun against the tree and took the cuffs from him.

I rolled onto my back and whipped my hand around, the steel hammer inverted in my grip so the hooked end of the handle sank right into her calf. I twisted and yanked, ripping out a plug of flesh about the size of a thumb. She howled and fell, clutching at her leg. Instead of lunging for the shotgun like a non-idiot, the guy swung his bat at me. He could have pulped my skull if he'd done a good hard overhand swing, like a guy splitting wood with an axe, but instead he did this half-assed sort of sidearm thing, and I jerked my head out of the way, catching the blow on my shoulder. My upper arm went numb, but I've got two arms, so fuck it.

I dropped the hammer and grabbed the bat, rolling over and yanking it out of his grip. Then I bounced up to my feet and grinned at him, doing my best to look like a scary returned-from-the-dead revenant. I suspected the pine needles in my hair spoiled the effect, but he seemed sufficiently wide-eyed and startled. Good. These people needed to be startled. I flipped the bat up into the air and caught it by the grip—a little show-boat-y, I know, but if you can't have a little drama in your life, what's the point?

"I'd rather not bash your brains out, since you're slaves and everything," I said. "How about you lay facedown for me, slugger?"

He glanced at the shotgun, so I swung the bat and cracked him right in the side of his knee. He fell, howling and clutching his cracked kneecap. He wasn't going to be a problem for a few minutes.

The girl was trying to scurry away, scooting backwards on her ass. I walked over to her and put my foot down on her wounded leg, just above the injury. "Handcuffs," I said. She looked up at me, wide-eyed, and then tossed the cuffs toward me. "And the key?" She winced, then tossed that to me, too. "Okay, sweetie, why don't you hug that tree there?"

She scooted over to the tree I'd indicated, one small enough that she could reach her arms around it, and embraced the trunk. I cuffed her wrists together. She'd be stuck there until someone came by with a key or a saw. "Don't suppose you have another set of cuffs?"

She shook her head mutely.

I looked at the guy, who'd subsided into whimpering. I thought about giving him a thump on the side of the head with a bat, but that whole knock-someone-unconscious thing mostly only works in the movies. In real life, if you hit somebody hard enough to put them under, you run a real risk of fucking up their brains forever. Instead, I picked up the hammer and used the hook to slice through the fabric of the girl's dress until I had a few long strips of cloth. She didn't even try to kick me. These people really were shit at improvising.

"Ready to get on your belly now, Babe Ruth, or do I need to take a crack at your other knee?"

He obediently rolled over, prone, but had to bite back a scream when the movement jostled his hurt knee. I hog-tied him with the strips of cloth, wrists to ankle behind his back—but because I am trying to Do Better, I only bent back and tied his uninjured leg. I didn't see him getting too far by pushing himself along with his busted knee, anyway, and why cause the guy unnecessary pain?

Once they were secured, I picked up the phone and called Pelly back.

"Sorry about that," I said when he answered—more promptly this time. "I had to deal with a couple of goons."

"Oh dear," he said. "I have located a place for you to take sanctuary. Can you make it to a main road? I can have someone pick you up."

"You're a prince, Pelly. Sure, I can get to a road." Luckily I have a good sense of direction, and figured I could get back to the endless enchanted loop that circled Moros. We discussed the details and timing.

"I hate to see you cut off from communication, Mrs. Mason, but you should probably dispose of the phone you're using. Such things can be tracked."

I swore. I was used to having phones enchanted to be untraceable. "Crap, right." I said my farewells, then removed the sim card and crunched it under my foot, took out the battery, and flung the pieces of the phone in opposite directions. I picked up the shotgun, leaving the baseball bat, then paused. "Do you guys even know what the Eater did to you?"

"The *Master* saved my life," the man said hoarsely. "I was a drug addict, a gambler, and he set me on the true path."

"I ran away from home, and I was living on the street, when he set *me* on the path," the girl said. "He shows us the way."

"Yeah, he's a humanitarian all right. The same way a vegetarian is a guy who eats vegetables." There was no point in talking to these people. They could only do one thing: serve the Eater. Every other option had been flayed away from them.

I hiked out, keeping a sharp ear and eye out for other patrols, but I didn't encounter anyone. Since I was so unpredictable, the Eater probably had his people searching the whole town and the surrounding areas, which would spread his flock a little thin. Eventually I emerged by the side of the road and crouched in the undergrowth, waiting for the car Pelham had told me to expect.

Eventually it came put-putting up, a modified dune buggy painted in blue-and-red tiger stripes, carrying a reek of used french fry oil from its badly-modified biodiesel engine. The guy behind the wheel looked like he'd gone to Burning Man one year and never come entirely back: shirtless and deeply tanned, ropy with muscle, a dozen necklaces of beads and chunky turquoise and carved wood around his neck, face scraggled with beard, hair an explosion of matted braids and dreadlocks woven with bows and ribbons in a way that reminded me uncomfortably of how Nicolette used to wear her hair, thick with charms.

"Hey, lady," he said. "You wanted a ride?" His voice was a gulf state drawl, but unquestionably welcoming, so I emerged from the bushes.

"You're Riegel?" I said.

"Your man Pelham sent me. Come on, I don't like getting this close to the Master's town."

I climbed into the passenger seat, an uncomfortable mass of busted springs and duct-taped vinyl, and he roared away before I could even start fumbling for my seatbelt. It was hard to converse with the wind ripping around my head, but I gave it a try: "You're a sorcerer?"

"Psychic." He tapped his temple. "Ever since I ate the wrong psychedelic mushroom when I was in college. Apparently it was some crazy rare kind of 'shroom, grew in mystical soil or the shit of a god or from a spore from another dimension or something, who knows—whatever it was, it permanently blew off my doors of perception. So I do work for people every now and then, you know—listen to see if people are telling the truth, stuff like that. I did some work for a guy who knows a guy who knows a guy who knows one of your guys, and here I am. Thanks for the big payday, by the way. Driving around is a lot easier than rooting around in some guy's head to find out whether or not he stole something, you know?"

"Whatever we paid you, you earned it," I said. "So you know about that town back there?"

"I know about all kinds of stuff I'm not supposed to. I can tell there are illusions wrapped around the place, and I can see through them, but I don't go poking around in places like that. I've heard the thoughts of some of the, I don't know—disciples? Students?"

"Cultists," I said.

"Right. Their thoughts are all full of worship for the Master, or the Opener, or the Pathfinder, all kinds of names, but I get that it's the same guy, some heavy magic dude." He shook his head. "Their minds have a really creepy feel."

"You reading my mind right now?" I asked.

He nodded. "Sure, man, of course. But you've got some kind of good shield going. Your thoughts are all about super boring shit—getting your nails done, picking up dry cleaning, going grocery shopping. Which I'm pretty sure you're *not* actually thinking about, but any psychic dipping into your stream of thought just for a second under normal circumstances would believe it, and go looking for something more interesting. How'd you do that, anyway? Usually people who are psychically shielded, it's just like you hit a wall, or maybe hear a snatch of nursery rhyme over and over and over—I've never seen a mind that was, like, camouflaged this way."

"I'm a woman of many talents." In truth I had no idea how I did it. Probably more goddess shit.

Me and myself really needed to have that talk.

"Your guy Pelham said you needed a safe place to hole up for a while, so you could do some kind of ritual?"

"Yeah. I might only need a few hours, but it's probably best to assume I'll need all night."

"I've got a place," he said, and abruptly turned off-road, the dune buggy bumping down a gentle slope, following a twisting track I could barely perceive that allowed passage through the trees. Either he'd done this before, or he had a bit of basic precognitive ability that allowed him to see far enough ahead to avoid crashing into things.

We proceeded that way for a while, then stopped by a stand of trees, near a trickling creek. "Here you go," he said.

I squinted. "Is that a tent?" There was a sort of pavilion or something in camo colors, browns and greens, draped among the trees.

"Yup. Camouflaged. But the outer tent is made of enchanted metal mesh, so the whole thing is a Faraday cage, it'll shield you from various kinds of detection. And there's a circle of warding around *that*, to add an extra level of protection from divination. If somebody wanders into the place in person, they'll find you, but otherwise you should be all right. And if somebody does show up, you've got a shotgun."

"What do you use this place for?" I said.

"Sometimes things just get too noisy." He tapped his temple again. "Up in here, I mean. So a sorcerer I did work for made this place for me, a quiet room. I go in there, and I don't hear any thoughts but my own, and shit, is that a relief. There are some snacks and water and stuff inside if you need them, and there's a composting toilet back there—outside the Faraday cage, but inside the warding circle, so it's still pretty safe. You can find your own way out when you're done?"

I climbed out of the dune buggy. "I can. Thanks, Riegel."

"No problem." He glanced at the rearview mirror, then back at me. "So, this master-opener-pathfinder guy… you've got some kind of beef with him?"

"He's got a couple of my friends brainwashed." That was close enough to the truth. "I want to get them out."

He nodded. "In that case, I might head over to Arizona for a few days. I don't know much about this guy, but I get the sense he's not somebody to mess with."

"True. But it turns out, neither am I. It couldn't hurt to stay out of the neighborhood for a little while, though, Riegel—you're right about that. And maybe don't drive back past the hidden town. They have people out looking for me, and they might snag anyone they see passing by, for questioning and who knows what else."

He winced. "Gotcha. Good luck." He got back in the buggy and drove off, and after the roar of his engine diminished, I was left alone, in silence. With no thoughts but my own, like he'd said.

Except not exactly *just* my own thoughts. Someone else's thoughts were in there, too, buried deep, and it was time I heard what she had to say.

A Meeting of Minds

The tent was big enough to stand up in, and had more of a dorm room feel than a camping one. A ratty patterned rug covered the ground tarp, and paper snowflakes dangled from the support poles at just the right height to hit me in the face. There was a sizable bong, a cooler full of bottled fruit-infused tea, and stacked milked crates jammed with unlabeled jerky, bags of homemade trail mix, and potato-chip-analogues made of flax seed and kale and other virtuous foods. The seating options were a cot and a beanbag chair, so I sat down on the latter. Night was falling, and my gut was grumbling, so I ate granola and drank a little water, just enough to make my body stop complaining, then turned on the battery-powered lantern on top of the milk crates. I considered hitting the bong—that little wooden box beside it almost certainly held some weed—but decided to save chemical aids for a last resort. Maybe I could get where I needed to go purely on my own.

I am not what you'd call a recreational meditator. Sitting quietly, doing nothing, thinking about nothing or red triangles or whatever, isn't really my idea of a good time. I am a do-er, a think-er, maybe an over-doer and over-thinker, even. But I do a fair bit of enchanting, and when you do enchanting you spend a lot of time sitting alone and concentrating *very hard*, so hard that time disappears and you cease to feel any connection to anything but the work, in that state some people call "flow," so I certainly had some idea of what to do.

I slid off the beanbag, sat down cross-legged on the rug, rested my hands palm-down on my knees, and closed my eyes. I took a deep breath, then let it out, then another breath, imagining the flow of air as a wheel turning inside me, through me, letting the world become my breath—

The Bride of Death was clearly just waiting for an opening, because she more than met me halfway. I imagined her as a leviathan lurking in the deep waters of my subconscious, and now she was rising up to the surface as I was sinking into the depths. The darkness behind my eyes became the darkness of a cavern, then the darkness of space, with twinkling distant lights, and then the dark fell away and I was sitting on a smooth black stone that just happened to be shaped like a chair, under that sky. Water chuckled nearby, a dark river running down to a sunless sea, and trees the color and approximate shape of skeletal fingers stood all around me. The air smelled of night-blooming jasmine and wet clay, and now and again the skies above were occluded as diaphanous but vast things flew across the sky with a swiftness that could scarcely be believed.

A door creaked, and I looked toward the sound in time to see the Bride emerge from a freestanding door that closed and promptly vanished. She looked at me for a moment, and hers was the face I'd seen in the mirror: skin whitish-blue like sea ice, eyes black, delicate pointed teeth in her smile. She wore a simple white robe made of some incredibly fine silk, and her hair was pulled back in a bun. (My hair, in my mortal form, is kept fairly short, so people can't grab it in a fight, but apparently in the underworld I had different fashion priorities.) A circlet of pale flowers rested on her brow, like she was some sort of Goth May Queen.

The Bride sat on a stone across from mine—I couldn't help noticing *her* rock chair was a little bigger, a little more chair-shaped, a little more like a high-backed throne. She crossed her legs, revealing bare feet, the toenails painted a black that was somehow also luminous.

"Hello, me," she said.

"Hello, you," I replied. "What's with the Kali face?"

She shrugged. "Goes with the job. Death isn't just *death*, you know—it's more than that. The entire cycle of life, death, and rebirth, rot and fertility, wildfire and new growth. The flowers die, the flowers come back, time and tide and seasons progress through their paths. I'm not a free agent, not like you—I am part of the machinery of time."

"That still doesn't explain the cannibal teeth and the black tongue. Been eating too much licorice?"

She leaned forward, showing her teeth, licking her lips with that pointed tongue. "Death and I… share responsibilities, according to our own individual strengths. He handles most of the fertility-god stuff, while I represent death in its more destructive aspect, mostly. Come on. I didn't even wear a necklace of skulls. I'm practically being demure here."

"This is weird. I have seen some weird shit, but none weirder than this." I shifted on my stone chair. "How can you be *me*? No offense, but you seem like a totally different person."

"I *am* you, or rather, who you are informs who I am.... Think of goddesshood as a vessel. A bottle. Your... spirit, for want of a better word... fills that vessel—but the vessel imposes a particular shape on the contents. I am you, and I am more than you. I am you when you become a goddess. Imagine an ant's consciousness suddenly given the resources of a human brain. Or a human suddenly developing the range of color vision available to a butterfly or a mantis shrimp. Everything would look *so different*, and it would change the way you perceive the world, and, thus, the way you react to the world."

"So I'm an ant now. Thanks."

She shrugged but didn't bother to apologize, or even look abashed. So maybe she *was* me.

"I was worried it was a trick, this loss of memory, that Death was fucking with me—I mean, we're married, we had a honeymoon, but it's not like I know the guy all *that* well. I *can't* know him all that well."

The Bride shook her head. Then she looked annoyed. "I wish you'd stop thinking of me as 'the Bride,' it's not like you to define yourself based on your relationship with a man—or a man-shaped fundamental force of nature, for that matter."

"Sorry, that's what the cultists call me, except it's really what they're calling *you*. It got stuck in my head."

"I guess it'll do for now. But, no, no trick by Death, and no brain damage from going into the underworld and back again—or rather, if there is brain damage, it gets repaired, so I haven't bothered to worry about it."

"I've been writing things down, in case I forgot them later. Guess I don't need to do that, huh?"

"No. You can stop writing."

(Obviously I haven't stopped writing. I don't know why. I got into the habit, is all, and found out I liked it. And even without my memory being magically erased, I can still *forget* things, just like anybody does, so maybe it's good to write them down. Notes for my future memoirs. Won't *that* be a bestseller.)

"Great. I did it to myself. Mea culpa. But the thing is—I think I *need* access to that stuff I forgot, now. The occasional handwave inferno or mass grave by accident isn't enough. I need to be able to *do stuff* if I'm going to stop the Eater."

"I understand. I can open things up, just a little. I can give you access to the few powers you're capable of wielding without destroying your physical body, or shattering your mind. In truth you've always *had* access, you just didn't remember, which is why some of your capabilities have slipped out at unexpected moments. I think I can open the vault of memories just a crack, to let you access what you need—"

"Wait," I said. "Why just a crack? Why not give me my memories back? I still haven't gotten a satisfying answer about why. Because there are things woman is not meant to know? Really? Will my brain *actually melt* from the unbearable hotness of true knowledge? Tell me it's a matter of preserving my life, because otherwise, I don't see the fucking point of locking up large swaths of my own mind from me."

She sighed. "No. Your brain wouldn't melt. Some things you wouldn't be able to comprehend, or hold in your head, but the knowledge wouldn't disable you—you just wouldn't notice them, the same way you can't directly detect magnetic fields or perceive ultraviolet light. But there *are* good reasons to hide the knowledge from you. I can't lie to myself, so all I can do is ask you—not to ask."

"Fuck you." I knew how ridiculous I was being, telling myself to fuck myself, but I was annoyed, and I said so. "I am the keeper of secrets, the holder of mysteries, so spill. Give me my fucking memories back."

"Are you sure you want that, Marla? We can deal with what needs to be dealt with, give you the capability to get revenge on the Eater and free the people of Moros and save Squat and Nicolette, without going into… all this."

"I always want to know everything," I said. "You *know* that."

"I do, but… This isn't someone else keeping a secret from you. This is *you* keeping a secret from you." I noticed she wasn't fidgeting or shifting on her chair at all. Apart from her lips moving, she might have been a statue—and I knew my cultists would fall down to worship such an idol. "And hiding things from yourself… well, it's hardly unprecedented. You have a history of choosing to forget things because they're too painful, or distracting, or because they do you no good, you know—you drank Lethe water and forget-me-lots potions to erase the memory of sex with the lovetalker Joshua Kindler, and the pain of losing Daniel—"

Who? "Sure, I made myself forget what it was like to sleep with Joshua, because otherwise no sexual experience I ever had after that would measure up, and I didn't want to sigh and pine away like victims of lovetalkers usually do when they stop getting supernaturally fucked. That was just good sense. But who the fuck is Daniel?" I'd known a Dan or two, but none that mattered all that much to me. I should've started writing down my life a long time ago, apparently.

"Exactly," the Bride said. "You don't remember him, because the pain of his absence was too debilitating, and you chose to take it away. The way I've suppressed your memories is *another* case of you sparing yourself pain. I only remember those things you chose to forget in life because I can't not remember. My understanding is necessarily more vast and complete than yours, because being a god is all about knowing things that are perhaps best forgotten—"

"Just tell me!" I said. "Give me back my memories! Why not?"

"Because if I do," she said, "Your friend Squat will not be saved. Nicolette will not be saved. The Eater will not be stopped."

I stared at her. "But… what… why? You said I could get the power to stop them even without having all my memories back, so…"

"Because if I let you remember all the things you know as a goddess," the Bride replied, "then you won't care about any of the pointless to-ing and fro-ing of these mortals. Shakespeare wrote, 'As flies to wanton boys are we to the gods. They kill us for their sport.' Death and I lack the cruelty Shakespeare ascribes to the gods… but I can't deny that when you can see all the teeming billions of human lives at once, plus all the countless trillions and trillions of *other* lives on this planet, each one a spark of greater or lesser brightness… they might as well be flies. Or specks of dust in a sunbeam. It becomes impossible to differentiate them. They blur together into a single faintly-glowing mass. Death and I deal with the gestalt, the ebb and flow of life on Earth as a whole, the cycles of the seasons and the ages and the epochs. It's not that we don't care about humanity, but we care about humanity as a whole—and much less about the individual parts. We tend vast fields, and when you do that, you simply can't spend time worrying about each individual blade of grass. From the point of view of the grass, that might make us monsters, and rightly so. But it's the truth. If I let you have the fullness of your memories, of even that fraction of my awareness available to you with a brain made of electrified meat, you wouldn't *bother* with your rescue plan. You'd just open a door and return to the underworld, where the work of the world awaits."

She might as well have punched me in the head. I leaned back, trying to work it out, trying to make sense of everything. "But… all this stuff, about 'Doing Better,' the tattoo on my wrist, the mission to kill the killers and hunt the hunters—I thought I was doing that because as a goddess I was more enlightened. Because you thought I needed to learn a lesson about treating people better, about doing good and making up for my crimes…"

"Death and I were trying to honor your wishes," the Bride said. "That's all. The bargain you struck, to remain mortal for half the year—it was so important to you to be a person, to not ascend entirely to godhood. To be half earth and half air, half gold and half clay. But once you became *me*, you stopped caring about being mortal at all. I—we—told Death to just forget about the bargain, to let me be a goddess forever, but he said that wasn't fair to the person I used to be—to the person you *are*. So we agreed the only way to let you be yourself was to remove the part of you that yearned to be something more."

"I don't believe this." I was apparently going for some kind of gold medal in stubbornness. "How could I stop caring about Rondeau? About Pelham?"

She shook her head. "It's not that you—that I—don't care about them, exactly, but… it's like they're people you knew in elementary school. Your best friends from first grade, say. Maybe you have a few fond memories, scraps of moments that occasionally flutter through your mind, but you never really *think* about them, and why should you? It's unlikely you have anything in common with them anymore. The people they are have nothing to do with the person you are, and you haven't been close to them in a very long time. It's not exactly like that, but I think that's the best way I can explain it. Or… you know how you don't have many friends who aren't sorcerers?"

"I don't have many friends at all, but… sure. Ordinaries can't possibly understand my life. The same way cops are mostly friends with other cops, and criminals with other criminals. Sometimes you need to be with someone who understands."

"Exactly. And when you're a god, humans can't possibly understand."

If she'd looked smug then, I might have punched her, even if she *was* just the manifestation of a repressed part of my psyche, but instead she looked serious, and maybe even a little sad.

"But it *does* matter." I spoke with great ferocity, leaning forward, wanting to jump up out of the chair and shout at her. "Individual people do matter, every one of them is a world unto themselves, center of their own universe, they contain multitudes, they're not just interchangeable parts—"

"Beetles can probably tell each other apart, too." She shrugged. "But to us, they're all just beetles. I'm not saying your perspective is wrong… just that, from my perspective, it's simply incomprehensible. Even when Death first meddled in your life, when you first met him, he found *you* interesting only because you defied him—the way you'd notice the individual insect that bites you, at least long enough to swat it. And that was before he'd ascended into his full power, when he was more human-scale. But even then, you saw the way he took lives indiscriminately—individuals didn't *mean* anything to him, not really. You've tempered him, taken the cruelty out of him, made him a better man and arguably a better god, but there is still a fundamental disconnect between his kind and yours. Your desire to meddle directly in human affairs is baffling to him, but he loves you, so he respects it because it's important to you, the way you might tolerate a spouse who tinkered with toy trains or collects stamps, even if the hobby makes no sense to you."

"Saving people is a hobby now?"

"When you put it that way," the Bride said, "I guess it does sound better than stamp collecting. At least you get to kill stuff. So, what will it be, Marla? Your full memories, as much as you can handle, anyway? Or just enough access to power to get the job done?"

Hell Hath

I'VE SAID IT BEFORE. I'm sure I'll say it again. There's nothing we aren't *meant* to know—but there are, maybe, things we'd be happier not knowing.

"Fuck it," I told myself. "I'll be a goddess again in a few weeks anyway. I guess I'll stick with being a woman for the time being."

She put her hands together, palm against palm, then drew them apart, revealing inch-by-inch a wand of pale polished bone, with rings of silver and gold and platinum and copper set along the shaft at irregular intervals. "Here," she said. "It's not a magic wand—it won't do anything for anyone else—but it is an external focus of power, to help you gather and direct your resources. Do you want physical invulnerability?"

I blinked. "Don't I already have that?"

She shook her head. "No, you have immortality and regeneration, but we—you—believed it was important to still be able to feel pain, both because you have this notion that you have crimes to atone for, and because you believed that pain is part of being alive, a necessary part of the human condition, at least for you. So you could still be *hurt*. But since the Eater has shown a tendency to blitz attack you, perhaps making you a bit more hardy would be a good idea?"

"I don't want to be numb," I said, "but I'd take some temporary indestructibility. Not *always*, because I think it would become a crutch and get me into bad habits—I already do shit that's way too foolhardy because I know I can't die, like strolling right up to the House of the Eater—but for a few hours... sure."

She handed over the wand, and I took it. "We're done here," she said. "See you—or, rather, *be you*—in a few weeks." The Bride rose, and a door opened beside her, and she stepped through, returning to the depths of my mind.

I closed my imaginary eyes, and a moment later, opened my real eyes, and I was back in the tent, sunlight filtering in through the mesh, my body stiff as hell because apparently I'd sat cross-legged for an entire night. Dreams seem to last a long time and last only moments in clock-time, but apparently communing with your inner goddess works the opposite way, and minutes become hours.

The wand was in my left hand, pressed between my palm and my knee, solid as anything. I groaned, guzzled water, stretched out and tried to un-cramp my legs, then crawled into the cot and slept, blessedly without dreams. (At least without any I know about. Maybe I dreamed about Daniel, whoever that is, and just can't remember it. I'm tempted to investigate that name, but maybe it's one of those better-off-without-knowing things again.)

I woke up in mid-afternoon and got moving and brought Hell along with me.

I walked back to Moros, and it was many miles over occasionally rough terrain, but my muscles didn't so much as twinge. (Indestructability was not as good as, say, the power of flight would have been, but I'll take what I can get.) I considered experimenting with the wand... but I didn't feel like I needed to, somehow. I kind of knew what I could do, and I was ready to do it.

I walked right down the main road toward Moros, with no more subterfuge than I'd used the last time. I saw a figure far up ahead, holding something long and greenish-gray, like a length of pipe, and I couldn't help but smile. Fuck yeah. Bring it.

There was a flash of light, a popping sound, and something streaking toward me at high speed. I wasn't even going to break stride, but it became clear the rocket wasn't actually going to hit me—somehow it was trivial to calculate trajectories all the sudden—so I moved to one side with as much speed as my invulnerable physical body could sustain, and caught the rocket square in the chest.

I won't say I didn't feel anything. It felt sort of like someone tapping me on the breastbone with a spoon. The explosion didn't even hurt my clothes, and I wasted a good microsecond wondering if I was wrapped in some kind of forcefield or something, then remembered that Death had given me these threads. They were probably just woven from the shadows of the underworld, or something, and thus indestructible—only the best for his bride.

I kicked the scrap metal remnants of the rocket aside and kept on walking. Suddenly there were a lot more figures milling in the distance, and the sound of small arms fire, though frankly I didn't even see any of the bullets, let alone feel them. A woman could get used to this. I could have rushed them—I was capable of quite ridiculous speeds—but I was sort of curious about what they'd do if I just kept coming at my leisurely walk.

By the time I reached the town there was quite a turnout, maybe the whole population, kids and old people and everything in between, all in massed ranks, forming a sort of human wall across the whole road. They were all armed, though not with bazookas and pistols now—with knives, mostly, that looked like they'd been liberated from kitchens.

Squat was there, and he stepped out to the front, and cleared his throat. "Marla. You should leave. We don't want you here. We're *happy* here."

I walked right up to him, stopping when I was less than a foot away. He started to stink immediately, a smell like rotten eggs and sliced raw onions, and my eyes began to water. "That's fine. After I kill the Eater, you're all welcome to stay here."

He flinched like I'd threatened his mother. "We… we'll kill ourselves if you don't leave." He raised a knife, and all the others did, too, scores of them, hundreds, holding the blades to their throats.

Well, shit. I'd foolishly thought that being invulnerable and armed with a wand of death would make this into a cakewalk, but if all these people offed themselves, killing the Eater would be sort of a hollow victory. I was fast, but not fast enough to disarm more than a few of them, and my instinctive knowledge of my powers knew that it didn't extend to stopping time. Too bad. I always liked seeing that power in video games and movies.

I tried to keep my tone light, because when threatened with mass suicide, what else are you going to do? "Squat, come on, you can't even die—"

He shook his head, not even stubbornly, just dismissively. "The rest of us can, and we'll start taking ourselves out, right down the line, unless you leave."

"Guys, obviously the Eater isn't infallible, because he didn't see me coming—" I shut up both because it was obvious I was wasting my voice and because one of the cultists stepped forward and put the knife against her throat.

It's not actually all that easy to cut a throat, at least not with a knife you picked up in your kitchen. That whole area is full of tough tendons and muscles, and if you don't know what you're doing, you'll probably just make a bloody mess to little effect, besides giving yourself some nasty scars and maybe fucking up your voicebox. But this little old gray-haired lady was sawing away with a will, using a long serrated bread knife, and it was clear she was going to keep on hacking even as blood fountained out and drenched her sweatshirt with the applique jewels. Half a dozen cultists in the front rank lifted their knives, like violinists raising their bows and waiting for their part in the symphony to start.

I took a step back, but it was too late, because they started hacking away at themselves, too, one of them even shoving the blade in point-first and wiggling it around, a meditative expression on his face. "No!" I shouted, and reached out with the wand in my hand—

And withdrew death from them. From *all* of them. The kept stabbing and sawing, but the blood didn't flow anymore, and their wounds began closing as soon as they opened. Withdrawing death, and letting life flow—I was showing them the kinder side of my true nature. I grinned, and my teeth felt strange, pointed, and my tongue did, too. They began to drop the knives, some of them sobbing, some howling, all baffled and confused, kids let down by their parent—and Squat just stood there, gaping at me, and said, "Your *eyes...*"

They couldn't be hurt, for the moment, any of them, so I gestured with the wand, and the earth beneath them erupted in two diverging waves, sweeping half of them off to the left, half off to the right, and leaving a path of churned soil and shattered asphalt two yards wide stretching out directly in front of me. Parting the human sea.

I walked—slow and stately as a bride down the aisle—toward the center of town, gesturing here and there as I went. I pointed at his church—it was empty of life, I could sense, not so much as a mouse—and it collapsed in on itself, dropping into a sinkhole of my own invention. I pointed the wand at the stoplight and it exploded, gestured at the closed bank and watched it implode like a giant had squeezed the building in its fist.

Making the Eater tremble in fear probably wouldn't occur to my goddess-self, but I was human, and petty, and I wanted revenge. I wanted him to know I was coming.

When I walked through the park, the grass blackened, and new green shoots rose up in their place, budding into snow-pale flowers. My motorcycle, still parked on the street where I'd left it, roared into life, motor revving as if cheering me on. I considered riding it up the steps and inside the building and right over the Eater, but there's such a thing as being *too* theatrical.

The doors of city hall—the House of the Eater, rather—were closed, locked, and warded by considerable magics. I lifted my foot and kicked the doors off their hinges.

I couldn't see through walls, precisely, but I could apprehend the whole of the place, and I knew the Eater in the main room where I'd been chained, at the end of this rather boring hall. There was other life, too. Half a dozen of the crab-squid-octopus guys, like the one I'd killed in the motel, none of them bothering with disguises this time. A couple of shapeshifters, growling and beginning to transform into part-wolverines or whatever. A man with his eyes and lips sewn shut, his body surrounded by swarms of biting flies, their aura of life force intermingled with his own. The Eater's heavy hitters, his unstoppable honor guard, the last resort in case someone with a mind of their own wandered in with a shotgun and mayhem in mind.

I just waved my wand and they all burned, bright as magnesium, winking out in an instant, leaving only a thin dusting of ash behind.

I continued down the corridor, dragging the end of my wand along the wall like a kid running a stick along a picket fence, leaving a line of dry rot and charred wood.

The doors to the main hall flew open when I approached, and the Eater waited inside, dressed in the same brown robes, looking not quite as young as he had after his dramatic transformation, but not quite as ancient and withered as he had when he first lowered his hood.

"Let them all go, and I'll let you live out what's left of your natural span," I said, surprised at myself for offering mercy.

"What *are* you?" he demanded. He held the moon-colored axe in one hand, but his grip was trembling.

"Yeah, what the fuck are you?" Nicolette called, and I realized she was there, too, her head resting on the throne. "I've been telling Emperor Palpatine here all kinds of tricks for killing you, but the magic coming off you is *insane* right now, I can't even tell what the hell I'm looking at."

"Hell is pretty close," I said. "What'll it be, Eater?"

"His real name is Garcia," Nicolette said. "He was actually Monseigneur Garcia, for a while, weirdly enough. Interesting guy."

"Shut up, Nicolette. I came to save you, you know."

"Who needs saving? At least this guy put me down on a nice throne. I'm not even in a cage."

"*Silence*!" the Eater shouted.

"Wow," Nicolette said after a moment's silence. "Guess he's not used to people talking amongst themselves in this town. Or maybe he's just a sexist asshole who doesn't want to see two women talking to each other about anything, even a man."

"I definitely don't get a progressive vibe off him," I said.

"Eh, fuck him, then," Nicolette said. "Take him out."

Chaos witches are so fickle. "Last chance," I said. "Free your people, Eater."

He licked his lips. "If I release their futures, give up the source of my power, they will be lost, confused—some of them have been here for years. Some have been here since they were babies, they don't know any other life—"

"They'll learn. So will you. I know a nice hospital for sorcerers who get out of control, and need to be locked up for their own protection. You can rest there, for however long you've got left."

He lowered his head for a moment, and when he lifted it again, I knew he wasn't going to be reasonable.

"Suicide by goddess," I muttered.

The Eater raised the axe and launched himself at me.

That axe is a powerful artifact. Somehow I knew, maybe through one of the cracks in the vault of my mind, that it had once belonged to a moon goddess—no doubt she'll come calling for it someday, when she notices it's gone—but it couldn't hurt me. In the hands of another god? Absolutely. Then we'd have been on equal footing, just like a couple of humans hacking away at each other. But despite the power filling the Eater from all those futures he'd devoured, he was no god.

I twitched the wand, and his magical protections—layers and layers of armor, built up over years of rituals—flashed away like water turning to steam. Another twitch, and his flesh turned bluish-gray, every bit of fluid in his body transformed to ice. He went still, tottered, and then fell over, shattering like a rose dipped in liquid nitrogen and struck with a hammer.

"That's going to be nasty when it thaws," Nicolette said. "Where did you get that wand? What kind of magic is that?"

"I called in a big favor." I started to put the wand away… but it dissolved in my hand, turning into smoke that smelled faintly of night-scented jasmine. Somewhere I heard the small *click* of a partially-opened door closing deep in my mind.

I was human again, and I suddenly felt every ache I hadn't noticed in the prior hours. I walked over to Nicolette's throne and looked down at her. "I'll pick you up, if you promise not to bite."

"Bite my *ass*," she said, and really, there was no sensible response to that, so I tucked her under my arm and went to look for my stuff.

Bride of Social Work

Oh, how I wanted to get on my motorcycle and ride off into the sunset, leaving people to say, "Who was that mysterious woman who saved us all?"

But I couldn't, because I am Doing Better, and there were several hundred profoundly confused and traumatized people in the wreckage of a town, and they all needed help. It wasn't like they'd lost their memories, either—they knew exactly what they'd done, they just couldn't figure out why on Earth it had seemed like the *right* thing to do. So I had to quit being an avenging angel and start being a social worker.

That first night was rough. Squat is not a comforting presence, and Nicolette is Nicolette, so it mostly fell to me. It was tempting to call the local cops and let them deal with everything, but I'd exploded these people's lives, so they were my responsibility. (Sure, I'd given them their lives back, but that upside to their situation tended to get lost in the hysteria.) I am obviously not a people person, but I *did* run a city for years, so it's not like I'm incapable of managing things like this.

I got everyone gathered together in the central park and announced that the Master had died in an accident that could be deemed either tragic or fortuitous. I told them they'd been under the influence of psychotropic drugs and brainwashing—which also served to explain their "hallucinations" about me taking bullets without falling and ripping up the earth and them stabbing themselves in the neck and so on. Not all of them bought my story, but people want to believe *some* kind of narrative that makes sense, and I offered them one.

I explained that I'd come to Moros to rescue my friend Squat, and that I didn't want to call the police because I'd broken laws along the way, and because many of the cultists had been accessories to crimes during their time with the Master. I just wanted to get them all on their way back to whatever lives they'd had before. We ended up having a sort of giant campout-slash-cookout in the park. It was actually pleasant, for a party where all the guests had PTSD.

Pelly and Rondeau arrived in the RV the following morning. They brought Riegel the dune-buggy-riding psychic with him, and he and Rondeau helped do some direct-to-mind counseling for some of the more messed-up victims of the Eater's attentions. Some memories were discreetly wiped when necessary, and Pelly handled contacting family members, especially for the minors who'd been kidnapped.

Squat helped when he could, but people naturally found him offputting, even when he was disguised, because of the curse—and because he reminded them, if only subconsciously, of the half-remembered monsters the cultists had seen attending and assisting the Eater. Squat seemed pretty shaken up by the whole experience, too—being mind-slaved, twisting my head around backwards, all that. I guess when your life is already fucked-up with a curse, having your sense of agency entirely removed, too, must be horrifying. Talk about a loss of control. Squat started spending most of his time with Nicolette in the remains of the House of the Eater, the one place the lapsed Eat-arians could be counted on to avoid totally, and so the safest place for a talking head and a repulsive monster-man to hang without fear of freaking out the normals.

I took some comfort in the fact that Squat's presence, by definition, must be making Nicolette miserable, but I felt bad that she was the only one Squat could really hang out with. I could handle his company okay—I hate most people anyway, so the fact that I find his presence profoundly offputting is no barrier to our friendship—but I was just too busy dealing with the human consequences of my rampage.

It took about two weeks to get everyone squared away, back to their families when possible, or sent away with some cash (courtesy of Rondeau) to help them start new lives. I wasn't too optimistic about the long-term prospects for some of those people, but we'd repaired the psychic damage when we could, and when the last of the Eater's people left with a bus ticket in her hand and a money belt around her waist and a set of plausible invented memories in her head, I felt a great weight lift from me.

I went into the RV and tried to sleep, and when I couldn't, I wrote about what happened. And here I am. I think, now that I've written it down, I'll be able to rest. That's worked before. I seem to have created a ritual for myself, with this pen, this page, these outpouring thoughts. This is like confession, maybe, if only confession to myself. Well, whatever. Rituals are worthwhile as long as they work. It doesn't matter why they work, not to me. I'm a pragmatist.

There are just a few days left until I return to the underworld. I suppose it's possible I could do some more good in that time... but I'm only human. For the rest of the week, anyway. I'm tired. We're going back to Vegas. I'm going to sleep a lot and eat steak and play checkers with Pelly and shoot the breeze with Rondeau and stick Nicolette in a closet and see if there's enough money in the world to get Squat laid. Then I can go back to my other job feeling somewhat refreshed, and ready to look at the big picture again.

For my first time walking the Earth and Doing Good (or at least Better), I'll admit there's room for improvement, but I think I Did Okay.

Valley of Death

FUCK. I DIDN'T EXPECT TO BE WRITING HERE AGAIN. Didn't that last bit of diary end on a nice triumphant rah-rah-rah note?

All good things must come to an end, and things have gone to crap in an alarming fashion, and I'm going to be leaving the world in less than an hour so I don't have time to do a damn thing about it. I'm writing about it here instead, because I do have time for that, and maybe it'll help me get my mind right to take up arms again when I return to life in a month's time.

I'm not going to lie. I didn't spend a lot of time thinking about the cult of the Bride of Death. They were probably all profoundly broken people—the truly well-adjusted don't dedicate themselves to death goddesses—and I probably should have tried to do something to help them, but I was focused more on problems I could fix with violence when I first woke up from my dirt nap in Death Valley. So instead of hiring a psychic to soothe their messed-up brains, or even giving them a mission to go forth and do some good in the world, I'd sent them on the equivalent of a snipe hunt, or on a run to the hardware store to buy a left-handed screwdriver. Busywork for fanatics.

At least, that's what I'd intended when I told them to look for the remnants of an ancient imaginary civilization in the caves below Death Valley. But it turned out it was more like I'd sent them to go play in traffic.

We returned to Death Valley this morning, in preparation for apotheosis. I was willing to go to bed in Vegas and just vanish from sight, but one way Pelham had kept the cultists from chasing me all over the Southwest was by promising them there'd be a ritual farewell for me. I gathered they were going to put me in a hole in the ground and cover it with a stone and then remove the stone to show that I had vanished from sight—no uncomfortable symbolism *there*.

Pelly drove the RV and I rode shotgun, with Rondeau snoozing and boozing in the back. Squat and Nicolette didn't know about my goddess-related condition so we didn't bring them with us, leaving them back in Vegas. As far as they knew, I was just "going away for a few weeks" to deal with some personal business.

Rondeau had promised to hook Squat up with some of the local sorcerers who might be in need of muscle and get him back on his feet, but hadn't decided what to do with Nicolette during my absence. He was leaning toward locking her in a soundproof safe for a month, but I told him that was cruel—soundproof closet with a TV to watch was more humane. Either way, she wasn't going to be my problem for a month. Halle-fuckin-lujah.

We pulled in to the camp, hidden in the cave where I'd come crawling out of the dirt a month ago. The cultists had made the cave their own, and when I walked inside I winced. The cave was lit with camping lanterns, mainly, but there were a couple of burned-out torches jammed into cracks in the wall too. They'd carved niches in the walls, and filled them with the skulls of various animals. "What the hell, Pelly?"

He sighed. "There's a website that sells both genuine and replica animal skulls. They insisted on purchasing these, saying they gave the room the proper 'ambiance.'"

"At least there aren't stuffed ravens and fake spiderwebs everywhere."

"I'll see if I can find the cultists," Pelly said. "They might be off exploring. They have come back with some disturbing reports of odd artifacts in the deep caves, but the examples they've brought me just look like twisted bits of stone, rendered magical by the power of wishful thinking and nothing more. They claim there are strange carvings in the walls, too, but..." He shrugged. "Your cultists are a very imaginative lot, Mrs. Mason."

"Lucky me." I wandered around their living quarters while Pelly went in search of my followers. They had a makeshift kitchen of the camp-stove and canned-beans variety—the farts in here must be monstrous, I thought, and felt bad about thinking it later—and they had sleeping bags and camping pads all heaped together in one room. At least my cultists were a friendly and cozy bunch. They certainly weren't emulating their goddess in that respect.

Pelly said my worshipers were happy enough here, fulfilled and content to be serving their goddess. I felt so weird about that. The Eater's devotees had been happy too, maybe, or at least thought they were. Sure, I wasn't compelling anyone, not intentionally, but maybe there was some kind of goddess-aura I put out—certainly *something* drew those people to me, and maybe it was no more their "choice" to serve me, in any meaningful sense, than it was the choice of those who served the Eater. But since they did choose to serve, maybe I could help them out a bit. Buy them a couple of couches, or even just cast a keep-away spell around their camp so they wouldn't get rousted by park rangers, which was, otherwise, an inevitability. Make some gesture, beyond this dumb ritual of letting them bury me in a hole, to show that I appreciated them. Even though I really didn't. Faking it is part of Doing Better, right?

Turns out it was all pretty moot, because they were dead. I was yelling at Rondeau for eating the cultist's marshmallows and graham crackers when Pelham reappeared, face pale. "Mrs. Mason, you… You should come and see this."

"Fuck. What? I'm really not in the market for surprises."

"I think the cultists must have found something in the caves beneath the valley after all," Pelham said. "Or, at least, something found *them*."

Turns out they'd found an entrance to the rumored cave complex below Death Valley, accessible from my own cavern. They'd widened what must have been a fairly small hole into a shaft big enough to descend, and lowered a twelve-foot metal ladder down there. I slid down the ladder after Pelly—Rondeau stayed upstairs—and followed a claustrophobic corridor, lit periodically with clusters of low-energy LEDs that would burn for ages before the batteries ran out. The passageway meandered for a hundred yards or so before opening out into a conference room-sized cavern lit by big industrial Klieg lights. Various tunnels led away from the space at random intervals, and there was a whiteboard propped against one wall with a hand-drawn map, presumably of the cave system, in blue and red marker, scribbled with incomprehensible notations. A wooden table held a heap of broken bits of stone, which might have passed for hand-carved idols of some kind if you had the right kind of fevered imagination and had read too much Lovecraft lately. But I didn't notice any of that right away.

I noticed the blood, and I noticed the hole.

There were no bodies, no meat, no bones, but there were plenty of blood-soaked rags of robes and streaks of blood. Not puddles, but smears, as if a great tongue had licked up as much of the human spillage as possible before taking off. A few twinkling objects were scattered amid the blood. I knelt and looked them over, feeling cold inside. "This is a gold tooth," I said. "And here are several fillings, and that's a titanium screw—a surgical screw."

"There is a glass eye, here, Mrs. Mason," Pelly said. "One of the cultists, a Tara Yoshikawa of Dearborn, Michigan, had it in her head when last I saw her. And here there is a pacemaker. Mrs. Carroway of Stowe, Vermont had one of those. And, ah…" He flushed, and I glanced over, and winced. It looked like a little letter "T"—somebody's IUD.

"Something *ate* these people," I said. "Their bones, their organs, their skin, their hair…"

"But it spat out all foreign objects, it seems."

"That's even creepier than just devouring someone whole. What could have done this?"

"Whatever it was, it seems to have departed."

We both looked at the hole, then. It was about ten feet across, punched straight through the rock ceiling above us, and at the top, there was a glimmer of blue sky. Whatever had killed the cultists had bored or burned or dissolved or simply punched right through several yards of earth and stone, and now it was out there in the world somewhere.

I'd killed one Eater, and inadvertently unleashed another, more literal Eater, it seemed.

"Perhaps we should investigate the tunnels, Mrs. Mason," he said. "And search for survivors."

"Perhaps we should get up above ground and *track* this thing—"

"You don't have time, Mrs. Mason," he said gently. "Your allotted period of mortality is almost up. In just a few hours, you must return to your throne."

"Maybe I could get Death to give me an extension, or…" I trailed off. Death and I had made a bargain, but it wasn't like a handshake agreement—more like a geas. Or a natural law. You can't negotiate the timing of the coming of winter. Our agreement was binding in all kinds of ways, and Death couldn't have changed it even if he'd wanted to.

Pelham consulted the map—it made more sense to him than it did to me—and then we set off into one of the tunnels, armed with flashlights the cultists had left behind. This tunnel was smaller, tighter, and a pain in the ass to squeeze through, and Pelham said the cultists had probably avoided it until recently in favor of checking out simpler routes. Eventually we reached a round, low-ceilinged room, with a deep black hole in the center, about ten feet across. Our flashlights couldn't begin to penetrate those depths. There were cracked bits of stone around the hole, as if there'd been a lid or cap on top of it, and something had shattered the seal. Pelham and I took that in grimly and without comment.

The walls were indeed decorated with crude images, of twisting serpents and stylized whorls that might have been wind or waves, and human figures.

"What's that next to the people?" Pelham said. "A bush?"

I squinted, shining my flashlight, then whistled. "No. I think that's a tree."

"But, if that's drawn to scale…"

"Then the person is taller than the tree," I said. "Damn it. There really *were* giants in the earth, hidden away in caves under Death Valley? That's like sending someone on a snipe hunt and they come back with the body of a dead snipe."

"These giants are considerably taller than nine feet," he said. "If this drawing is to be believed, at least."

"Could be very small trees. So you think the cultists found a giant and woke it up, somehow?"

"It is a hypothesis," he said. "Or perhaps the lost race of giants imprisoned something here, long ago, and *that* is what the cultists released."

I thought of the Beast of Sunlight Shores. Whatever had killed the cultists—*my* cultists—was even more vicious than that creature had been, and may have been trapped under a similar seal. I hate coincidences. I've been around too many gods in my life to entirely believe in random chance.

"When did you last hear from the cultists?" I asked.

"They have a satellite phone, and their leader Ambrose called me just yesterday, to tell me they'd found something remarkable—but that was a claim I'd heard before, only to be confronted with a fist-sized piece of misshapen rock, or something that might have been the blade of a flint knife. Perhaps I should have taken them more seriously."

"It's not your fault, Pelly. None of us took it seriously, because we didn't think it was serious. But now… you have to move on this thing. Get Rondeau to help you—he can consult oracles—and make Nicolette help, too, tell her if she doesn't cooperate I'll make her life miserable when I get back in town. *Find* this thing, whatever it is. My hope is that it only ate all the cultists because it had been trapped for who knows how long, and it was starving. If we're lucky, it won't need to feed again for a while, and it's just curled up somewhere in the valley. At least we're not in the middle of Manhattan or something."

"And if we can track this creature?"

I chewed my lip. "There aren't a lot of people left who owe me favors, huh? Perren River, on the council of sorcerers in Felport, was always fond of me, and still has gang connections with the Honeyed Knots, if we need muscle or trackers. I already owe the Bay Witch a favor, but she's unpredictable, and she might help out if we asked sweetly. Try to track down whatever assistance you can, but in a pinch, send in Squat to fight the thing. He's immortal, at least. If all else fails, hold the line and wait for me, and when I get back…" I shrugged. "I'll do what I can. This thing getting loose is my fuck-up, and I should be the one to fix it."

It was hard not to notice that the death toll among my cultists was *way* higher than that among the Eater's cultists. In the Eater's fucked-up way, he took care of his people.

I really need to do better.

I will remember the ones who fell in my service. I didn't honor them in life, but I can honor their memories. And when the time comes, if I can, I will avenge them.

Here I am, in the room where I rose from the dead one month ago today. A few days ago I thought I'd done pretty good, but now, once again, I have to face the fact that I've cost people their lives by being thoughtless. Not so long ago I would have refused all responsibility—I didn't *ask* these people to worship me, they chose that for themselves, it's no business of mine if they got themselves killed—but I can admit my own part in it now. Their deaths are not wholly my responsibility, no, but I could have prevented them, if I'd taken a little more care.

I don't have much longer, maybe just a few minutes, and—

Well, hell. There's the door, appearing out of nowhere, but looking like it's been there forever. Swinging open now.

And death is a door that, when it opens, you have no choice but to walk through.

From the Desk of Nicolette

(Pelham and Rondeau, you boot-licking fuckwits, if you find this, make sure Marla gets it when she drags herself out of the dirt next month.)

Dear Marla,

Forgive my handwriting, ha, but it's not actually *mine*, obviously. I've compelled one of the maids in this shitty Vegas hotel to take dictation. I lured her in with magic—tickled her brain with the idea that there was a kid crying in here, scared and alone, she's the compassionate kind—and once she got here, I snared her with a charm. She's only mine for half an hour, but that's plenty of time.

So, you're a death goddess, huh? Yeah, I know. You thought you could keep it a secret from me? You're so stupid. How do you literally become a god and still be *so stupid*? I may be just a head, but my hearing's fine, and you let a few things slip, and more importantly, Tweedle-Rondeau and Pelham-Dum are crap at keeping secrets. They think because they put me on a shelf in a closet that I lost the ability to *listen*. Plus there was the fact that you should have died all those times and didn't and, oh, yeah, the fact that you somehow kept me alive even though *I'm just a head*. It all kind of added up, and then I got confirmation.

Oh, and hey, I'm real proud of you. My nemesis is a goddess? They say you can judge a person by the quality of their enemies, and you are one primo enemy, so that just elevates me even higher.

By the time you read this I'll be gone. Squat and I are hitting the road. Yeah, I brought him over to my side. First I just told him some of this shit you've done—the deaths you've caused, your ruthless political moves, how you snapped the neck of your last lover, how you caused the death of some of your closest friends, how even your old friend Dr. Husch wanted to murder you—I just told him what an asshole you are, basically.

I hardly even had to lie! Of course I did lie, also, because, why not? Once I had Squat basically on my side I got him to sneak around and spy a bit and, whaddya know, he found your stupid little journal. He was really worried about getting caught, so he read just far enough to find out I was right about you being a goddess, and about your month-on, month-off arrangement. (I wish I'd had time to read the whole thing. I bet it's full of laughs.)

But Squat also read some of that shit about you trying to be a better person, blah blah blah, and I had to explain the concept of an "unreliable narrator" to him, to convince him you were really a total shit. He was resistant, though, leaning toward thinking you were maybe sort of okay, so then I told Squat something great: I explained how, because you're a goddess, you could *totally* cure him of his curse if you wanted to, but that you preferred to use him for his muscle, and because it's handy to have immortal cannon fodder around. (Was that even a lie? I mean, you are a goddess. People pray to goddesses for intercession and the healing of wounds. I know you're a death goddess, not one of the traditional caring professions, but shit, power is power, right?) He hates you *so much* right now. Before you just kind of scared him, especially after the shit he saw you do in Moros, but now it's pure hate. Funny, huh? A guy who's cursed so no one can stand to be around him can't stand to be around *you*.

Then I told Squat that, as a one-time disciple of the witch who cursed him, maybe *I* could cure him, if he helped me get my power back. And shut up, I *did* work with Elsie Jarrow for a while there, she taught me a lot—we bonded. The fact that she cut off my head doesn't mean she didn't *like* me. She was a chaos witch—we do crazy shit sometimes. I told Squat that if he got me out of here, preferably while you were off on your little field trip, I'd devote my energies to making him an ordinary human again.

I could probably do it, too, but fuck that—he's immortal and as strong as a dump truck full of orangutans! I bet I can string him along for years.

He stole me a few charms from your bag, little things, stuff you'd hardly miss— and I ate them. I can't eat *food*, and to sate the thing I have in place of hunger I need disorder and disaster, but I *can* absorb magic. Having no hands means I can't do every spell I used to, and enchanting is a bit beyond me, but there are plenty of incantations I can still manage. I've been pretending to be a lot more helpless than I am. (Of course, you're so self-absorbed, I probably didn't need to bother with pretense.)

I bet you're wondering what I'm going to do, with this month of free play I've got while you're in the depths. There are so many possibilities, especially with Squat by my side. Maybe I'll reunite the Marla Mason

Revenge Squad—you left one or two of them alive, yeah? Or maybe I'll find a way to destroy something you love. Or maybe I'll do some serious research into how you kill gods—there's gotta be a way, right?

You never respected me as an adversary. You probably think, now that you're a goddess, you're even *more* out of my league. But you'll see. If you think being a deity makes you hot shit, you're only half right, and it's not the "hot" part.

Now, I know what you're thinking. You're thinking, "Dumb ol' Nicolette, she's missed the obvious thing—I gave her life, and I can take it away."

And sure. You *could* just withdraw my immortality, and maybe you'll do that—but maybe you should take a look at what I did during your month underground, first. I've got some plans that might make you hesitate to get rid of me. A month is a lot of time—time enough to make the consequences of you killing me even more awful than the legitimately super-awful consequences of keeping me around.

But you've never been sensible, and maybe you'll kill me anyway, even if I do arrange it so my death will wreak all kinds of havoc. I'll just have to live with the uncertainty. Hey, hurray! Uncertainty just makes me stronger. Worst case, I get a month to sow horror and discord to make your precious vacation from being a *goddess* into a total shit-pit of misery. A little welcome-home present for you.

Either way, Marla, it's been fun. I'll miss smelling your farts while I'm stuck on the back of your ugly-ass motorcycle. Until next we meet, screw you and the pale horse you rode in on.

See you next month, your goddessness.

Thugs and pisses,

Nicolette

The End

Acknowledgments

I HAVE A LOT OF PEOPLE TO THANK for this one. My wife Heather Shaw, of course, is first, for her tremendous support in helping me find the time (between parenting and a full-time job) to write this book. Thanks to Lindsey Look for painting the stunning cover, to Zack Stella for drawing the kickass interiors, and to Jenn Reese of Tiger Bright Studios for the cover design. John Teehan of Merry Blacksmith Press has agreed, once again, to produce the trade paperback print version. My gratitude to Elektra Hammond for her excellent copyediting, and to Besha Grey for catching assorted errors in the text. Many of my friends and longtime readers spread the word about this novel, for which I'm eternally grateful.

But my biggest thanks go to the backers who made this possible. This book would not exist without the generous individuals who gave money to me directly, or through my Kickstarter campaign. Thank you to: @dxfl, A Anthony James, A Girl Named Pinky, Aaron McConnell, Adam Caldwell, Al Clay, Alasdair Stuart and Marguerite Kenner, Alex Lang, Alexa Gulliford, Alexa S., Alexander the Drake, Allen L. Edwards, Alpha Chen, Alumiere, Amanda Fisher, Amanda Stevens, Amy Kim, Andrea Leeson, Andreas Gustafsson, Andrew Barton, Andrew J Clark IV, Andrew Lin, Andrew Qualls, Andrew Wilson, Angela Korra'ti, Ann Lemay, Annabeth Leong, Anton Nath, Arachne Jericho, Arashi Veronica Lilith, Arlene E. Parker, Armi Gerilla, Arun Jiwa, Arun Jiwa, Athena Holter-Mehren, Athena Holter-Mehren, Atleb, Atlee Breland, Balazs Oroszlany, Bananasplit.us, Barb Moermond, Ben Esacove, Ben Meginnis, Beth Hoffman, Beth Rheaume, Beth Wodzinski, Brenda Hovdenes, Brian Callahan, Brian Ketelsen, Brittany, Brumley D. Pritchett, Bryan Sims, Bryant Durrell, C. Joshua Villines, C.C. Finlay, Carl Rigney, Casey Fiesler, Cat Rambo, catherine james, Catherine Waters, CE Murphy, Chad Price,

Chamber Four, Charles Crowe, Chelle Parker, Chris 'Zero S' Parslow, Chris McLaren, Chris Schwarz, Christian Decomain, Christian Stegmann, Christine Chen, Christopher Todd Kjergaard, Cinnamon Davis, Claire Connelly, Claudia S., Cliff Winnig, Colette Reap, Colin Anderson, Collin Smith, Craig Hackl, Craig Marquis, Crystal Landry, D. Potter, Dan Percival, Dana cate, Dani Daly, Daniel and Trista Robichaud, Daniel McInerney, Danielle Benson, Dave Lawson, Dave Thompson, David Bell, David Harrison, David Harrison, David Martinez, David Rains, Dean M Roddick, Deanna Stanley, Deb "Seattlejo" Schumacher, Debbie Solomon, Deborah Vause, Deirdre Behan, Denise Murray, Duck Dodgers, Duncan McNiff, E. Tubert, Eain, Ed Fuqua, Ed Matuskey, Edward Greaves, Edward J Smola III, Elaine Williams, Eldritch, Eleanor Penley, Elektra, Elias F. Combarro, Ellen Sandberg, Elsa, Emma Bull, Emrya, Enrica P, Erica Stevenson, Erin Kowalski, Evan Ladouceur, Falcdragon, Ferran, Fran Friel, Fred Kiesche, Fuchsi, Gabe Krabbe, Gann Bierner, Gary Singer., Gessika Rovario-Cole, Glennis LeBlanc, Glyph, Gonzalo Bruno, Greg Levick, Greg van Eekhout, GrumpySteen, Guillaume Actif, Gunnar Högberg, H. Bledstein, Heather Richardson, Holly Kay, Hugh Berkson, I would like to remain anonymous, Ian Mond, Ira Green, Irina Ashel, Iysha Evelyn, J Kalinowski, J. Quincy Sperber, James Burbidge, James M. Yager, Janne T, Jason Italic, Jason Skaare, jason wilson, Jay Turpin, Jay Wilson, Jeff Huse, Jeffrey Reed, Jen Sparenberg, Jen W, Jenn Reese, Jenn Snively, Jennifer Berk, Jennifer Corbett, Jennifer Sander, Jennifer Scott, Jeremiah Tolbert, Jeremy Rosehart, Jerry Gaiser, Jessica Bay, Jim Crose, Jim Ryan, JM Templet, John Blankenship, John Dees, John Devenny, John Johnson, Johnathon Miller, Jon Eichten, Jon Hansen, Jon Lundy, Jon Lupa, José Rafael Martínez Pina, Josh Lowman, Juli McDermott, Julie Gammad, Justine Baker, K Greene, Karen Graham, Karen Mahoney, Karen Meisner, Karen Tucker, Kate Smith, Katherine Douglas, Kathleen Hanrahan, Kei Weinzerl, Keith Bissett, Keith Garcia, Keith Hall, Keith Teklits, Kelly Angelina Hong, Kendall P. Bullen, Keslynn, Kevin Hogan, Keyan Bowes, Kiara Pyrenei, Konstantin Gorelyy, Kris Downs, Kristin B., Kyle Mack, Laura Cox, Laura D., Lee Delarm, Leigh-Ann, Lexie C, Lianne, Lisa Wilson, LJ, Lori L. Gildersleeve, Lori Lum, Lunchtime Studios, Lunchtime Studios, Margaret Klee, Margaret Klee, Maria Lima, Marius Gedminas, Mark A. Buckmaster, Mark Kadas, Mark Loggins, Mark Rowe, Mark Teppo, Matt Leitzen, Matthew Galloway, Max Kaehn, Maynard Garrett, Melissa Tabon, Michael "Maikeruu" Pierno, Michael Bernardi, Michael Cross, Michael D. Blanchard, Michael Jacob, Michael Jasper, Michael M. Jones, Michelle, Mikael Olsson, Mikael Vikström,

Mike and Jen Schwartz, Mike Bavister, Mike Wilson, Misha Narov, MK Carroll, Mo Soar, Morgan McCauley, Mur Lafferty, NA, Nancy Lebovitz, Natalie Luhrs, Nathan, nathan gendzier, Nayad Monroe, Nellie Batz, Nicole Dutton, Nicole Pinder, Olna Jenn Smith, Ori Shifrin, P. Kerim Friedman, Patrick Bennett, Paul "Anorak" Record, Paul Bulmer, Paul Echeverri, Paul R Smith, Pedro Manuel Arjona Argüelles, Peter Macinkovic, Phil Adler, Phillip Jones, pockets, Rachael Squires, Rachel Sanders, Ragi Gonçalves, Rasmus Bode, Rebecca Harbison, Reed Lindner, Renee D. LeBeau, Rian de Laat, Richard Leaver, Richard Scott, Rick Cambere, Ro Molina, Rob Steinberger, Robert Hilton, Robert Mark Waugh, Robin in Vermont, Roger Silverstein, Ron Jarrell, Rowan A., Russ Wilcox, Ryan Rapp, S K Stidolph, S. Nasiri, S.J. Elliott, Sam Brock, Samuel Montgomery-Blinn, Sandy, Sara Puls, Sarah Livingston Heitz, Scott Drummond, Scott Serafin, Sean Havins, Sebastian d'Hinnisdael, shadow, Shanna Germain, Shanyi Gu, Sharon B., Sharon Wood, Shef Reynolds, Shirley D, Siobhan Porter, Skyler Spurgeon, Sraedi ScatterbuG, Stephen Reid, Steve Smoot, Steven Desjardins, Steven Saus, Su, summervillain, Susan Marie Groppi, Sy Bram, szazszorszapathy, T4b, Tammy DeGray, Tammy Thaggert, Tania Clucas, Tara Rowan, Tara Yoshikawa, Taylor S Kendall, Ted Brown, Thomas, Thomas Wells, Tiffany Bridge, Tim Uruski, Tina M. Kirk, Tobias S. Buckell, Topher Hughes, Travis Dunn, Vincent Meijer, Von Welch, William P. Hassinger, Winston Worrell, Yaron Davidson, Yolanda Ray, Yoshio Kobayashi, and Zen Dog.